MAFIOSA PRINCESS- HONOR

LIZA MALLOY

To Mimi
Thank you for always believing in my dreams and for supporting this awesome series...and for babysitting the kids so I can write.

FREE COPY OF FIRST BOOK IN SERIES

The Mafiosa Princess series is best enjoyed from the beginning. If you've picked up Mafiosa Princess-Honor without reading the first two books (Mafiosa Princess and Mafiosa Princess- Sacrifice), stop!

You can get a FREE digital copy of the first book, Mafiosa Princess, simply by joining my email list at this link: https://www.lizamalloy.com/mafiosaprincess

Don't worry—I won't ever share your contact information with anyone else, and if you decide you don't enjoy the freebies and other content I send, you can unsubscribe at any time.

Enjoy!

- Liza

CHAPTER 1

Giada

The explosions boomed relentlessly, piercing my ears as I prayed for the noise to stop. When it ultimately did, relief washed over me, but the reprieve was fleeting. I surveyed the room, my sight finally landing on Luca. His eyes were empty and sad.

I waited a moment before approaching him. Just as my fingers grazed his tee-shirt, Luca jumped, pulling me into his arms and tickling me while I shrieked.

"Don't do that!" I scolded. "You scared me!"

"I'm sorry," he said, peppering my arm with kisses. "It's good to see how much you care."

He brushed a hair out of my face and gazed into my eyes, his expression filled with so much adoration that I felt I might burst with pride at the fact that this beautiful, funny, athletic, smart and oh so popular boy loved me. He could have any girl he wanted, and he chose me.

Luca's lips pressed against mine, his tongue caressing mine with a tenderness that sent chills up my spine. I let my body sink into his, wishing we could stay like that forever, certain I'd never feel happier or safer than I did in his arms.

But then he abruptly pulled away, wiping his thumb under my eye. "Gia, you're crying. Babe, wake up," he said.

His arm jostled me, and his voice grew louder. "It's only a dream, Gia. Wake up."

I slowly peeled open my eyes, burdened by the weight of my own eyelids. When I focused on the figure beside me, icy blue eyes peered back at me instead of the warm chocolate eyes I'd gazed into moments before. My breath caught in my throat, and I shivered, coldness overtaking me as it all rushed back at me.

I was with Adrian.

Luca was dead.

And it was all my fault.

I'd been having the dreams for days now, and they were always the same. They started with the end, then juxtaposed that with the beginning of my relationship with Luca. As some sort of cruel punishment for letting Luca die in my stead, my brain was forcing me to relive the start of our complex relationship over, and over, and over.

I weighed my options, considering avoidance of sleep just to spare myself the horrifically vivid replay of those last minutes, but that would be pointless. The bad moments played on a loop through my mind regardless of whether I was asleep or awake.

At least when I slept, I could relish the good times again. Being with Luca in my dreams felt so real. I could see him, hear him, touch him, smell him, taste him. He was there, and he was smiling.

In my dreams, we were in love.

Adrian

Once I'd calmed Giada again, I stepped out of the room to make her some tea. She hadn't eaten more than a few bites since the shooting, and she'd forsaken her beloved coffee altogether. I couldn't tell if she wanted to punish herself for something or if she just feared the caffeine would make the nightmares worse. She was taking sleeping pills her mother had supplied, though they didn't seem to help. She spent all her time in bed but rarely slept.

I didn't blame Gia for being distraught. She'd had a rough couple of weeks. Earlier in the spring, her father, Marco, had apparently gotten on the bad side of a Colombian drug cartel. One of the guys had shot Giada's brother Matteo, and Luca had retaliated by killing the shooter. After that, Giada's father had become even more overprotective, something I wouldn't have thought possible. Marco pushed Giada into the open arms of Luca, thinking that publicly pairing up his only daughter with a well-known mobster like Luca would ensure her safety.

Maybe his logic was sound, but I would never see Giada's brief engagement to Luca as anything but a colossal mistake. After he cheated on her—with hookers, for the record, she broke the engagement and came back to me. But we'd barely gotten back to normal when another one of those drug dealers made an attempt on Gia's life. That time though, Luca dove in front of the bullet, literally shielding her with his own body.

I couldn't deny it was a brave or classy thing to do, but I also had to admit I resented Luca for his actions. Maybe even envied him a bit. Not that I wanted to get shot, certainly not killed, but it sure would've been nice to be Giada's hero, especially now that I was the only one left. I felt her pulling away, knew she struggled with guilt over how she'd ended things with Luca. She possibly even blamed herself for his death. But there was nothing I could do except pray that time truly did heal all wounds.

I'd been so busy comforting Gia that I hadn't really had a

chance to fully process all my own emotions about that day. Before that fateful afternoon, I'd literally never heard, let alone seen, an actual gunshot. I'd been around guns, thanks to Giada's family, but they'd never actually been used in my presence. And now, well, now I'd witnessed a full on shoot-out. I'd watched multiple people get shot at and one man die. I could've been shot.

Fleetingly, I let myself consider what would've happened if I had been shot. How shocked would my parents have been to know their perfect son was even involved with thugs like the Contis? Was a non-fatal bullet wound as painful as it looked?

The other type of what-ifs—the ones filled with regret—were worse. What if we hadn't gone to the warehouse that day? What if Giada had questioned it when someone texted her from a blocked number and asked her to meet him at an abandoned warehouse? Sure, the person claimed to be her beloved brother, and yeah, the person knew Matteo had been shot.

But why the fuck did she just assume they were telling the truth? Why hadn't she called the number to hear her brother's voice? Why hadn't she confirmed the plan with her other brother, or father, or anyone? Why hadn't Enzo asked her more questions about our destination or motivation for going there? Why hadn't I?

Jesus. I knew Gia was gullible. She'd believe anything, no matter how implausible or unlikely, as long as it supported the narrative she'd created for her life where her family was normal, law-abiding, and good. Gia staunchly defended the goodness in everyone, even when life repeatedly proved her wrong.

But I didn't share her rose-colored glasses.

Before that day, I'd thought I was different — smarter, less naïve, maybe even savvy about the world. Clearly, I was wrong. I'd known for nearly a day that Gia believed Matteo had orchestrated some birthday surprise for her, and I hadn't checked into any of the logistics. Luca knew for a matter of minutes and somehow not only realized he needed to confirm the details but also figured out it was a setup and got there in time to save her.

Obviously, Gia's father had been right to push her into Luca's arms for her own safety. Luca may have been a bastard, but he was the one who kept her safe when it mattered. Not that I would have to send him a thank you card.

There was a knock on the door right as the tea kettle whistled. I switched off the burner before heading to the door. I peered into the peephole, then unlocked it to allow Giada's oldest brother to enter my apartment. At twenty-seven, Angelo was roughly two inches taller than me and maybe ten pounds heavier, but he was a hell of a lot more intimidating— even if you ignored his obvious mafia connections, as his sister tended to do. His eyes were alarmingly expressive, clearly displaying anger when he felt it but equally revealing of other, less frequently-harbored, emotions.

At the moment, he looked sad, tired, and worried. All of that contrasted sharply with his put-together appearance. He wore a tailored black suit and tie, fitting for the somber occasion.

"She's still a mess," I said, turning to pour the water into a mug for her. "I'm not sure it's good for her to go."

"She's not skipping it. It would be disrespectful."

Before I could decide if I had the balls to stand up to Angelo, Giada appeared in the doorway. "I'll be ready in fifteen minutes," she said to her brother, her tone apologetic.

He nodded and sat, uninvited, on my couch. I followed Giada towards the bathroom and handed her the mug of tea.

"Are you sure you're feeling up to this?"

"I need to be there," she replied.

"If you want me to go with you..." I began, uncertain of how I'd finish that sentence. The Conti family had already made it perfectly clear that they didn't think my presence at Giada's ex-boyfriend's funeral was a good idea. I supposed I could've waited in a car for her.

"The whole family will be there, Adrian. It's fine."

She shut the door in my face before I could protest further.

I reluctantly turned back to Angelo, who was eying me warily.

"She's been taking sleeping pills, and she has all these night-mares," I explained. "And she isn't eating."

"She'll eat when she's hungry."

I glanced at the bathroom, confirming the door was still shut, rendering Giada out of earshot. "She's always been frightened of Mr. Marino. You don't think he'll be upset that she's there, do you?"

"No one would expect her to miss this, and she'll be with me the entire time. And Matteo and our father and Lorenzo. She'll be fine."

I pursed my lips together in lieu of pointing out that nothing about Giada's current mindset was "fine." Maybe she wouldn't literally die today, but did her psychological health or mindset matter at all? Because that may never recover.

I couldn't help but wonder if Angelo subconsciously blamed his sister for what happened to Luca, or perhaps blamed me. In the immediate aftermath of the shooting, when Lorenzo had driven us directly to the Conti mansion, Giada had huddled in her bedroom with her mother. Her brothers, father, and uncle had all interrogated me. They didn't understand how I hadn't been suspicious of the text claiming to be from Matteo. I'd pointed out that they all seemed to change cell phones more often than most people and that it made sense for Matteo to have lost his phone when he was shot, but their questions remained legit. I should have at least called Matteo to confirm especially since Giada had asked her family not to make a big deal out of her birthday. Hindsight was always twenty-twenty, I supposed.

Angelo glanced up from his phone casually, as though just remembering something he'd forgotten. "The Marinos haven't decided how they'd like to handle the official side of all this, so don't say anything to anyone."

I nodded lamely, still traumatized from the way he'd barked the same order at me before, shortly after the horrific incident. Angelo had made it clear that Giada and I had never been to the docks that day, hadn't seen Luca or anyone else, and had no idea what had happened to him.

I wasn't well-versed in the ways of the mafia, but I did at least know they preferred to handle justice on their own, outside of the traditional, legal avenues. If Luca's father had involved the coroner rather than "handling" the body on his own, whatever that meant, I supposed there would have been an in-depth police investigation. Presumably, that would've made it harder for the Marino family to go after the perps themselves. And if the police actually caught the bad guys, it would likely be a challenge for the Marinos to exact their revenge on the guys in jail. Still, there were certain necessities they couldn't dodge.

"They'll have to get a death certificate, and then there will be questions," I said.

Angelo hissed in response, the look in his eyes almost making me wish I hadn't been born. "There's no body, no evidence anything happened at all, so no reason for a death certificate. If and when Mr. Marino wants things official, he can get it then."

"How do you explain the funeral?" Just because *I* didn't like the deceased didn't mean there wouldn't be a ton of other people mourning his passing. As befitting of someone with the nickname "the Prince," Luca had a following like true royalty.

"It's a memorial service. For Luca's uncle, Samuele. He passed several years ago, but the Marinos like to observe the anniversary of his death out of respect."

I started to open my mouth again, then stopped.

"If anyone asks you questions, play dumb. That shouldn't be hard for you, Patras. You haven't seen Luca. You don't know anything about him being dead. Can you handle that? Just keep your fucking mouth shut."

I nodded grimly.

Gia stepped out of the bathroom just then, having transformed herself in record time. Her hair was pulled into a tight bun and small diamond studs decorated her ears. She wore a simple black dress with no sleeves, but she'd wrapped a gauzy black scarf around the shoulders. The dress hung looser at the waist than it was intended, thanks to her avoidance of all nutrients the past several days. She wore a diamond bracelet and necklace, both of which I assumed were gifts from Luca, along with the earrings. Giada retrieved her phone off the counter, slipped it into a tiny black clutch, and wiggled her feet into a pair of black heels. Her brother stood and nodded to me before walking to the door.

I wanted to let her know I'd be thinking of her, or at least offer her some words of support or encouragement, but my mind was blank. There was no Hallmark card that said "I'm sorry your evil ex-boyfriend took a bullet for you and died." So instead, I just pulled her in for an awkward hug, kissed her forehead, then watched them leave along with two other men in suits who had been waiting outside my door.

~

Giada

I kept my head down as we entered the church, grateful for Matteo's firm grip on my arm. I wasn't certain my legs would support me otherwise. We made our way straight into a pew, and I stared directly at the back of the row in front of us, unwilling to glance around and greet people. Angelo shook many hands and expressed condolences to dozens of people before finally sitting on my other side.

It was rude for me not to at least offer sympathy to Luca's closest family and friends, but I just couldn't. My heart felt like it was breaking, and I was certain I'd forget to breathe if I lost focus on that for even a moment. Besides, I couldn't let myself cry. If I were to start, I might never be able to stop, and I had no right to mourn. There were people here who'd loved Luca in good times and bad; people who didn't assume the worst of him and leave him for another man; people whose last words to him hadn't been that they wished he were dead.

I couldn't listen to the priest as he spoke, but instead repeated the Lord's Prayer over and over in my head, squeezing my rosary so tightly that the beads left painful imprints on my fingers. When it was time for communion, my brothers both helped me up the aisle. As we returned to our seats, I caught a glimpse of Camilla Marino, and it was like a punch to the gut. I'd assumed Luca's mother would be distraught, but I'd never seen a person look so miserable. Beside her, Luca's father sat stone-like. As nearly everything his son achieved during life disappointed the man, it didn't surprise me to see him equally displeased with his son in death. While I viewed Luca's last act as brave and heroic, his father surely felt it proved Luca was weak, sacrificing his life for a woman who didn't even choose him.

Officially, no one was to know Luca was gone, but Matteo told me the Marinos didn't want anyone who actually knew Luca to question his passing. Knowing the sort of shit Luca and his family had been involved in, it seemed like they'd be better off letting their enemies think he was still alive and out to get him. Had I not witnessed the shooting and his last breaths, I would've happily entertained thoughts that this was all an elaborate ruse and that across the Atlantic, Luca was happily living out the rest of his days along the Amalfi Coast.

As it were, though, I couldn't even delude myself into imagining such an alternate reality, at least as long as the look of Luca's empty, lifeless eyes still pierced into my soul with every breath I took.

After the service, my father and Angelo went to the wake at the Marino's house, but Enzo drove Matteo and me back to Adrian's apartment. My brother offered to come in and stay for a while, but I declined. Adrian was home, so I wouldn't be alone, no matter how much I wanted to be. Besides, all I wanted to do was shower. I wanted to scrub at my skin with bar after bar of soap until I felt clean and blameless.

CHAPTER 2

Adrian

I didn't dare leave Giada alone the day after the funeral, but the following day, I had no choice. I had been set to start a new job at the public defender's office the prior week, and I couldn't postpone it longer. I'd blamed a family emergency for my absence since I couldn't exactly tell the truth without risking Angelo's wrath, but I couldn't keep up the ruse any longer.

I arranged for Giada's best friend, Gabriella, to come over and babysit while I worked. It wasn't that I worried Gia would try to hurt herself, but I just didn't have a good feeling about her current mood. From the moment I'd met Giada nearly two years prior, her optimism and perpetual perkiness were some of her defining characteristics. Even when faced with the normal type of college student stress, like finals, she approached the challenge with cheer.

So now, her unending moroseness was… unnerving, at best.

Gabriella texted me shortly after lunch, claiming Giada

kicked her out so she could nap, so I packed up as much stuff as I could in hopes of finishing my work from home.

As I approached my apartment, I noticed the door was cracked, with two men in suits standing in the entry. Based solely on the attire, I guessed they were associates of Marco or Angelo or some other random mobsters Giada knew, but I picked up my pace regardless. As I neared, it was obvious they weren't Italian.

I cleared my throat loudly, unable to enter with two strangers blocking my apartment. They turned to me hesitantly. Giada was visibly flustered but seemed relieved by my arrival.

"What's going on?" I asked.

"They're um…law enforcement. They had some questions for me," she said.

The men introduced themselves and quickly flashed badges, but I was too riveted by the fact that there were cops at the door to look too closely. I wasn't exactly sure how to recognize a true badge, either.

"Do you have a business card?" I asked.

The one who'd introduced himself as Martin Sedgewick frowned, but the other reached into his jacket pocket and handed me a small card identifying himself as Paul Kibbler, an agent with the F.B.I.

I stuck the card into my pocket without asking if I could keep it. Regardless of why they were here, it couldn't be good.

"And you are…?" Martin asked.

Not such a great investigator, I decided. "Adrian Patras. This is my apartment. What do you need?"

"We just had a few questions."

"Alright, well, this isn't really a good time. I have your card, so should we just call and make an appointment, or…"

Paul chuckled. "We really only needed Ms. Conti here. Can we come in?"

Gia stepped back to let them into the apartment, but I dashed through ahead of them, blocking the path so they could only step in a few inches.

"What are your questions about?"

"They're asking about Luca," she said.

"We understand you were involved romantically."

"Ages ago," I answered. "I don't think she'd have any information about him relevant to you now."

The men exchanged a glance.

"Perhaps we could speak with Ms. Conti alone," Martin said.

"Not in my apartment, you can't. I'm sure she does not recall anything relevant, but if you want her to make an appointment to go down to the station…" I stared at Gia while I spoke, hoping she was hearing my words, or at least the part about not remembering anything.

"When was your most recent conversation with Luca Marino?"

"I don't recall," she said after a pause.

I sighed with relief.

"When did you last see him?"

"I'm sure she doesn't recall that either," I hurriedly said.

She frowned but shook her head.

"We've heard rumors that he is deceased, but the official paperwork hasn't been filed."

Giada made a face like she was going to vomit.

"Why don't you go grab a drink of water?" I suggested to her before turning back to the men.

"You don't really think he's dead, do you?" I asked them.

Martin raised an eyebrow. "Your girlfriend attended his funeral earlier this week. Our detectives have photos of her at the cemetery."

"She attended a memorial for Luca's uncle. The man died years ago, though."

"No one has seen Mr. Marino for over a week now," Martin continued.

"He's back in Italy," Giada said, glancing at me as though ashamed for having kept that a secret.

"You're sure?"

Her shoulders bobbed. "I'm guessing. Or maybe somewhere else in Europe. He has an on-again-off-again sort of thing with some Swedish model."

Paul reached into his pocket and retrieved several photos. I recognized all of them as associates of Luca's. "Can you identify any of these men?"

Giada stared at the picture. "I think they look like some of Luca's friends, maybe."

"You don't know their names?"

She shrugged.

"Luca had a drug problem, right?"

Now Gia's reaction was genuine. "No. Not that I know of. He was too much of a control freak. I can't even imagine him ever trying drugs."

"Was?" Martin said.

I winced, having hoped he wouldn't pick up on her use of the past tense. "He probably still is, but since she hasn't seen him recently, how would she know?"

Martin rolled his eyes but Paul pushed onward with the questions. "You never saw him with drugs? Maybe for his friends?"

She shook her head.

"See any gambling or prostitution in that crowd?"

"Prostitution?" Her eyes widened further.

I couldn't tell now if she was faking ignorance now or truly shocked by the questions.

"Were you familiar with his dad, Salvatore Marino?"

"We met. He speaks Italian, and I don't. So I couldn't tell you much about him."

"But he and Luca were close, right?"

"Not as far as I know."

Martin looked dejected, but Paul remained determined.

"Your brothers—would you describe them as close to Luca?"

"Not particularly."

"They didn't get along?" Paul pressed.

Giada shrugged again. "I wouldn't say they were friends, but they got along fine."

"Speaking of her brothers, why don't you talk with them? Surely they recall more than Gia," I interrupted.

Martin gazed dryly at me, clearly onto my plan. "Her brothers are surprisingly difficult men to catch up with, as I'm sure you can imagine."

"I hadn't noticed." I pulled out my cellphone to check the time and contemplated calling Marco. "If that's all—"

"One more thing," Paul said. He pulled another photo out of his pocket. "I apologize for the graphic nature of this next picture, but I'm wondering if you could tell me if you've ever seen either of these men." He handed Giada a photo.

She gasped, and her eyes widened. She snatched the photo out of the man's hand as her jaw fell open.

I peered over at the photo and cringed, my heart dropping into my belly. The image was two men that I'd never forget—the ones who shot at Giada on her birthday. Except when I'd seen them last, they were running away. In this picture, they were both laid out side by side, a single bullet hole in each of their foreheads. I turned away from it quickly, biting my cheeks in a desperate attempt to keep my expression more neutral than Giada's.

Regardless of her oral answer, Gia had without a doubt conveyed to the agents that she recognized these men, she was glad they were dead, and she knew why they were dead.

"These men are dead?" she asked, her eyes not leaving the photo.

"Shot at point-blank, execution style."

Giada stared at the picture a moment longer. I reached to tug it out of her hands to return it to the men, but she clutched it tightly. I caught the pointed glance the agents exchanged.

"How old is this?" she asked.

"This photo was taken on Monday. Forensics estimated the deceased had passed about twelve hours prior," Paul said.

That sounded about right, I decided. I knew Giada was putting it together in her mind, too, the fact that her father lifted the security restrictions on her the day these men died, suddenly letting her come stay with me after insisting she remain at home the first few days.

"Cause of death wasn't the bullet to the brain, though," Martin said. "These men were suffocated. Judging from the traces of chemicals on their lips and in their lungs, their faces were coated with plastic wrap. Someone wanted them to watch them suffer."

I gazed to Gia, hoping to see some measure of disgust, but her expression remained neutral at best. A cynic might have even noticed a hint of a smile on her face.

"I don't know these men," she said abruptly, snapping out of her trance and returning the photo.

"You've never before seen them?" Paul asked.

"I see a lot of people, but I don't recall these two in particular."

"Don't know anyone who would want these men dead?"

"No," Gia said. "If I had to guess, I'd say they probably weren't good men, and bad men tend to have a lot of enemies."

Paul tucked the photos back into the pocket of his suit coat. "I bet you're right," he said. "We handle a lot of murder investigations, and the victim is rarely a good man."

If that dig offended Gia, she didn't show it.

I held my breath until the men were out of my apartment and the door was safely locked behind them. I turned to Gia, ready to comfort her and rehash the entire interrogation, but she simply walked away.

"I'm tired. I'm going to lay down," she said.

I opened my mouth to say something, but by the time the

words came to me, she'd already closed the bedroom door behind her. "I'm gonna call your dad, just to give him a heads up," I called through the closed door.

She didn't respond. I shuddered, thinking of the picture of those men. Sure, I was relieved to know they wouldn't come after Gia again. Obviously, I didn't think they were good guys, either, but the details about the plastic wrap…well, that was too much for me. I didn't have the stomach for torture, and I never would've guessed Gia did either. But now, I wasn't so certain.

~

Giada

With Adrian back at work, I had no distractions to fill my days, so I spent my time at church. It had always been the place I'd go for comfort, and I needed it now more than ever. Over the years, I'd found a church home wherever I needed it—in Italy, in my small college town, even in Staten Island near Luca's family home. One of the most comforting aspects of the church was that it wasn't dependent on the physical building or location or even the language of the service. The general trappings of the mass were always the same, and that predictability housed a magical soothing quality for me. But even outside of mass, simply sitting in a sanctuary, my rosary beads in hand, calmed me regardless of where I was or what had happened.

Since Luca's funeral, though, I hadn't found that tranquility, even for a moment. I kept returning to the church in search of even a hint of inner peace, but all I felt was resentment. The questions with no answers haunted me. *Why Luca? Why now?*

None of it made sense. Obviously, God was punishing me. I wasn't sure exactly what crime I'd committed, but it probably had to do with the way I'd flitted selfishly back and forth between

Adrian and Luca. Now, I was destined to spend the rest of my life overwhelmed with guilt.

I couldn't even pinpoint the strongest source of my guilt. There was the obvious—the fact that my stupidity literally brought on Luca's death. I mean, if I hadn't been so gullible as to show up to the docks that day, he'd still be alive. Or was my stubbornness more to blame? If I'd actually answered the phone that day, he could've warned me before either of us was in danger. Instead, I'd assumed he was just stalking me. Hubris, therefore, was at fault.

Luca hadn't been a saint by any means; he had more than his fair share of sins to justify his fate, but I couldn't shake the feeling that it had something to do with me, in the greater scheme of things. If he'd died in any other way—doing anything but saving my life—I could've accepted that God was punishing him, and not me. But as it was…

Compounding my guilt was the timing of it all. To a casual onlooker, it would seem like it should be easier for me to get over Luca since we weren't together. But instead, that made everything a million times worse. Now, I felt like I was betraying Adrian every second I mourned Luca. But I also realized the magnitude of Luca's final act was even grander because we weren't together when he made the ultimate sacrifice for me. I'd chosen Adrian, and still, Luca was willing to die for me.

It was all maddening.

I had no answers; only questions. And after a lifetime of trying to be a loyal servant to my God, I deserved an explanation. I fully intended to sit in a pew day after day until I got the answers. He owed me.

Adrian

I hadn't been in the best mood when I arrived, but somehow after one drink with Ryan, I felt better. We talked about work, classes, and sports, but when our second round of drinks arrived, there was a natural lull in the conversation.

"I have to get home after this one," I said. "Giada's all alone at the apartment."

Ryan grinned and wiggled his eyebrows. "Yeah, I get it. I'd ditch you, too, if I had a hot girl waiting in my apartment for me."

"No, it's not like that," I assured him, shaking my head. Ryan gave me a funny look, and I realized instantly what he must be thinking.

I blew out a sigh, cringing. "It should be like that, but um…" I didn't know how to explain everything with Luca without breaking any of Angelo's rules. "She's not in a good place right now."

"How so?"

"Well, you know her ex? You met him here one night."

Ryan nodded. "Yeah, kind of hard to forget him. Thick accent, pompous ass, told you he was going to propose?"

"Right, that's the guy. Anyway, he did propose, and she said yes, but then she told me it was really just to appease her family, and she didn't really intend to ever marry him, but I don't know."

"Well, she left him for you, right? So clearly, she wasn't that into him."

"Yeah. I mean, he cheated on her. She finally realized what kind of a man he was, so thankfully, he's out of her life for good." I paused, catching my breath and then taking a long swig of my beer to buy more time. "Everything was going well with us, but then her ex had this accident, and now she feels really horrible. It wasn't her fault, but she thinks everyone blames her, and she's dealing with a lot of guilt."

"What do you mean accident? Like what kind of accident? Is he okay?"

I reached for my beer again, avoiding eye contact. "I don't know details. He's, um, definitely out of the picture for good now. Back in Italy or something, I guess, so she won't ever see him again."

"Isn't that a good thing?"

I nodded. "For sure, but I think she wanted it to be her choice, not something unavoidable. Anyway, her family has been through a lot lately too, and so she's just really stressed. Giada's usually this happy, optimistic person who just makes everything more fun, but now, she's just...not herself."

Ryan wrinkled his nose. "I'm sorry, man. That sucks. You finally got the girl you wanted all to yourself, and now she's not the same girl."

My lips parted as I cocked my head to the side. Somehow, he'd just identified my precise problem, even though I hadn't even been able to fully disclose all the facts. "Yes, exactly. I just...I keep telling myself I should be happy. I got everything I've ever wanted, but I don't feel that way."

"I get it. We want what we can't have. Once we get it, we miss the fun of the chase."

"I don't think that's it."

He shrugged.

"Although, maybe it is, for her. I guess I'll never really understand how the same woman who claims to love me could ever see anything redeemable in him. That jerk and I had nothing in common."

"Yeah, sounds like she just couldn't let go of the history she had with him. Hopefully things are back to normal with you guys soon," Ryan said.

I nodded and patted him on the shoulder blade as I stood. We headed out in different directions, and I started off at a fairly quick clip.

My gait slowed as I neared my apartment, a fact that filled me with immense guilt. I loved Giada more than I'd ever loved anyone. I should be excited to return home to her. Instead, I dreaded it. She was miserable, still. Everything I said or did to try to make her feel better only made it worse.

After the first few days, when she'd alternated between sleeping and sobbing, I'd been so desperate for a change in her demeanor. I'd soon gotten my wish, since now Gia never cried or showed any emotion whatsoever. Except, the joke was on me. Seeing her so filled with hurt—but now simply hiding it from me —was worse.

Giada barely resembled the woman I'd fallen for. What had attracted me to her initially was her positivity, the carefree happiness with which she faced every challenge. Sure, she'd been naïve when we met, but she'd also been optimistic and content.

Now she'd lost the naivete and her joy for life, but instead of admitting it, she put on a mask. She didn't cry when I was home, but she also didn't smile, sleep, or eat. The sparkle was gone from her dark brown eyes, and instead of letting me close enough to see, she just pushed me away.

I wanted her to believe she could trust me enough to support her through her sorrow. Hell, *I* wanted to believe I could do that. But I struggled because the man she was mourning was the precise man who tore us apart time and time again. Now, even in death, he was manipulating Gia.

The apartment was silent as I turned my key, and for a brief moment, I considered that maybe she wasn't home. Maybe she was still at church, where she'd been spending most of her days.

I peered into the living room to see Giada seated on the couch with her feet tucked under her and a book in her hand. Her gaze was fixed on the window across the room, just above the book. I couldn't help but wonder how long she'd been frozen in that pose.

I bent over to kiss her head, and she reached up her hand, softly touching my cheek without turning to me.

"I'll make you some tea," I said, slipping out of my shoes and heading into the kitchen. "What sounds good for dinner?" I asked, fully cognizant of the futility of my question. Whatever I made, she'd poke at it, take maybe two bites, then praise my cooking before pushing the plate to the side.

"I made soup," she said.

My cellphone slid right out of my hand at the unexpected statement. Surely the fact that she was cooking was a good sign. I filled the kettle and ignited the burner to heat water for her tea, then glanced in the gently simmering pot. I knew without asking that it was minestrone, as that was virtually the only thing other than pasta that Gia could cook.

I popped the cap off a beer, swallowing two large mouthfuls before even shutting the fridge. Then I tossed a tea bag into a mug while I waited for the water to boil. I'd drained my entire beverage by the time Gia's was ready.

I sat beside her on the couch, forcing the tea into her hand since I doubted she'd drink it otherwise.

"You didn't have to cook," I said.

"I bought some bread, too."

"Sounds good. How are you feeling today?"

"Fine."

She hadn't touched the tea, and her eyes remained fixed on the window. Nothing about her was "fine."

"Gia," I began tentatively, terrified of making things worse. "I love having you here, but without a job or any friends or family in town, I'm worried you'll get lonely or bored with me working all day."

She turned abruptly to face me. "You want me to get a job?"

My lips parted at her unintended interpretation of my statement. She was in no condition to work right now. "I want you to be happy, and sitting around here isn't helping."

She nodded, then glanced down at her hands, seeming surprised to see the mug.

"What if you moved back home for a little while? It might be comforting to have all that activity in your old house and to see everyone. You and I could still talk every night, and then on the weekends, we can spend every minute together."

Gia's eyes flitted shut as she sipped her tea. I held my breath as I awaited her response.

"Okay," she said. "You might be right."

I exhaled the tension that had accumulated. "I want you back here as soon as you're feeling like yourself again," I said.

She nodded then turned back to the window. "I bought some bread to go with the soup," she said.

I sighed, tugged the book out of her hands, and began telling her about my day, certain she wasn't hearing a word of it.

CHAPTER 3

Giada

Gabriella, my best friend since freshman Italian class at the university, came along to help me with the move. Well, technically, my aunts unpacked everything and recreated my childhood room in a matter of hours while I dozed on a lounge chair by the pool, but Gabby tagged along as emotional support. She herself was moving to New York City in a matter of days to begin her life as an actual adult, so it was our last time together for a while.

We spent the afternoon in the pool, with Matteo joining us for a bit. It was nice to have a distraction, even if the sight of my brother flirting with my best friend was more than a little nause-ating. Gabby joined the family for dinner, and then we retreated to my bedroom and changed into pajamas.

"So now that we're alone, will you tell me how you're really doing?" she asked, smoothing a blue corn facial mask across her cheekbones and forehead.

I rinsed the residue of my own mask off my fingers and dried my hands on a fluffy pink towel that reminded me of cotton candy. I set the timer on my phone so we'd know when to rinse, then made my way back into the bedroom. I curled up on the chaise beside the bed, and Gabby followed suit, plopping onto the side of the bed.

"Well, let's see. I graduated college but have no job prospects. My best friend is headed to NYC to pursue her dreams, and I just moved back home into a room that looks like it was designed for a third grader. My whole family treats me like a child. Oh, and my fiancé is dead."

Gabriella frowned and slowly opened her mouth. "Ex-fiancé," she said hesitantly.

"Shit," I mumbled, hiding my face against the grey pillow on the chaise. "Shit!" I said again, louder, as the blue residue of my mask stained the expensive fabric.

Gabby stood, scurrying into the bathroom with the pillow. When she returned a moment later, a damp but clean spot was the only remnant of my mistake.

I willed myself not to cry, certain that would cause my face to melt all over the entire piece of furniture and not just the pillow.

"So... things not going well with Adrian?" she asked.

I shrugged. "I don't even know. He was so great to take me back after I'd picked Luca over him. I mean, I am the luckiest girl alive to have a man like that. But now..."

"Luca was a big part of your life for a long time. It's natural for you to be upset. Adrian understands that."

I nodded, because she was right. Adrian was the most understanding boyfriend there ever was. The more I screwed up, the more perfect he became. In that way, he was the opposite of Luca. Well, in most ways, actually, they were polar opposites.

Not that any of that mattered now.

"It didn't feel right to be sleeping beside one man and crying over another."

"That's why you came back home?"

I nodded. "Well, that and I had no reason to stay on campus.

Adrian started a new job, so he's busy. I'm not in school anymore, I don't have any friends there anymore, and I don't have a job there."

"You could come with me to New York. You know I was serious about that."

"You have a roommate."

"I could use another."

I rolled my eyes. "I hardly believe sharing a bed with your college roommate is how you imagined your start in the big city."

"We're sharing a bed tonight."

"That's different," I said, opting not to remind her of how tiny her bed in the city was in comparison to my king-sized bed. "And what happens when you want a guy to sleep over?"

"There aren't any hot guys in New York," she replied with a grin.

I laughed. After dating the same guy for the majority of our sophomore and junior years at college, Gabriella had ended the relationship, gone on a few dates, then become incredibly picky about men. She said she was done settling and that she didn't want to waste any more time with someone who wasn't The One, but I couldn't help but wonder if she was just hung up on someone else.

I didn't want to push it. "I'd feel bad dragging Enzo to New York."

"It's too bad you couldn't just date him," Gabby said. "Then you wouldn't feel like you were putting him out whenever your dad made him follow you everywhere."

It took nearly a full minute after the words left her mouth before she cringed, clearly having momentarily forgotten the little incident nearly two years ago where I'd almost hooked up with Enzo.

"Shit, I'm sorry, Giada. I didn't mean to bring that up. I just meant, well, he is hot. Maybe *I* should date him?"

I giggled and swung the still-damp pillow at her. The timer

went off then, so we took a break in the conversation to finish our spa-like skincare ritual.

"You do have a license, don't you?" she asked suddenly, once we'd returned to my room.

"Yeah. I mean, I did. It may have expired. I could count on one hand the number of times I've ever driven myself somewhere."

"That's so weird."

"A lot of people in the Big Apple have drivers."

"You're in Connecticut. And in the suburbs."

I shrugged. She was right. The only reason I had a driver was because my father wanted me to have a babysitter.

"Lots of people don't start working right after graduation, and lots of people live at home for a while. Your brothers both still live here," Gabby reminded me. "But if you want to feel more independent, maybe get Enzo to give you a driving refresher, and then convince your dad to let you drive yourself. You'll feel less like a child if you're at least able to handle your own transportation to visit Adrian and me."

She was right. I hated feeling like a burden to everyone around me. I understood that my father did have legitimate concerns about my safety, but the life I was leading didn't feel worthy of the sacrifices everyone around me had to make. It was past time for me to go out on my own.

~

Adrian

Waking up alone and seeing Giada's side of the bed completely untouched immediately jogged my memory about her moving back home. I missed the immense warmth that always emanated from her and the adorable squeaky groans she made as she stretched first thing in the morning. But I also felt immeasurable relief. I'd been walking on eggshells—to no avail—since Luca's death, and it was exhausting. As much as I couldn't believe I'd helped Giada move out of my apartment—after over a year of pining over her and doing everything I could to bring her closer to me—I felt lighter as I stepped out of bed.

With no one around to offend by appearing happy, I blasted upbeat music as I dressed, shaking my hips as I flipped my veggie omelet onto a plate, then caught up on email while I ate. I'd applied to serve as a research assistant to another professor at the school, having way too much guilt over the crap Giada's family had forced me to pull with the last professor I worked for to keep up that gig. While the workload was somewhere between minimal and nonexistent over the summer, I didn't want to slack, so I made a point to stay on top of all communications in case he needed something.

I rolled into the public defender's office a half-hour early, making a point to ensure my boss noted my early arrival. I'd always been a hard worker, but thanks to Luca's untimely sacrifice, I'd missed the majority of my first week of work and cut many workdays short the second week. Now, I was determined to make up for lost time and establish my reputation. Even though my dad was also an attorney, I didn't want to ride on his connections. And I sure as shit didn't want any "help" from Gia's dad. No, I wanted to make my own way in this world.

Having spent the previous summer at the prosecutor's office, I went into this job skeptical. Yeah, I knew the accused had a right to counsel, but from what I'd seen on the other side of the courtroom, the deck was already stacked against law and order. Besides, if everything with Luca and Giada's family was any indication, the criminals of this world were doing just fine fending for themselves.

Still, even if I ultimately returned to work for the good guys after graduation, it couldn't hurt to have some experience defending criminal matters. And at least while I was here, there was nothing Marco Conti could ask me to do to muddle with a case.

I took the long route back to my apartment after work, having nothing to rush home to. Torrential rain was forecasted for later, but at the moment, it was a gorgeous evening, with the temperature cooler than the past several days thanks to the storm blowing in. As I neared campus, I spotted a food truck. I ordered the ancho beef street tacos, and after a short wait, I walked around the corner to sit on a bench and eat. I was about to tuck into the third and final taco when a musty smell overwhelmed my nostrils. I turned in the direction of the offending odor and jumped so high I nearly dropped my taco.

The animal standing before me looked like a cross between a German shepherd and a coyote. Its matted fur was the color of sludge, and in some places, full patches were missing. I prepared myself for an attack since the beast must be suffering from rabies or some parasite, but instead, it calmly sat in front of me and angled its head up. I could make out gentle brown eyes beneath tufts of fur and a small pink snout that twitched as it leaned closer to my dinner.

Sighing, I reached my hand out and stroked the pet's head. His tail thumped cheerfully in response, so I extended the foil packet containing the taco. I expected the animal to wolf the food and scamper off, but instead, he gazed from the taco to me and back again.

"Go on, you can have it," I said, my tone light and encouraging. The dog began to chew, so delicately devouring the dinner that I laughed out loud. "You're a scruffy thing, aren't you?"

When it finished eating, it remained at my feet, gazing at me expectantly. I checked for a collar but wasn't surprised when I found none. I walked back towards the food truck, and the dog followed. The man working the counter chuckled when he spotted us.

"Let me guess. He tricked you out of some of your dinner?"

I nodded. "Yeah, but it's fine. Do you know if he has an owner?"

The guy shook his head. "Naa, definitely a stray."

I checked my phone for contact info for the nearest animal shelter and dialed, but of course, they were closed until the following morning. As I slid my phone back into my pocket, a few drops of cool rain splashed my arm.

"Well, that's my cue to head home," I said to the dog, raising my gaze to the sky, which had filled with dark, menacing clouds just waiting to explode. I started towards my apartment, and the dog followed. Right as I reached the door, a clap of thunder shook the world, and then the rain burst free of the clouds in massive, hard sheets.

I wasn't sure about my apartment's pet policy, but I wasn't about to leave the poor creature shivering on my doorstep during that storm.

"One night won't hurt anything," I said, motioning for the dog to follow me inside.

~

Giada

*G*abby stayed for three nights before heading out to New York. I promised to give her a week to get settled and adjust to her new job, and then I'd come visit. In the meantime, I broached the topic of driving myself with my father. To my surprise, he was more receptive than I'd anticipated. I'd noticed that over the past week, security had thinned up around our house, and the mood had lightened considerably. I assumed that was because Luca's killers had been caught, but I couldn't actually bring myself to ask or to mention the photo the detectives had shown me.

Matteo was the one to assume the role of driving instructor, and while he feigned terror at my driving ability, I was impressed with how much I'd retained over the years during which I'd rarely used my driving skills.

A little over a month after my twenty-second birthday, my father presented me with a belated gift—a dark metallic blue Audi. I wasn't a car expert, but I couldn't have been more thrilled with the present—and what it symbolized. I wondered if my father would pay someone to follow me the first few times I drove, but really, I didn't care.

My first trip in my new car was to visit Adrian. I'd hoped that the time apart would've given me a chance to fully process every-thing that had happened and return to the way things used to be with Adrian, but of course, it didn't. For some reason, being with Adrian made me feel the absence of Luca more acutely. It didn't help that he'd brought home some mangey mutt. He claimed to have given it a bath, but the whole apartment stunk like the animal, although that could have been the random spots of urine it left on the carpet.

"You're going to lose your security deposit," I told him.

"I'll have the carpets cleaned before I move out anyway. And it's just until the shelter has an opening," he insisted. He explained that the local animal shelter had reached capacity, probably thanks to its staunch "no-kill" stance. They'd added this grotesque monster to the wait list and promised they would find it a home if Adrian could just "foster" it until they had room.

It all sounded shady.

"You have to admit he's sweet," Adrian said, letting it crawl between us on the couch.

The only thing I appreciated about the mutt was that it offered a nice distraction from how awkward things had become between Adrian and me. I wrinkled my nose and then yawned, feigning sleepiness to escape the fur monster. At least Adrian wasn't letting it into the bedroom with us.

I did my best to pretend nothing was wrong, to act the part of the loving girlfriend the full weekend I spent with him, but when I returned home on Sunday, I couldn't ignore the overwhelming relief I'd felt.

I visited Gabriella that week, but when my father insisted Enzo drive me, I hadn't resisted. Even though it was only an hour-long drive, I wasn't eager to assume the stress that came with navigating big city streets, let alone finding parking in Brooklyn. And since they'd let me drive myself back to campus, I at least knew they had some faith in me. I spent two nights with Gabby, but felt much as I had with Adrian. I assumed it was because of the history New York held for Luca and me. He'd grown up in the city and lived there during much of our relationship. We'd gotten engaged in New York, too. Everything about the city reminded me of him.

When I returned home, my parents encouraged me to head to Italy for the rest of the summer. The notion repulsed me. I claimed it was because I didn't want to leave Adrian, but in reality, it had nothing to do with Adrian and everything to do with Luca. If the memories of Luca were plentiful in New York, they'd be smothering in Italy. In fact, I didn't have a single adult memory in Italy that wasn't inextricably woven together with Luca.

That left me with one option, wandering my childhood home day in and day out. I loosely considered different career options, but nothing spoke to me. I was rudderless, but I had no clue how to fix it. Besides, I was still in mourning. Some days, I tried to hide it, but other times, I flaunted it as an excuse to wallow in my solitude. The family tolerated my moroseness, but that wouldn't continue indefinitely. At some point, they'd expect me to perk up and rejoin the functioning, productive members of society.

In the meantime, I opted to take a nap.

When I awoke from my nap, the house was eerily quiet. Generally, the rooms were bustling with activity, and thanks to the absence of carpeting anywhere on the first floor, most noises echoed and resonated throughout the entire home. I rubbed my bleary eyes, then started down the stairs, bracing myself to hear that some new tragedy had occurred. As I approached my father's office, I heard whispers and giggling.

I paused by the door, not recognizing the voices, then peered inside. There, beside my father's desk, stood Angelo. The doorway was just to the side of his line of sight, so he could've seen me, except his attention was fully focused on a woman. Her back was to me, but I felt confident I'd never seen her before. She was tall, though still several inches shorter than my brother, and her hair was pulled into a low ponytail that reminded me of a bundle of straw.

Angelo said something else to her, and while I couldn't decipher his quiet words, I could see the way his eyes lit up. I'd never seen my brother look so peaceful or happy. It was weird and unsettling.

The woman laughed again, then pawed at his chest with atrociously fake nails.

Everything about the scene nauseated me, but as I was about to walk away and let them enjoy their privacy, I heard the woman speak.

I couldn't hear the whole sentence, but there was no mistaking it when the words "Luca Marino" slipped through her thin lips.

I cleared my throat loudly, acting on pure emotion.

Angelo dropped her hand and turned abruptly, looking like a kid caught with his hand in the cookie jar.

"Giada! What are you doing?" he asked, stepping in front of the woman. "I thought you were napping."

I didn't answer his question, certain we both knew he was the one who had more explaining to do. I also didn't ask why he was in our father's office or who the hussy by his side was. Instead, I skipped directly to what I wanted to know.

"What about Luca?"

Angelo frowned and shook his head. I continued before he had a chance to disgrace himself by offering a lie.

"I heard her say his name."

Angelo blew out a sigh and glanced at his lady friend. "Giada, this is Julia."

She stepped closer and smiled, offering her hand towards me. "Your brother has told me a lot about you. It's a pleasure to finally meet you."

My hands remained pinned at my side. "Why were you talking about Luca?" I repeated.

My brother shot an apologetic glance to Julia then crossed the room to me. He tapped my bicep and nudged me out of the room and down the hall till we reached the kitchen.

"What is wrong with you?" he asked.

"Me? I asked you a straightforward question, and you can't seem to answer."

"That was rude. Julia was only being polite."

"I don't give a fuck about Julia. I want to know why you were talking about Luca."

Angelo's jaw tightened so abruptly that I stepped backwards, flinching in anticipation of the blow that never came.

"I was telling Julia that business has been going well. She suggested that perhaps it had to do with the Marinos no longer carrying on business here."

"Why would that have anything to do with it?"

"It doesn't."

I frowned. "Don't treat me like an idiot, Angelo. I know our fathers did business together."

"If the Marinos had been competitors, then having them out of the picture would've been good for business. But they weren't. That wasn't how things worked between our families. Julia just didn't understand that, and if you hadn't barged in and started interrogating us, I could've explained that to her."

"Why would you explain anything about our family or Luca to that woman? Are you sleeping with your secretary now?"

"Julia isn't my secretary. She's my girlfriend."

"Since when?"

He flung his hands in the air. "February."

I felt my jaw drop. My brother had a girlfriend for six months and hadn't bothered to tell me?

He ran his fingers over his short, dark hair.

"There was never a good time to tell you. You were upset about breaking up with Adrian, then with Luca. Then you were engaged... I didn't want to take the attention away from you when you were happy, and I didn't want to rub it in your face when you were going through a breakup."

I shook my head, still frowning so hard it made my eyebrows ache. I understood why he hadn't mentioned it the past month. I hadn't exactly been in a position to appreciate, or even tolerate, other people's joy since Luca was killed, but before that?

"I don't like her," I said, almost embarrassed by the petulance of my tone.

"I don't care if you like her or not, but you will treat her with respect."

"Or what?"

"Giada—"

We both turned towards a sudden noise behind us. Enzo stepped in through the back patio door, then froze like a deer in headlights, clearly aware he'd walked into something tense.

"Is there something urgent?" Angelo asked, his tone clipped.

Enzo shook his head. "No, I just...no."

"Leave us, please." Angelo barked.

I shot Enzo a look, pleading with him to stay, but he quickly let himself back out the door, leaving me alone with Angelo.

"Giada, you had a chance to really help this family with the Marinos, but the way you handled things with Luca... you have no right to be sad now. You left Luca, for Adrian, of all people."

He shook his head as though my behavior disgusted him. "So I'm a little sick of you moping around here like you're somehow the victim in all of this. We've given you more than enough leeway. I, for one, am done walking on eggshells around you just because you're pissed that you no longer have two men fighting for your attention while you walk all over them."

I opened my mouth to say something but no words came out.

"And I see how Dad is wrapped around your little finger, but he's not going to be in charge forever and if you expect to mooch off this family for the rest of your life, you better shape up and treat me with some respect. You're not a little princess anymore and without Luca here, there's no one left to treat you that way."

"Fuck you!" I spit at him, so wrapped up in my own anger that I didn't even realize I'd also slapped him until my palm began stinging with pain.

Angelo's hand rose to his cheek while his other fingers clenched in a fist. I braced myself, fully expecting him to retaliate. He had when we were kids, and there were countless times I worried he'd actually kill me before Matteo or one of my uncles stepped in and dragged us apart.

"Giada Francesca Conti, that is the last time you will lay a hand on me. Do you understand?" He paused but fortunately, wasn't delusional enough to think I'd really respond with anything but the middle finger. "If you can't grow up and treat me with the respect I deserve, you will be leaving for Italy with Zia Sofia this weekend."

"You can't banish me."

"I can, and I will. Don't test me."

I held my breath, certain he meant every word and not doubting his ability to follow through with the threat. Still, that didn't mean I was going to relent.

"You've been dying for a chance to get rid of me since we were little," I finally said. "And don't worry, I'm moving to New

York next week. I was waiting to tell you all until I'd worked out all the details, but now you can start the celebration."

"You are not moving to New York."

I rolled my eyes. "Don't tell me that isn't far enough."

His glare deepened, his features tightening.

"And while we're on the topic of Luca, I understand your little girlfriend may not have meant anything by her comment about Luca, but don't think for a moment I'm oblivious to the way you reacted to his death."

"What are you talking about?"

"You've always been jealous of him, and me. If I'd married Luca, I could've done more for this family in one hour than you'll do your entire life. And you will never be half the man he was."

Angelo's fingers clenched my arm so tightly that I had to bite my lip to avoid crying out.

"Enough," he said, the look in his eyes terrifyingly cold. "Something has to change, and it isn't going to be me."

There was another noise at the backdoor as Enzo reappeared. From the frantic look on his face, it was apparent he'd been watching us through the window. The poor guy was probably panicking trying to envision telling our dad that one of his children had killed the other.

"Giada, can I borrow you for a minute?" he asked timidly, addressing me but looking at my brother for permission.

Angelo's grip tightened even further for a moment, and then he released me with an abrupt shove. He didn't answer Enzo but stalked out of the room.

I flipped my finger up to his back as he walked away. Enzo nudged my hand down to my side with a stern warning glance.

"You okay?" he asked as soon as Angelo was out of earshot.

"Terrific," I snarled, gently massaging the purple bruises that already circled my arm like a bracelet. "Was anyone going to tell me Angelo had a girlfriend?"

Enzo shrugged. "I'm surprised you hadn't already figured it

out. It's the first time since I've known Angelo that I've ever seen him happy."

"Yeah, well, if that's what my brother is like when he's happy, remind me not to piss him off."

Enzo laughed, and I followed him outside.

We walked around the property for the better part of an hour. I appreciated Enzo's company, but I was more grateful that he didn't try to talk. I needed the silence, needed to think more than anything.

Angelo was right. Something had to change. Avoiding everything that reminded me of Luca wasn't working. If I was ever going to heal my heart and move on, I needed a different approach. I needed to fully immerse myself in my memories of him, to encounter it all head-on and either let it kill me, or fight through it and come out stronger. I needed to find that cabin we'd visited together.

CHAPTER 4

Giada

The next day, the sun shone brightly and the celadon sky lacked a single cloud, yet I shivered as I approached the cabin. Objectively, nothing had changed. The symmetrical log structure still stood proud, though dwarfed by its surroundings. Subjectively, though, it was night and day. Before, the cabin represented pure joy. The time I'd spent there with Luca remained some of the best of my life, and since then, I'd associated the cabin with happiness, serenity, and peace. Now, I felt nothing but sorrow and regret as I gazed upon it.

I pressed the button to lock the car out of habit, even though there wasn't another soul for miles. I'd left my purse on the leather seat but clutched my phone in my hand. I approached slowly, surprised by how loudly the gravel crunched beneath my feet. Before, when I'd been here with Luca, I hadn't noticed the silence. Now, aside from the occasional bird chirping, there was only me—my ragged breath, my clothing rustling, my shoes snapping twigs and crumbling old leaves.

My eyes locked on the porch swing and my breath caught in

my throat. I could still see Luca there, squinting against the sunlight, smiling and waving as I approached. I remembered snuggling against him as the sun dipped beneath the horizon, talking for hours about everything we could have done, would have done, in our alternate reality. I smelled the pancakes we burned, tasted the spiked cider on his lips, felt the scratchy wool of the blanket he draped over me.

A loud thunk snapped me out of my thoughts, and as I bent to collect the cell phone I'd dropped, I realized my cheeks were damp. I wiped my tears and walked closer, gripping the splintered rail as I climbed the steps onto the porch. Bracing myself for the onslaught of memories that were sure to assault me the moment I stepped inside, I paused with my hand on the doorknob. I turned it slowly, then stopped.

It was locked.

Of course it was locked. What had I expected? Luca may have trusted me with his deepest secret, but he had not left me a key. I crept around to the window, rising onto my toes to peer inside. I assumed I'd find cobwebs guarding the window, but there were none. Everything appeared well preserved and tidy. The lighting made it hard to see detail inside, but from what I could observe, the cabin was doing just fine. A blanket lay across the sofa, and a book was open on the coffee table. The kitchen area was even harder to see, but I could've sworn dishes filled the sink. It was almost as if someone was still there.

A bird squawked in the distance, and I flew back from the window, scanning my surroundings. What if I wasn't alone? What if someone else was out here?

I focused on my breathing and shook my head. Obviously, no one else was here. The cabin was as close to the middle of nowhere as one could go, and if I was the only living person who knew about it, well, I was alone. I'd known there was a chance I'd get creeped out when I arrived, but I'd felt compelled to come check it out anyway.

I still had no clue what to do about it all, though. Should I tell Mr. Marino? I figured he was legally entitled to the property now, but morally, I suspected that violated Luca's wishes the most. It didn't feel right to keep it as my own either, especially since I didn't have a key.

Who would have the key anyway? I assumed Luca's parents had gone through his belongings, but would they think anything at all of a random key amidst all worldly possessions? Why hadn't Luca devised some plan for what would happen to his things if he were gone?

I gritted my teeth, annoyed at myself for even wondering that. I knew why, because twenty-four-year-olds didn't write wills. How was he to know he'd be shot? He just woke up, expecting another boring day, maybe looking forward to a drink with Alessio in the evening, wondering who would win the soccer match, and then bam! It all ended in one explosive bang.

My tears were falling freely, and I was too upset to drive, but I couldn't stand by the cabin either. The quiet was too oppressive now, the cabin too empty, and the trees too spooky. I made my way around the back of the cabin, walking towards the clearing. I couldn't picture the route in my head, but my body clearly remembered as I ended up right where I'd hoped to after several minutes of walking. I stood at the top of the hill, gazing down at the trees and feeling so utterly small in the grand scheme of things. And then I turned back to the woods and walked down towards the stream.

It was cooler surrounded by trees, and a symphony of bugs and woodland critters filled the air with calming sounds. I spotted a boulder by the water and brushed it off before sitting. It had been a dry week, so the creek was shallow and relatively still, but the sight of the water soothed me.

I jammed my phone in my pocket and cried until I had nothing left to release. Then, suddenly exhausted, I slumped over my legs, resting my forehead on my arms.

I entertained fleeting thoughts of a wandering hunter mistaking me for a deer, or worse yet, some total psycho stumbling onto me by luck, but I was too tired to care. I didn't fall asleep, but I stayed there, my eyes squeezed shut, until my thoughts stilled to a beautiful nothing.

Suddenly, a stick snapped, and terror filled my limbs. I opened my eyes with dread, painfully aware I was not alone.

"Giada? What are you doing here?"

I flew to my feet and turned towards the voice, equally terrified and soothed by its familiarity. I was no less conflicted by what I saw. Either I was hallucinating or Luca had a twin, because less than five yards away stood his clone.

I squeezed my eyes shut and opened them repeatedly, trying to clear my vision. The man walked closer, his face as confused and conflicted as I suspected mine was. It was too real to be a hallucination. It had to be...

"Luca?" My voice came out as barely a croak, so I hardly recognized that I had even spoken.

"Yeah," he said. "It's me."

In an instant, the trees swayed around me, the crickets' chirps increased to a roar, and then everything went black.

Luca

*D*eath was too good for me, I supposed. In the moments that passed right before that monster shot at Giada, a lifetime of regrets flashed by my eyes. I hated myself for the countless times I'd hurt her, and somehow, even saving her life hadn't seemed like enough to make it up to her.

When I'd woken, later, and realized my body had technically survived, it wasn't hard for my father to convince me to pretend otherwise. I couldn't possibly live, even for a few hours, without undoing any redemption I'd earned with Giada for blocking the bullets. It was better this way, to go out on a high note. And by the time I made my return, if ever, she'd be settled once and for all with Adrian. Or maybe even some other guy who was a decent, good person like Adrian but decidedly less annoying and pretentious.

There was considerable freedom that came with death, but also, especially after the first few weeks, immense boredom. Always a man of action, thinking had never been my strong suit. But now, I had nothing but time to think. A fair portion of those thoughts were about Giada. I wondered what she was doing at any particular moment, pictured our life together if things had gone differently, wondered how she would have changed if we ever met again.

The thoughts grew obsessive to the point where I actually caught myself on occasion talking aloud to her. I realized that was definitive proof that I'd lost my mind, so I accepted the likelihood of delusions obscuring my brain, too.

When I first saw Giada that breezy summer day, seemingly unconscious in the middle of the woods near my cabin, I assumed I was seeing things. I watched her silently for several minutes, appreciating the small piece of heaven unexpectedly dropped into the middle of my personal hell.

Giada

I smelled the fire and felt the heat settling over me like a blanket before I opened my eyes. I glanced around me and immediately recognized the interior of the cabin. My muscles clenched, then Luca crouched on the floor by my side.

"Giada? Oh, thank god, Amore. I thought…" he sighed and ran his fingers through his dark hair. It was longer than the last time I'd seen him. It made him look younger and more carefree.

"What happened?"

"I think you fainted. I carried you back here because I wasn't sure… I mean, I caught you. You didn't hit your head. But you should've woken up faster, right? Do you need to go to a doctor? I could drive you…"

"Luca?"

"Yes?"

"Is that you? You're Luca?"

He frowned. He looked like Luca, and he sounded like Luca. He wasn't exactly acting like Luca, though, babbling and uncertain of himself.

"Yes. It's me, Giada," he finally said. "I should take you to a doctor."

"Am I dead?"

He bit his lip as though trying not to laugh. "No, tesoro. You are alive, but…"

"Then how are you here? Or how am I here with you?" I pushed back against the sofa to sit upright.

His dark eyes locked on me, slowly scanning up and then down. "We are both alive. You're at the cabin. My cabin. You remembered—"

"Of course I remembered."

"Why are you here?"

What a loaded question. I had no rational answer. I couldn't not come here. I had to see it. What would make sense? I opted not to answer at all. "I thought you were dead."

"So why come here if you thought I was dead?"

"I figured someone should. You told me no one else knew about the place."

"I can't believe you remembered."

I shrugged. He rose to sit beside me on the couch, still eying me like he didn't know what to do with me. I took the opportunity to inspect him as well, noting that he looked just fine, as alive as could be and completely without injury. Then, I remembered the hour or so of heavy crying I'd done in the woods, and the self-consciousness kicked in. I started to wipe under my eyes, certain mascara had smeared across my face. But then I stopped and focused on the fact that I'd been crying over him. Not just that day, but every day. For weeks.

I'd questioned everything I'd ever done in my life the past few weeks, all because of him. I'd blamed myself, hated myself, blamed him, hated him, blamed Adrian, blamed Angelo, blamed my father, blamed Luca's father. I had been through hell, and all along, Luca had just been camping.

What the fuck?

My hand slapped the side of his face, the pain stinging through my fingers before I even realized what I'd done. "I thought you were dead," I repeated.

"I'm sorry."

"You're sorry?" I stood, wobbling slightly. Luca shot up to steady me, but I swatted his hand away. "I thought you were dead, Luca. *Dead.* I watched you get shot. I saw you bleeding. I saw you! You were dead." I swallowed, blinking back new tears now, remembering the nausea and pain that had swept over me in the instant he was shot, only to settle in my core for weeks without rest.

"I couldn't wash the blood out. I literally had to cut my fingernails to get rid of it," I continued, glancing to my hands and half expecting to still see remnants of his blood.

Luca reached for me again. And again, I swatted him away. I heard words still flowing out of my mouth, angry, incoherent rants about the hell he'd put me through.

He let me say it all. He took it all, and then he reached for me yet again. Finally, I let him.

He wrapped his arms around me and held me so tightly that

all I could focus on was the effort it took to breathe. His shirt was wet, and I realized it was from my tears, but I couldn't stop. It didn't make sense. Nothing felt real.

When he finally released me, the cabin was dark, illuminated only by the dying embers of the fire.

I stared at him long and hard, memorizing every detail of the face I thought I'd never see again. He was so familiar, and yet I felt like I was seeing him for the first time. An overwhelming sense of gratitude filled me.

"I'm so sorry, Giada. It killed me not to tell you," he said, wincing at the same time I did over his choice of words. "But I thought you'd be better off without me."

"How could you ever think that?"

"You chose Adrian, not me."

I shook my head furiously. "That doesn't mean I wanted you dead."

He laughed sardonically. "Literally, your last words to me were 'I wish you were dead'."

I sunk to the couch, certain my wobbly legs couldn't support me another minute. I took a breath and then another, but I was still suffocating. No matter how quickly I inhaled, I wasn't getting enough oxygen.

Luca crouched beside me and rubbed my back. "Giada, stop. Look at me!"

He nudged my chin upwards, giving me no choice in the matter.

"Take a deep breath and hold it."

I tried, but my muscles forced the air out instantly.

"You're going to hyperventilate, Giada. Focus. Breathe in for two, out for two, in for two, out for two…"

I forced myself to comply, and by the time I realized his counting had slowed, I was breathing normally.

"You were mad," he said. "I know you didn't mean it."

I shook my head. "I told myself you wouldn't remember that."

Luca shrugged. "If I were dead, I guess I wouldn't."

I squeezed my eyes shut. He wasn't helping. I would've never forgiven myself if those had actually been my last words to him. It wasn't even the truth. "I didn't mean it. I loved you, Luca."

"And then you hated me," he said, taunting me with his smile. "And then you loved me again, and then you hated me. And now from the way you're looking at me, I'd say you're back to loving me."

"Shut up," I said, rolling my eyes.

"I get it, Giada. I never blamed you, I never believed you wanted me to die. That's just, you know, how it is with us. We have strong feelings for each other, you and I. It's either all, or it's nothing. It's either sizzling or frozen." He chuckled again. "It must be all that Italian passion."

I rolled my eyes again, but he was right. I stood and turned away, feeling too confused to look at him right then. When it came to Luca, I felt everything, and I felt it fiercely. I'd never hated or loved anyone as much as him. At times, I'd been terrified for him and other times terrified of him. I had always let myself feel freely and just went with it.

I'd never pressured myself to rationalize my feelings for him or work through it all because I'd never realized we were on a timeline. When we'd broken up the last time, sure I'd said it was the last time, but a part of me assumed it wouldn't have to be if I changed my mind.

It took Luca dying for me to realize I was out of chances to run back to him, that I couldn't control when we had our final chapter. When I thought he was gone, that was when I realized all the things I still wanted to say to him that I'd never had the chance—or the courage—to say before. That was when I realized there were many more things I wanted to see with him, experience with him, and do with him. Mostly I'd just thought about kissing him.

For weeks, I'd been telling myself it would all be okay if I could just stare him in the eyes, tell him I was sorry, and kiss him. One last time.

"I'm so sorry," I said, turning back to face him. "For everything."

Before he could reply, my lips were on his. I half expected him to shove me away, but instead, his hands came to my hips, holding me close. I let my hands rest at his waist, then worked them up his back, so grateful to even be able to touch him again. My fingers roamed his hair, which was even softer now that he'd grown it out and ditched the product, and then my hands stopped on his cheeks. He had a day's worth of stubble, maybe more, but I'd been so engrossed in the kiss that I hadn't felt it with my lips. Now I could focus on nothing else, but it tickled me pleasantly.

I nudged him back an inch and gazed into his eyes. They were as serious, as fierce, as vulnerable, and as needy as ever, and I couldn't deny everything I felt for him.

"I will always love you, Luca. Even when I hate you."

He breathed a laugh and planted a kiss on my forehead. "I know, amore mio. I know."

"Don't leave me again."

He nodded solemnly, and then my stomach growled loudly.

Luca bit back a smile. "Take a shower, and then I'll feed you. You're too skinny."

"I haven't had much of an appetite since you died," I admitted. I considered protesting his implication that I needed to bathe, but I felt gross. I'd been in the woods, and I'd bawled. I couldn't possibly look pretty, and I sure didn't feel it. Besides, with the fire roaring in the tiny cabin, I was starting to sweat, feeling like a half-roasted marshmallow. I had no clean clothes or hairdryer, but I did have makeup and a brush in my purse, so I'd survive.

"Why is the fire going?"

"You were freezing when I found you in the woods," he said, turning to poke at the fire with a metal stick. "It'll burn out soon."

"What time is it?" I asked, realizing my phone was no longer in my pocket.

"Eight thirty."

"At night?" I asked, instantly realizing the idiocy of my question. I'd driven there late morning, so...

Luca frowned. "Who knew where you were going?"

"No one."

"You drove off into the middle of the woods without telling anyone where you were going?"

I couldn't tell if his disbelief was due to the stupidity of my actions or the sheer implausibility, but either way, a nod of my head answered.

"Who is going to worry if you're not back?"

"No one."

Luca cocked his head to the side.

"Lorenzo?" he asked.

"Maybe."

Luca hesitated. "Adrian?"

I sighed. "Maybe."

He gestured towards my phone on the table. "Text them. Make up something they'll believe, and tell them you'll see them tomorrow."

"Wait, you have cell service here now?" I asked, followed quickly by, "I'm staying the night?"

"Yes to both. They built a cell tower a few miles down the road after our last visit here." His tone was so confident that I couldn't even muster a joke about how presumptive he was.

I thought for a moment, then started texting. I told Enzo I made it safely to Gabriella's and not to bug me or tell my father or brother I'd driven myself. I told Adrian I was exhausted and that I'd call him the next day. With how things had been going between us lately, he wouldn't bat an eyelash at that.

I dropped my phone on the table and walked towards the bathroom.

"You're still together, you and Adrian?"

I stopped and shrugged, then turned to face him. "Yes," I said, although who knew, really. A few hours ago, Luca was dead, and I was with Adrian. Now that Luca was alive, I didn't know what I was anymore.

CHAPTER 5

Adrian

My sister flew in to spend the weekend with me. The entire time I'd been in New York, Annie had only come from Chicago to visit once. But the timing of this visit couldn't be better. I needed the distraction and definitely needed some time with a familiar, friendly face.

I met Annie at the airport, and we explored campus for a while before heading back to my apartment. I'd offered her my room for the weekend, happy to stay on the couch, so I carried her bags back and dumped them on my bed.

Annie's grimace when she noticed the dog was so extreme it was almost comical.

"What is that?" she asked.

"I told you I found a dog."

"That's not a dog. That's like…a drowned rat on steroids." She shook her head and crouched down. "Is he missing an eye?"

I fluffed the hair off of his forehead so my sister could see that his organs were all completely intact. "He just needs a trim."

"And a bath," she said, her nose wrinkled. "He stinks."

"Well, yeah. I bathed him once, but I think there's something stuck in his fur. But once I get him trimmed up, he'll be fine."

"The shelter doesn't have a groomer on staff?"

I shuffled my feet back and forth. "I don't know. They might. I called and said I found a stray, but they're almost at capacity, and they don't have a lot of people wanting to adopt right now, so…"

"Oh God. Are you thinking you'll keep him?"

"No! Of course not. I mean, only until he gets back on his feet again."

Annie stifled a laugh. "Back on his feet? Adrian, he's a dog, not a war veteran."

"He's got a little cough, and he's not really eating. I'm going to get him to a groomer and a vet, and maybe work on his training and help get him housebroken, and then he'll find the perfect home."

"He isn't housebroken?"

"He is," I began. "I mean, he goes to the bathroom outside. Sometimes. It's just, you know it's hard when you move to a new home, and…"

My sister shook her head and backed away from the dog. "This is even worse than that time you brought home that pregnant cat."

"Lola was there for mom when she was at her sickest during chemo. If I hadn't rescued her—"

"Adrian, no. This is insane."

I could tell she wasn't going to change her mind about Scruffy, at least not before she really got to know him, so I switched topics. We planned out our itinerary for the weekend, and then I grabbed us each a beer. I settled onto the couch, and Scruffy joined me. Anne perched on the chair across from us, still scowling at his haggard appearance.

"I think he has mange," she said.

I ignored her but made a mental note to Google that condition later, just in case. "Here, Scruffy, lay down," I encouraged. He sunk onto my lap.

Annie laughed out loud. "Well, at least his name fits."

"It's not a final name, I mean, he just needed something…" I began, sighing and shaking my head.

"How's Giada?" Annie asked, tucking her feet beneath her.

I cringed despite my best efforts not to. Annie's eyes widened.

"Ouch. You looked calmer when you were talking about that mangey fur monster. What happened? I thought things were going well with you guys."

"Yeah," I said, regaining my composure. "Absolutely. She stayed with me for a while but then she went back home, and… I mean, she came to visit last weekend, but she doesn't like dogs, so…" I sighed and scratched behind Scruffy's ears. "Things are fine."

"So you brought home a dog that your girlfriend doesn't like, and now things are strained between you guys?"

I cringed, trying to decide how to explain the deeper issues.

"I don't blame her for not liking this dog."

"It's not this dog. She just doesn't like any dogs."

"What kind of person doesn't like dogs? Is she allergic?"

Annie was kidding, probably, but I answered anyway. "She doesn't like any animals. Dogs, cats, fish, birds…"

"That should've been a red flag," she replied.

I chucked a random sock from the couch at her, and she laughed.

"You know how we had sort of an on-and-off-again relationship for a while?"

"Yes. Your love life is like a Mexican soap opera."

"Well, Luca, the other guy that she was seeing, he's totally out of the picture now."

Annie frowned. "Adrian, you've said that before. Every time, you're sure she's the one. Then you break up, and she goes back to him. You're an amazing catch, baby brother. You can get a girl who is positive you're the one for her."

I shook my head, wishing I could explain to my sister how I knew it was different this time, but I couldn't. The less she knew about the Marino's business, the safer she was. I hated not being able to defend Giada's complex emotions about it all, but I didn't want to put Annie in harm's way. "He's gone for good this time. I'm positive."

My sister's shoulders raised. "Okay, well, he's gone, and you still cringed when I asked about Gia. You're twenty-four. You should be living your best life and playing the field, not sticking it out in a relationship where you're not happy."

"I am happy."

"Promise?"

"Yes." I paused. "Giada's just having a really tough time now. It's hard to watch, and I don't know how to help her."

"What's going on?"

I couldn't exactly explain that her ex-boyfriend was murdered in a mob hit intended for her, so I went with a more general response. "Her ex wasn't a good guy. He left her with some baggage. And her family, they've got a complicated situation. She just doesn't know how to be in a normal, healthy relationship."

Annie eyed me warily, sipping half her drink before answering. "Look, can I give you some sisterly advice since I'm older and infinitely wiser?"

I nodded but prepared myself for the worst.

"The world is filled with problems. You can't fix them all. Just because you can take in a stray doesn't mean you should. It is not your job to rescue every hurting creature that crosses your path."

I replayed her words in my mind then sought confirmation. "Are you comparing my girlfriend to a stray dog?"

Her face told me that was exactly what she'd done. Annie

continued unapologetically. "Giada is much more beautiful. I'll give her that. I'm only saying that you have a hero complex. The more something or someone needs help, the less likely you are to walk away. But at some point, you've got to put yourself first."

~

Giada

I was too stunned to talk about anything serious while we ate, so instead, Luca told me about all the reading he'd done lately, and how he'd practiced fishing and hunting, and that some days he was so bored he talked to animals. But as we cleaned up, all the questions flooded back into my brain.

"How did you survive?" I asked.

He shrugged. "I don't think anyone has ever literally died of boredom."

"No, I mean, the shooting."

"Oh."

I wasn't oblivious to his discomfort, but I had to know. "I watched you get hit three times. And there was blood."

"The blood was from my shoulder," he said. He turned and rolled up the sleeve of his tee-shirt. The skin was discolored, and there was a red scar about an inch from his armpit. Luca lifted his elbow and showed me a different scar on the back side of his arm. Both looked painful, but the scar on the front was larger and redder, while the other one already seemed to be fading.

"The bullet went straight through?"

He nodded. "Nicked the bone but missed the brachial artery. They tell me I was very lucky."

"They?"

"The doctors. Alessio and Thomas took me to the hospital."

"Didn't the doctors ask questions?"

Luca set down the dishtowel and sunk into a chair at the table. "The guys called my papà on the way to the hospital. He told Thomas to take my wallet and disappear, and Alessio used a fake ID to sign me in. He said he was my brother, and that I was mugged. He gave an accurate description of the actual guys who did it but everything else was fake."

"Did your father come visit you in the hospital?"

"No. But Alessio updated him."

I frowned. All of this was hard to piece together. And the timeline just didn't make sense. "How long were you in the hospital?"

"I was discharged on the third day."

"They told me you died on the scene," I said, shaking my head.

"My papà told people what he wanted them to know. Officially, I never died, but my papà made sure anyone who knew me —or knew of me—believed I died."

"But they were at your funeral, Thomas and Alessio. They saw me crying and said nothing."

His expression changed. "You went to my funeral?"

"Of course."

"But my guys, they all thought…"

"Yeah, they all looked at me like I was pond scum. And they made it pretty clear I wasn't welcome anywhere near your family. Not that I would've tried anyway."

"I'm sorry. It's not your fault."

"Not my fault that you got shot or that they hate me?"

"The first one," he said. Then he smiled. "My guys have hated you for years."

"What? Why?"

"You've always been my weakness, Giada."

I didn't know what to say to that. "What about the other bullets? They didn't hit any major arteries?"

"Kevlar," he said, walking towards the bedroom. He opened a

drawer, pulled out a pair of boxer shorts and a cotton tee shirt, and tossed them to me.

I caught the clothes but was still confused. I'd heard of Kevlar before, but couldn't fathom why he'd be wearing it. "Like a bulletproof vest?"

"Yeah. The kind cops wear."

"You knew someone was going to shoot at me?"

"Giada, I didn't even know I'd see you that day. But I'd had some business at the docks early that morning, and I like to be prepared."

I watched as he turned his back to me and stretched, lifting his shirt up over his head.

"People shoot at you?"

He sighed as he moved to face me again. "No, I mean, it's not a regular occurrence or anything, but you know what I do, what it's like. You know there's risks."

My eyes dropped down to his chest, which was every bit as smooth and sculpted as I remembered. I stepped closer and noticed a faint mark on his left pec. Without thinking, I reached my hand out to touch it lightly. The skin was smooth, but it was definitely a fading scar.

"That's where one hit?" I asked.

He nodded.

"The other?"

Luca glanced down, and instead of pointing to the matching scar on his abdomen just a few inches below the first one, he moved my own hand to it. That one was also faint, but I couldn't help tracing the outline then smoothing my fingers over it.

"It doesn't hurt?"

"Not anymore. The impact left pretty big bruises. They did some scans to make sure it didn't hurt my liver or gallbladder or anything, but like I said, I was lucky."

"You took three bullets for me after I dumped you for another guy and said I hoped you died. I think maybe I'm the lucky one," I said.

I glanced down and realized both of my hands had made their way to his abdomen. I slid them along his smooth torso up to his chest then around to his back before settling on his hips. "Thank you for that, by the way. I owe you."

I planted a gentle kiss on each scar before letting myself look at his face. I braced myself in case he was eying me with the same hatred his crew had after I caused him to get shot. But he wasn't. The look in Luca's eyes was as far from cold or hatred as possible. He was looking at me with red hot desire.

I didn't give him time to change his mind. My lips smashed into his with such force that he stumbled backwards a step. I tightened my grip on his hips then shivered as his hands slipped under my shirt, settling on my own hips for just a moment before tugging my shirt up over my head. My bra disappeared even faster, and I relished the feel of the skin to skin contact.

Luca had always been a good kisser, but this—kissing him after I thought I'd lost him—this was even more intense. It was fierce and passionate and desperate, a messy tangle of tongues and lips and teeth. I needed more from Luca, needed to be closer. I wanted to be with him in the way I would've the night before he was taken from me had I known what was about to happen.

I nudged him back towards the bed, ready for more. When his knees hit the foot of the bed, he willingly sat, pulling me onto him. I shrieked but was about to continue the kiss when he rolled us onto our sides. He pressed his hand against my arm, holding me at a distance, then scooted himself backwards and propped his head on his hand.

"You're with Adrian, Giada. You chose him."

I shifted onto my back and sighed, focusing my eyes on a dark knot in the wood along ceiling so I wouldn't be tempted to look back at the gorgeous man beside me.

Given that Luca never billed himself as a man of high moral

character, I should've been offended that he was the one putting on the brakes with me. I considered reminding him that it wasn't exactly cheating since he was dead but decided that wasn't the best route.

"You didn't give me much choice," I reminded him. "Besides, things with Adrian and I aren't great. We haven't been close since I thought I lost you."

"Why not?"

"Because you jumped in front of a gun and took three bullets for me, Luca. I picked Adrian before because I didn't think you cared, but then you showed me you were willing to die for me. I thought you *did* die for me. Every day since then, all I've been thinking about is how I completely misjudged you and how I chose wrong. I could've been with you that whole time, and instead, I wasn't. Then it was too late because you were dead."

Luca leaned over me, planting his hand on the opposite side of my head. He pressed a soft kiss onto each of my eyelids, and I realized I'd started crying. Again. God, I was a mess.

"Don't cry, Giada. I'm sorry. I didn't mean to suggest..." He paused and shook his head. "You just seem really emotional tonight and I've been alone on a fucking mountain for a month. I don't want to take advantage of you."

I started to giggle. I couldn't help it. It was all just too ridiculous. After all the times I'd slept with Luca when my heart truly wasn't in it and now when I really wanted him, maybe more than I'd ever wanted him, he was saying no. I wasn't sure what kind of ironic karma this was, but it was bullshit.

A funny smile crossed Luca's face. "You think this is funny?"

"I think this is crazy. You're supposed to be dead. I want nothing more than to be with you right now, and for once, you don't want me."

"I want you very much. But you're not mine to have."

"That's never stopped you before."

"But it does stop *you*," he said, sitting up. "I don't want a pity fuck because you feel bad that I got shot. I don't want you to hate me again tomorrow morning."

Okay, ouch.

"I am not good for you, Giada. You were right to dump me. That's what I wanted you to do."

"What does that mean?"

He hesitated. "I didn't sleep with those girls, the ones that showed up the day you threw the ring at my head. I never intended to. I only invited them over so that you would see them and realize what kind of a man I am before it was too late for you to choose Adrian. They were supposed to arrive when they did." He paused. "I had some second thoughts when they actually showed up, and I saw the look on your face, but I had orchestrated the whole thing so that you would dump me."

I rubbed my forehead, worried my brain might explode from the plethora of revelations tonight. I didn't doubt that he was telling me the truth now. No one would ever accuse Luca of being the most morally upstanding guy, but he was always harder on himself than he should've been. "But why go through all that trouble instead of just telling me you wanted to break up?"

"Because I didn't want to break up with you. You've always been good for me, but I will never be right for you. I wanted to make you see that. I needed something that I could never take back, something you wouldn't forgive."

It was all too much. Shaking my head, I stood up and looked around for the tee shirt he'd brought me and pulled it over my head. I took the shorts into the bathroom, changed, and climbed under the covers.

Luca watched me return, then when he seemed to realize I was planning to sleep in his bed, he stood and collected some blankets. "I can sleep on the couch."

"Oh my God, Luca. You can sleep in your own damn bed. I promise not to molest you in your sleep."

He eyed me warily, then stepped out of his jeans and joined me under the covers.

I turned so my back was to him. I needed space to process what had just happened. It was mortifying, being rejected. Worse yet, I wanted to feel bad about Adrian, but I just didn't. If there were ever a time for a free pass to guilt-free sex with an ex, this had to be it.

"I can break up with Adrian tomorrow."

"No, you can't break up with him. He'll be suspicious."

"I won't tell him why."

"What would there be to tell him anyway? There is no reason for you to break up with him."

"Umm…you just said you won't be with me as long as I'm with him."

"That's not exactly what I said, but it doesn't matter anyway. I'm dead, Giada. It's not like I can suddenly reappear and go back to normal. And once you leave, you can't ever come back here without raising suspicion."

I considered this, then flopped onto my back so I could see him. "Wait, I finally get you back, and you're telling me we only have tonight?"

His face fell as though he too was just processing his own words. "Yes. I'm sorry. If there were any other way—"

"If we only have one night together, I don't want to spend it talking."

I saw the hesitation in his face and prayed he didn't reject me again. I couldn't take it a second time.

"Luca, please. I need you. I need to feel you inside me."

He launched himself over me, stripped off our clothes, and covered my body in kisses. My nipples hardened into firm peaks as his hands caressed my breasts. As he worked his mouth down past my abdomen and settled between my legs, the desire that had been so tightly coiled within me began to throb. I didn't want to come that way, though. I meant it when I said I needed him inside me.

I tugged him up and arched my back to meet him. Sensing my urgency, he thrust fully into me with one powerful roll of his hips. He slammed into the sensitive bundle of nerves deep inside me, and I cried out loudly, shattering around him with dizzying force. He kept going, his relentless pace quickly rebuilding the tension within me. Over and over, he thrust into me, filling me and stretching me and making me feel whole in a way I hadn't since he'd been shot.

"Come again with me, Giada," he pleaded, his voice hoarse. Then he dipped his head lower, nipping at my breasts and rendering me powerless to do anything but what he'd commanded. I felt him swell within me, and right as he found his release, I reached my own again as well.

We didn't talk for a moment, both of us too focused on catching our breath. I shouldn't have been surprised, really. Even when I wanted to strangle Luca, the sex was fantastic. So it made sense that when I felt loving towards him, it was even better. Selfishly, I wanted to believe that it was us, and not just that he was some sexpert. I needed to think that the sex with us was better for him than sex with others and that it wasn't just me feeling the superiority of our physical connection.

Luca draped his arm around my waist. He scooted himself closer and then relaxed. In this position, I couldn't deny that he'd spoken the truth—he did want me. I could feel the evidence of his desire pressing against me. Still, Luca had never been a snuggler, so this felt wrong to me. It was almost like he was still trying to protect me.

"You're not hiding from someone out here, are you?"

"I'm hiding from everyone out here. Aside from us, only four people know I'm alive."

"Thomas, Alessio, and your parents?"

"No. Giovanni, Thomas, Alessio and my papà."

"What about your mother?"

"She thinks I'm dead. I told you my papà's a bastard. He doesn't trust her."

"Wow. Yeah." I turned over and nudged Luca onto his back, resting my head against his chest. I couldn't imagine his mother's pain, not knowing her son was alive. What a cruel thing to do to a person!

"Are you safe now? I mean, no one is after you now, right?"

"No one was ever after me. It was you they shot at."

I lifted my head. He had a casual expression on his face like he was teasing, although it was the truth. "Enzo said I'm safe now. He assured me they're not a threat anymore."

"They're not."

I hesitated, then told him about the visit from the F.B.I.

"But how can you be so certain there's no one else after us, other than just those two guys?"

"Because they're all dead."

"What? Seriously?"

He nodded.

"Did your father...I mean, did he have it done?"

Luca frowned, and his eyes flitted back and forth as though he were engaged in a terse conversation with someone else. "My papà didn't kill them, Giada. Yours did."

"My dad had someone killed?" I kept my head lifted so I could better read his expression.

"No, Giada. He had someone bring them to him, both of them. He had them tortured. And then he shot them each, point-blank in the head."

I sat upright, suddenly needing more space. "Why would you say that?"

"Because it's the truth."

"And how would you know that?"

"Because he let my papà come watch. And my papà recorded

it and showed me so that I'd never come out of hiding to try to hunt down the guys who threatened you."

"You saw an actual video of my father shooting someone?"

He nodded solemnly. "Giada, I'm sorry, but your papà is no different from mine."

I opened my mouth to argue with him, but no words came. I knew without discussion that what he said was the truth. Maybe I'd known it all along and just hadn't been ready to admit it.

"I'm sorry," Luca repeated. "It's not my place to tell you. What your papà and your brothers do is their business, not mine."

"My brothers? You're saying my brothers know that my dad is…in the mafia?" I nearly laughed at the ridiculousness of the statement.

Luca made a face like he'd just sucked a lemon. "Giada, your brothers are… well, I mean Angelo especially, he's…"

I blew out a sigh. *Of course.* They didn't know about it; they were involved in it. God, I was a fool. Luca rubbed my back supportively while all the clues played through my mind like a movie reel.

"Shit. Adrian has been telling me this all along. Why didn't I ever listen to him?"

"Maybe you weren't ready to hear it."

I shook my head. So Adrian had been honest with me all along while Luca had lied for years in a misguided attempt to shelter me. What did I do? I cheated on Adrian with Luca. Clearly, I was a stellar judge of character.

"You can't lie to me anymore. I don't care if you're doing it to protect me or whatever. I need to know the truth."

He paused only for a minute. "Okay."

"Okay? You're just agreeing like that? You'd say anything just to shut me up now that it's four o'clock in the morning, wouldn't you?"

"Jesus, it's four?"

I confirmed on the clock then nodded.

"Shit."

"Sorry. I'll let you sleep now."

He squeezed my hand and raised it to his lips, kissing it softly. "I don't want to sleep. I can sleep whenever. I've had a month to sleep. I only have a few hours left with you, and I want to make the most of it."

I wondered if the lack of sleep was making him delirious, but I couldn't argue with his logic. Besides, it was really romantic.

"Well, then what should we do with our remaining hours?"

Luca raised an eyebrow. "I think we've already exhausted all topics of discussion, so…" He quickly ducked under the covers, kissing his way down my body as I giggled and shrieked.

~

*L*uca

After the second round of mind-blowing sex with Giada, I had to pinch myself to make sure I wasn't dreaming. I had fantasized about this exact scenario countless times over the past month, and I wasn't stupid enough to believe any version of karma entitled me to such happiness.

"See? You can't deny we're good together," Giada said suddenly, tracing her finger along the path of the thin gold chain around my neck.

I laughed.

"What? It's the truth."

"Good sexual chemistry doesn't mean we are good together. History has shown time and time again that we're not."

"So you think we have good chemistry in bed?"

I rolled my eyes. "In bed, in the car, in the shower, in the middle of the woods…" I paused, trying to think of all the places I'd made her come. "You can't even pretend to deny it. I barely touch you, and you're wet and begging for it."

Her jaw dropped. "I can't believe you just said that."

"It's true."

She sighed. "You probably say that to all of your women."

I cocked my head to the side, unsure of how to respond. No one would ever believe me if I tried to claim Giada had been my only lover, but being with her wasn't even in the same category as sex with other women. With Giada it was… different. We were always in sync sexually. She knew just how to please me, and I knew just how to return the favor. But it wasn't just mutually satisfying on a physical level, it was always like we connected on a more spiritual level too. I definitely wasn't saying that to her, though.

"It's different with other women. You're the only woman I've ever been with who makes me feel that way."

She gently brushed her fingers along my jaw then through my hair, almost as though she were trying to memorize every detail about me. "Why are you telling me all of this now?"

"I don't know," I admitted. "Maybe death brings out the honesty in me. Or maybe I've just been so desperate to see you that now I want to say everything I should've told you before."

"Do you work for my dad?" she asked suddenly.

"No. My papà is the boss of our family. When he dies, I'll take over, assuming I don't fuck up in the meantime."

"Who does my dad work for?"

"No one. He's a boss. Your brothers are both captains, like me. Angelo will take over for your father when he…retires." I winced at the terminology but couldn't stand the thought of alluding to her papà's death.

"Are we competitors then, your family and mine?"

I chuckled at her naivety. "No, sweetheart. I think the hope was always that our families would merge someday because of us."

"So my uncles, and Enzo, and…"

I shushed her. "Giada, every man who's set foot in your house works for your papà. They all have different ranks, and it's not my place to tell you all of it, but they're all involved."

"Adrian?"

I cringed. "Well, no. Although if Angelo has his way…"

"What does Angelo want with Adrian?"

The panic on her face at this thought was unsettling and undermined her claims that she was over him. "Nothing. Your papà trusts Adrian, but Angelo doesn't trust anyone that he can't control."

"That sounds like him."

Giada was quiet for a moment, then continued. "What about my aunts?"

"Women aren't involved. Some of the men's wives know more than others, but we try not to involve the fairer sex at all."

"That's sexist."

"Or chivalrous. You can't pretend you wouldn't be happier not knowing any of this. And you certainly can't tell me you'd want to be involved. If you'd been born a male, you wouldn't have had a choice."

"There's always a choice."

I snorted. "Yeah, tell that to Matteo," I said, quickly naming the least-suited person for the lifestyle I could think of.

Her brows wrinkled together, and she stifled a yawn.

"Sleep, Giada," I whispered.

"I don't want to. If we only have tonight…" she yawned again before finishing her sentence. I shifted her against me and watched her eyes drift shut as I slowly smoothed my hand up and down her back.

Giada

*D*espite my best efforts, I fell asleep at some point. When I woke, I was alone. I glanced out the window and spotted Luca on the front porch, so I slipped on the boxer shorts he'd given me the night before and then pulled his sweatshirt over my head.

When I stepped outside, Luca froze like a deer in headlights.

"I'm sorry. I didn't mean to wake you," he said.

"You didn't, and besides, I didn't intend to fall asleep." I eyed him warily as he crouched down to pour a cup of coffee. "What are you doing?"

He laughed. "I watched you sleep for a while, but then I needed coffee, and I didn't want to wake you, so I brought the coffee maker out here."

"Ah. Perfectly logical," I said, biting back a laugh.

He handed me the cup of coffee, and I sat on the swing. He sat beside me and pulled my feet over his lap.

"You really didn't sleep at all?"

He shook his head.

I gazed around. "It's gorgeous here in the morning."

Luca quickly scanned our surroundings before nodding. "It is, but you get used to it after a while."

"It seems like you could use company more often."

"It's hard work playing dead."

"How long are you keeping up the charade?"

"I don't know. Indefinitely."

"Not forever."

He shrugged. "No, despite the fantasy, I don't think I could survive that. But, the situation is still pretty volatile now, so from a business and strategic point of view, it is better if I don't make my grand reappearance quite yet. Maybe a few years."

"Years?" I nearly dropped my coffee cup. "You can't stay here all alone for years. I can't wait for years."

"No one's asking you to wait."

"Luca, don't start. I don't want Adrian. I want you."

He grinned, and it was comforting to see that despite everything, he was still a cocky bastard.

"You don't think he'd notice if you disappeared for one night every few weeks?" he asked.

I wasn't sure if he meant Adrian or who exactly, but my answer was the same regardless. "No. I can get away, and no one will ask questions."

Luca seemed less certain. He set down his coffee and thrust his hands in his hair. The strands looked so soft and touchable that I couldn't resist. I reached my hand up and ran my fingers through his hair, too. He glanced up at me and raised an eyebrow.

"It's longer now. I like it." I slid my hand down to his cheek. I traced my thumb back and forth across the beginnings of his beard and then kissed him. Before his "death," he'd shaved daily. Sometimes more than once if he'd shaved early in the morning and then had an evening meeting that required professionalism. And he never let his hair grow out. He hadn't looked this casual and carefree since high school when I'd first fallen in love with him.

"I don't want you to risk anything. You can't raise suspicions, and you can't chance getting caught. If anyone asks questions, or if you think anyone will wonder where you're going, just don't come."

I pouted. "Gee, you really know how to make a girl feel welcome."

"Giada, I'm telling you, it's not safe for the two of us to be together now. If I can't trust you to take precautions and be serious about this—"

"I promise," I interrupted.

He retrieved his coffee mug and took a long swig right as I added my last condition.

"But I'm not waiting weeks. I'll come back Saturday morning."

A slight grin tugged his lips upwards.

"Can I call you between now and then?"

"You probably shouldn't."

"What if it's an emergency? You're not completely off the grid."

He hesitated. "Buy a burner phone, something disposable. Never use it for anything else except calling me. Don't leave me a message, and don't ever text anything with either of our real names. Can you handle that?"

I nodded. "What's your number?"

"I'll write it down before you leave."

I smiled contentedly. I wasn't sure how it happened, but it appeared I'd gotten everything I wanted—not just a solitary night with Luca, but the promise of more time alone together, at our own private love shack.

I turned back to Luca and realized he looked uncomfortable.

"Oh God, have you brought other women back here?" I asked, cringing at my premature naming of the cabin as our love shack.

"No. Never. You are still the only other person who even knows it exists."

"Oh. Then why were you making that face?"

"What face?"

"I don't know. Your stressed-out face, like you need to tell me something I won't like."

He instantly made a more pronounced version of the face. "I was going to say that I don't want you driving out here without a gun. You shouldn't be all alone in these woods without protection."

"I don't have a gun."

"Get one. Before next weekend. And I want you to get a permit. As soon as you can legally buy one, do it so you can keep it in your car when you come here." He stood abruptly and darted into the cabin, returning a moment later with a small black handgun. "Until then, you can borrow this," he said, dropping it on my lap. "But don't get caught with it because the ID numbers are all scratched off."

I eyed the gun warily, afraid to breathe or shift in my seat and accidentally set it off.

"Oh geez. Tell me you know how to shoot, Giada."

"Get it off of me."

"Baby, the safety is on." He picked it up and tilted it to the side. "I can't believe no one ever taught you how to use a gun."

"I've had a bodyguard since I was seventeen. It's never been a necessity."

"Well, it is now. Finish your coffee and come eat something. I'm teaching you this morning."

We went inside, and I snooped through his fridge and cabinets. "I can make pancakes," I said.

"Since when do you cook?"

I shrugged. "Pancakes aren't that hard."

"Do you cook anything else?"

"A few things."

Luca looked impressed. "Where did you learn?"

"It's a long story."

"Oh, well, I have a meeting in twenty minutes. So I guess there's no time to hear it," he said.

I shot him a quizzical look, then realized he was messing with me. I hesitated, then fessed up. "Adrian taught me."

"Oh," Luca said. "Huh, well, turns out that wasn't such a long story."

An hour later, we were in the woods behind the cabin, finishing up my beginner lesson on gun safety.

"Is it wrong that it really turns me on seeing you wearing my shirt and holding my gun?" Luca asked.

I glanced sideways at him.

"Hey, eyes on the target, Giada!"

"Then stop distracting me."

The full lesson consisted of a fifteen-minute lecture on gun safety, an additional ten minutes on the mechanics of the gun, like checking if it was loaded and whether the safety was on, then a few minutes on aim. He didn't let me actually shoot anything.

I had to admit I felt pretty badass standing there on a mountaintop with a loaded weapon. In the past, guns had always frightened and mystified me to an extent, but now, I felt powerful.

"Here," Luca said, nudging my elbow upwards. "You want your dominant arm in control."

I held the position for a moment before realizing he was distracted. Keeping my arms in position, I glanced at him. He was frowning at my bicep. He took the gun, wedged it into his waistband, and then placed his fingers on my arm. As he repositioned his hand, I realized what he was so focused on—the now purple bruise from my little tiff with Angelo.

"Did I do this?" he asked, even though the hand that made the mark was clearly bigger than his.

"No. Of course not."

Instead of looking reassured, though, now his concern turned to anger. "Then who did?"

I hesitated, debating whether I could pawn it off as an accidental injury, but the distinct shape of fingers was pretty well embedded into my flesh.

"It wasn't Adrian…" Luca phrased it like a statement, but his eyebrows rose to signal the hint of doubt.

"No," I scowled at the ridiculousness of that notion. "Angelo."

"What?" Luca's question echoed through the woods like a roar.

"He was mad. I'm sure he didn't mean it."

"Did you tell your father?"

Now I outright chuckled. "We aren't kids anymore. Just because I still live at home doesn't mean I can run to Daddy every time my big brother bullies me. Besides, it's fine. I can handle him."

"I don't doubt that, but…" He ran his fingers over the marks.

"I bruise easily."

Luca rolled his eyes. "What did you do?"

"After? I walked away. Well, technically, Enzo dragged me away, but…"

"No, before. What provoked him?"

"Oh, so it's my fault? Sure, blame the victim."

"Jesus, Giada, you know what I mean."

I did, and just because I had, technically, incited my brother to the point of violence didn't make it any less offensive for Luca to suggest I brought it on myself. "I overheard his new girlfriend say something about how business must be better now with you out of the picture."

He wrinkled his nose. "Julie?"

"Julia," I corrected. "But how do you know this girl when I'm just now meeting her? You've been dead for a month!"

Luca laughed, placing his hand behind by back to escort me towards the cabin. "He's been seeing her for a while. I assume you don't like her?"

"Not in the slightest." I paused. "I mean, I barely said hello to her, but everything about her rubbed me the wrong way."

"Can you do me a favor?"

I nodded, eager to do whatever would speed along the process of bringing Luca back to life.

"Find out a little more about what your brother is working on now. Don't snoop too deeply or anything. Just try to figure out what all your father has let him take the reins on for now."

"How do I do that without snooping?"

"Ask questions. Play dumb." He paused and smirked. "You're good at that."

I swatted his arm.

"Seriously. You know so much more than Marco and Angelo think you know, so just keep up the innocent act and be curious. Talk with Matteo some, too. Just don't get on Angelo's bad side."

"I'm not afraid of Angelo. He's always been a grumpy jerk, but at the end of the day, he's harmless."

Luca lifted my arm and lightly brushed his lips across the bruise, contradicting my words in the sweetest possible way. "Be careful around Angelo, Giada. He may be your brother, and your father may be controlling his every major move, but don't assume that just because he's on a leash, he's all bark and no bite. Angelo is a dangerous man."

"You never seemed scared of him before."

"I'm not scared of him now. But without me in your life, he has a lot more power than he did before, and the only person left to keep him in check is your father."

"Maybe you just need to come back from the dead then."

Luca silenced me with a kiss.

CHAPTER 6

Giada

My thoughts kept me busy as I drove home, but once I reached my destination, exhaustion swept over me. It wasn't just the missed night's sleep, but the weight of my new, blissful discovery wearing me down. I thought of a billion more questions I should've asked Luca, but I reassured myself that I would have another chance to ask. I would see him again, and soon.

Luca was not dead.

Luckily, that revelation helped me tolerate the other new information I'd gained overnight. I certainly hadn't forgotten what Luca had said about my father—and brothers and uncles—but I wasn't focusing on that now. Right now, I had a bigger issue to confront—Adrian.

When I'd chosen Adrian over Luca months before, I'd sworn I was done with Luca for good. At the time, I'd meant it, and when Luca had died shortly after, it was a moot point anyway. I was positive Luca wasn't the man I thought he was, and I really did love Adrian. I still did, to be honest, but in a different way than I loved Luca.

But now that Luca was alive, well, that changed everything. Luca was the man I loved with all my heart, but that didn't mean I felt nothing for Adrian. I respected him too much to string him along now that I knew Luca was alive.

Besides, the entire reason I'd broken up with Luca was faulty. He hadn't slept with prostitutes, and I was a fool for ever thinking otherwise. Luca wasn't perfect, but given the monster who'd raised him, I wouldn't expect perfection. And besides, Luca was the type of man who would literally risk his life to save me, even after I chose another man over him. How could I not love him?

I decided I'd drive up to see Adrian the next day, but first, I needed to rest. Luckily, my sleep had been erratic enough lately that no one in my family questioned me taking a three-hour nap that afternoon. I woke in time for dinner, then drove into town and bought a burner phone. Next, I went to the least shady-looking shop that my internet search indicated sold guns.

The mere concept of touching a gun rendered me uneasy, so walking into a store filled with firearms sent my pulse through the roof. Luckily, it wasn't crowded. The shop owner, who fit every stereotype of a gun zealot—from his leather vest to his giant, colorful tattoos of nude females—was more than happy to help. I supposed I should've been relieved to learn that the process of buying a handgun wasn't as simple as buying a new purse, but it was disheartening to know I'd have to wait. Apparently, I needed permits and licenses before I could legally own a gun. To even get those, I had to take a basic gun safety course.

Still, I made a sizable dent in my progress towards following Luca's instructions before I returned home. In the morning, I completed the safety course, having told my mom I was headed to a spa, then dropped off my paperwork at the police station. I wondered if Luca had followed this process for obtaining his weapons or if all these legalities were a joke to guys like him. And pondering that made me think about my father. And Angelo. And poor, sweet Matteo. I trusted Luca, but I couldn't really picture Matteo complicit with any type of organized crime.

I couldn't let myself think about all that now, though. Adrian was expecting me. I told him I'd be at his apartment by the time he got off work. I hurried upstairs to fix my makeup then stopped off in the kitchen to grab a snack before I left. I was so nervous about what I was about to do, terrified by the mere prospect of breaking Adrian's heart—yet again, that my hands were already shaky. The lengthy drive back from campus would be a nightmare, especially with nothing to distract me.

"Whoa!" Enzo cautioned as I darted around the corner and slammed into him. His hands shot out to steady me so I didn't fall over.

"Sorry," I mumbled, looking at my feet. If Enzo saw my face, he'd know I wasn't okay. I brushed past him to the fridge, peering in and trying to decide what my stomach could actually tolerate at this point. I settled for a ginger ale and then grabbed a mini bag of pretzels.

"You alright?" he asked.

"Fine," I lied, retrieving my keys from my purse.

Enzo snatched them out of my hand and narrowed his gaze at me. "Something is going on with you."

"No. But I need my keys to drive."

"Where are you headed?"

"Adrian's."

He peered around me. "Where's your stuff?"

"I'm not staying overnight. I just need to talk to him." I winced, realizing how that sounded. "He's cooking dinner for me."

Enzo frowned, probably wondering why I'd drive so far just for a short visit. Of course, Adrian assumed I was staying overnight too. Maybe I should've just told him over the phone that we couldn't be together. I convinced myself I couldn't do that because he deserved more, but maybe it wasn't Adrian who needed more. Maybe the in-person meeting was for my benefit more than his. I needed closure, and I needed to make sure he was going to be okay.

Enzo dropped my keys onto the counter and nodded towards the door. "Come on. I'll drive you."

My feet carried me towards the door even as I protested. "I'd rather drive myself. I'm sure you have something else to do."

"Your father told me to keep an eye on you till he returned, and I can't let you drive anywhere like this. You're shaking." He paused and held open the passenger side door to his car. "You didn't take any pills or anything, did you?"

I rolled my eyes. "No, Lorenzo. I didn't. I just have low blood sugar. Hence the snack." I held up my soda as proof. "Where is my dad anyway?"

"Business," he said, shutting my door and then walking around to the driver's side.

"What kind of business?" I asked once he'd started the ignition.

"What kind of a question is that?" Enzo made a face.

"I'm just wondering what he does on these trips."

"Well, as you can see, I don't accompany him on these trips. I stay here to babysit you. So maybe you should ask someone else," he snapped.

"I'm not riding the whole way with you if you're going to be a jerk to me."

He blew out a sigh and turned to me. "I'm sorry, Giada. Honestly, I've just been worried about you lately, and in the past I felt like I could keep tabs on how you were doing since I drove you everywhere, but now…"

I gazed out my window, not having realized how my request to start driving myself had basically put him out of a job. "I'm feeling more like myself every day," I finally said. "You don't need to worry."

He glanced at me but didn't answer. Instead, he cranked up the radio.

~

Adrian

*E*ven though Giada was likely already at my apartment waiting, I didn't leave work early. I'd really hit my grove lately at the office and didn't want to jeopardize that. Besides, I wasn't sure what to expect with her. When she'd called me the day before and said she was coming out to see me, I tried to get excited by the surprise visit. Except judging from her voice, she was still depressed.

As I neared my apartment, I spotted Enzo's car alongside the curb. That was strange, but he appeared to be on a call, so I headed on up to talk to Giada instead. Since she'd been driving herself more lately, I wasn't sure why he was there anyway. He couldn't possibly be planning to spend the night outside in his car.

I knocked once then let myself into the apartment. "Gia?"

She was on the couch, clutching a mostly-full glass of wine and staring at Scruffy as though she expected the dog to rip out her throat at any moment. Her voice was cool as she greeted me, and she didn't turn. Scruffy flew off the couch and tackled me, so I spent a minute paying attention to him.

I washed my hands then joined her on the couch, needing to gauge her mood before deciding how to approach the evening. She had been all over the place since Luca died. I never knew in advance when I was walking into a minefield.

"How was your day?" I asked, kissing her cheek.

She shrugged. "Okay. Yours?"

"Good. What's up?"

"We should talk."

"Okay."

"I don't think this is working, you and me."

I frowned. Her words were cut and dry, but her tone was calm. For someone who'd been so full of every emotion nonstop as of late, it was almost eerie to hear a complete absence of any feeling in her voice now.

"Okay," I finally said. "What's this about?"

She didn't answer right away. When she did, her response felt like a knife to the abdomen. "Luca."

"Luca," I repeated, almost scared to say his name. Though I knew he was all she thought about since the shooting, his name was taboo. No one else could mention him without setting her off.

I got it, to some extent. They had a lot of history, sure. In any circumstances, I'd expect her to mourn the death of someone who'd been such a big part of her adolescence. And it didn't help that he didn't just die randomly, but died actively saving her life. The guilt was eating her alive. I saw that. I just wasn't sure how to help.

"Gia, maybe counseling would help?"

She wrinkled her face in disgust. "Like couples counseling?"

"No, I mean for you. You lost someone who was once a big part of your life. It's natural for you to be upset."

"Adrian, look. I know I've been a mess these last few weeks, and I really appreciate you putting up with me and with all of this, but it just isn't right. Everything that happened has put things in perspective for me, and I shouldn't be stringing you along when I have feelings for someone else."

I grabbed her wine glass and took a long swig, nearly emptying the glass. I replayed her words in my brain, trying to decipher what in the actual fuck she was saying. Surely she wasn't telling me she'd met someone new, but that meant…

"You're breaking up with me because you have feelings for your dead ex-boyfriend?"

I cringed when I heard how harsh my words sounded, but it was the truth. And it was warranted.

Gia turned to me, her eyebrows furrowed and her eyes glossing over. But all she said was "Adrian…"

"I'm sorry. I just don't get it. I know this is your thing, you go back and forth between us like we're some fucking game of tennis, but four months ago, you said all that was done. You said you made your choice, and you wanted me."

"I did want you, Adrian. I'm sorry. I just… things have changed. I'm not saying this to hurt you. I'm trying to be honest."

She was starting to cry, but I was too worked up to back off. "Okay, so now you're saying you changed your mind again, and you still don't want me even though I'm the only fucking player left in the game?"

"It's not a game, Adrian!"

"No, you're right. It isn't. It's my life, and I deserve some explanation. Am I really that shitty of a boyfriend? You'd rather love a dead man than me?"

"Stop saying that, Adrian!"

I'd overstepped. I clenched my teeth together to stop myself from being even more of an ass. I stared into her eyes, trying to read her expression, but all I could tell was that she wasn't telling me the whole story. There was something she was keeping from me.

"He saved my life, Adrian. He got shot three times to protect me."

What a fucking hero, I thought. I was tempted to remind her of all the times he'd endangered her and others, but I didn't. What was the point? I didn't want to be with her if I had to beg for her to stay. I wasn't *that* pathetic.

Suddenly, it came to me. This wasn't about her wanting him,

but about her not wanting me. "You're mad," I said. "It should've been me, not him, and you can't forgive me."

Gia frowned and then shook her head. "No. That's not what I meant. I've never once wished it were you."

"I don't believe you. I'm your boyfriend, and I should've been the one to take a bullet for you." I swallowed the lump in my throat, hating the way my words sounded as they fell into the cold room. It was the truth, and we both knew it. I'd replayed that day over and over in my head on an endless loop, trying to figure out when I should've known they were going to shoot, how I should've shoved her out of the way, why I didn't put it all together before Luca did.

I'd half expected her father to kill me when he heard the full story, or at least to write me off. I apologized, acknowledged that it should've been me, and he'd forgiven me. He'd patted me on the back and said, "No, son. It wasn't your fault." He meant it, too.

"You can't forgive me," I said, realizing that was where she differed from her father. "You look at me and think it's my fault he's dead. Well, you're right, and I'm sorry. I can't change that."

Gia clutched my hand suddenly. "Adrian, I've never once blamed you. I am so, so grateful it wasn't you that got shot. I know it's been hard for you to watch me mourning Luca, but you have to realize it would be even worse if I'd lost you."

She seemed sincere, but it didn't make sense.

"If you don't blame me, then what's changed? Before…the shooting, you hated him. Ever since, it's like you're in love with him all over again."

Gia was quiet, and then she nodded. "Adrian, the entire time we've been together, I've always believed that you would sacrifice yourself for me if you had to. I don't doubt you would've jumped in front of those bullets. But until Luca did just that, it never occurred to me he would. I always thought Luca only wanted me for bragging rights or to impress his father. I never believed Luca truly cared about me more than himself. At least, I never believed he loved me enough to die for me, without even thinking about it."

She paused again, swallowing loudly. "Had I known that before, I would've chosen differently. I'm sorry."

She stood abruptly and took her wine glass to the kitchen. I assumed that was my cue to shut up, but I couldn't, not just yet.

"Okay, so now you know he loved you, but that doesn't really change anything with us. Luca isn't here now, and I am."

Gia turned to face me. "I can't be with you when I feel this way about him. It feels like I'm betraying you both. I'm sorry."

I shook my head as I made my way to the door. I needed to leave before I said something I'd regret. I was determined to be mature, sensitive to her feelings, respectful of her loss. But I couldn't ignore the acute pain that she'd caused me, yet again, by virtue of her yo-yo style of love.

"I'm not going to wait for you this time, Gia. One day you're going to realize what you're giving up, and I won't be there to give you another chance," I said. I clipped a leash to Scruffy's collar and slammed the door behind us. He seemed confused about why we were leaving the apartment without Giada, but I simply tugged him along. Once outside, I marched up to Enzo's car.

He was off the phone and turned to me as soon as I approached. He rolled down the passenger window but didn't smile. I sighed.

"I assume you already knew Giada was breaking up with me," I said, now understanding why he was there in the first place. Although, did she seriously think she needed her bodyguard? Like, that I would make a scene or refuse to let her leave or something?

Enzo's face showed no emotion and offered no confirmation of whether I was right in my assumption or any hint of whether he approved of her decision. Typical.

"She's still in my apartment. Just tell her to leave my key on the kitchen table when she leaves."

He nodded.

I paused in case he wanted to say something, but he remained silent. I stormed off down the street.

~

Giada

I waited for Adrian to return, but he didn't. After a half-hour passed, there was a knock on the door, but when I peered out the peephole, I saw Enzo.

"He said to leave his key on the table," he said.

"I'm waiting for him to come back. We weren't done talking."

"He said you broke up with him. He's not coming back, Giada. Leave the key, and let's go."

I sighed but did as he said and then followed him out to the car.

"You want to talk?" he asked as he started the car.

"Nope," I said. I assumed anything I said to Enzo, along with whatever Adrian had already told him, would simply be passed along to my father. So instead, I just silently stared out the window, watching the trees blur together as we sped along the interstate.

CHAPTER 7

Giada

I still had enough of my sleeping pills left to knock me out that night. Then, I spent the next day by the pool. I couldn't take my mind off Luca, though. I was starting to think I'd imagined it all, that he wasn't really alive. By evening I couldn't wait any longer. I had to see him. But since that was impossible, I'd settle for talking.

Butterflies filled my stomach as I dialed. I told myself he had nothing to do aside from answering his phone, but since I couldn't leave a message, I felt a lot riding on the call. It rang twice, then stopped. There was a pause, then he answered.

"Pronto."

I exhaled with relief. "Hi," I said. "I hoped you'd answer."

"Yeah, well, I have so much other stuff to do," he teased.

"You had no way of knowing it was me."

"Very few people have this number. The others don't call it."

"Ahh. Is this ok? I mean, it's not an emergency or anything. I just wanted to hear your voice. I started to worry I'd imagined it all."

He took his time answering. I pictured him settling down on the couch, running his fingers through his dark hair. "It's fine."

"I used to talk to you at night when I couldn't sleep."

"Huh?"

"The last month. I mean, you didn't answer, obviously. But I figured if there really was a heaven, maybe you could hear me."

"You pictured me in heaven?" Luca laughed heartily.

I ignored the implication. "I told you all the stuff I wished I'd said before. Everything I ran out of time to say."

"Like?"

I felt my cheeks flush even though he couldn't see me. Somehow, it felt too personal to repeat it all now that he wasn't dead. "Like thank you. And I'm sorry. And I love you. I forgive you," I added after a pause.

Luca didn't answer right away. "I think I would've liked to hear that last one the most."

Suddenly, the days remaining before the weekend stretched on for an eternity. I didn't know if I could last that long without seeing him, touching him.

I slept in the next morning, then divided my day between the gym and the pool. Since Luca had "died," I'd lost nearly eight pounds thanks to my daily routine of forgoing food in favor of sleep. I'd become a pale, scrawny shadow of my former self. Meanwhile, Luca had taken the time to get even hotter. Now I was determined to rebuild the muscle I'd lost and add the glow back to my complexion.

Having a goal, even an entirely cosmetic one, felt good. Still, I needed something else to occupy my time. I couldn't visit Luca as often as I wanted without arising suspicion, and now that I wasn't involved with Adrian anymore, it looked like I'd be staying at home for a while. I decided to spend my time updating my childhood bedroom.

I snapped some pictures of my bedroom and took the basic measurements. I drew a plan of the room, then used materials from my interior design class to design my dream bedroom. My mother was so thrilled to see me with a plan, albeit a pathetic one that implied I'd never leave home, that she fully embraced my ideas and offered me a ridiculously high decorating budget.

In class, we'd learned to work with a variety of budgets, so as I browsed my options, I tried to reign in the budget a bit. I settled on a primarily grey color scheme with touches of lavender and metallic silver accents. I wanted the room to look sophisticated yet feminine.

I hoped that sooner rather than later, Luca would resolve whatever issues were keeping him in the land of the dead, so to speak, and that I could move away with him. When I did, this room could become another guest room in my childhood home. But until then, I might as well love where I was sleeping.

My new project cheered me up, but I had some lingering guilt over the way I'd ended things with Adrian after reuniting with Luca, so I made my way over to church in the late afternoon. I hit up the confessional first, then plunked down in the third pew for some quiet reflection. Ever since I'd been a child, the church was my safe place. Inside the dimly lit, ornately adorned sanctuary, I found shelter from whatever was tormenting me, be it internal or some outside force. Outside my sanctuary, I could attain almost the same level of calmness with my rosary. Stroking the smooth slopes of the beads instantly tamed my anxieties, and speaking the words of the rosary prayers intensified the calming effect.

On days like today, where the church was empty aside from myself and Father John, I spoke the prayers aloud, my soft whispers piercing the silence of the cavernous room. The effect was powerful, reminding me of how small I was, comparatively speaking. My problems were nothing in the grand scheme of things.

I finished with the rosary but remained seated, enjoying the rare peacefulness I felt. I reached for my phone to text Enzo and let him know I'd be ready to leave soon, then stopped when my fingers brushed against my car keys. I still didn't understand what prompted my father to suddenly loosen the reins on me and let me drive, but I wasn't about to look a gift horse in the mouth.

The sanctuary door opened and closed loudly, but I didn't turn to see the newcomer, having learned from experience that people attending church on a weekday afternoon usually didn't do so for the company. Worshippers who were compelled to attend outside of mass, like me, were generally here to atone for something.

I noticed Father John scurry across the room, abandoning his booth in favor of a side hall. Judging from the loud footsteps, the newcomer joined him. My curiosity over the situation blossomed, and I wished I had been nosy earlier. As the men's voices grew louder, I could tell they were both agitated, but I couldn't distinguish any words, just a general tone.

Realizing I was now too distracted to absorb any of the benefits of my surroundings, I stood to leave. Right as I neared the back hall, where the massive solid wood doors opened into the grand entry steps, the door to the side hall burst open, and my brother Angelo appeared.

His jaw was set firmly, his fists clenched and his brow furrowed, so I instinctively jumped out of his way. Despite his steadfast focus on whatever had pissed him off, he noticed the motion and turned to me.

"Giada? What are you doing here?"

He lurched forward, closing the distance between us in one purposeful step. His gaze narrowed. "Did you follow me here?"

In a single breath, my mouth ran dry, and I was reminded of Luca's caution. I hesitated, trying to ignore the murderous look in my brother's eyes and remind myself that he was, in fact, my brother. I was silly to feel intimidated.

At that moment, Father John joined us in the hall.

"Your sister has been here the better part of an hour," he said, his voice as relaxed as ever. "I assumed you'd driven her."

"I drive myself now," I said, raising up the keys I'd been clutching in my hand.

Angelo glared at Father John, then at me, and then turned to the door. "I'll see you at home then, Giada. We have dinner guests coming, so don't be late."

I flashed Father John an apologetic glance then took off after my brother. I practically had to run to catch up.

"What were you doing at church, Angelo?"

He took several brisk steps before swiveling towards me. "What kind of question is that? What does anyone do at church?"

"It seemed like you only showed up to yell at the priest and leave."

"What I discuss with the Father is private. You, of all people, should appreciate that. God knows all the shit you've confessed over the years."

I rolled my eyes, instantly resuming my role as the petulant little sister. "Yes, God does know, but I talk to Father John in the confessional, like a normal person."

Angelo took one slow, measured breath. "Go home, Giada."

He climbed into his Navigator and zipped out of the parking lot before I even took another step. I glanced back at the church steps, where Father John stood watching us warily. I waved, then made my way to my own car.

I barely had time to change clothes before my parents called me down for dinner. I had no interest in sitting through a whole meal with Julia, but after my chance encounter with Angelo, I was too curious about his behavior to feign exhaustion now.

"I called Adrian to invite him as well, but he said he couldn't join us tonight," my father said, cutting into his chicken.

"You called Adrian? Why?" I asked, nearly choking on my water.

He gave me a peculiar grin. "Angelo's girlfriend is here, so I thought it would be nice if your boyfriend was as well."

My stomach sank. I had completely forgotten to tell my

parents about the breakup. Enzo knew, but I trusted he wouldn't have told unless it somehow affected my personal safety or my dad's business. I slowly gazed up at my parents, trying to gauge from their expressions whether they now knew.

"So, um, what exactly did he say?"

"Uh, just that he couldn't make it. Nothing else, really. He sounded busy."

"Yeah, he's swamped. Still working as a teachers' assistant but also doing that internship with the public defender's office full time. Plus, it's a really far drive."

"He's a hard worker," my father agreed.

I opened my mouth, certain now was my chance to casually mention that I wasn't seeing Adrian anymore, but before I worked up the nerve, my dad continued.

"He's a good man. I had my doubts at first, but you chose the right man for sure. He's been a good influence on you."

My mom immediately jumped on the bandwagon to sing Adrian's praises as well. Neither of them went so far as to truly disparage Luca, but they both made it clear that they thought I was a better person when I was with Adrian and not Luca. *Great.*

I took a healthy swig of my wine and turned to Julia, eager to shift the focus off of myself. "So what do you do, Julia? I mean, other than my brother."

The clang of my mother's fork on the plate signaled that my words hadn't come out exactly as I'd intended. Okay, well, maybe I'd sort of meant it that way, but...

"I mean when you're not with Angelo," I clarified, feeling my cheeks heat up. "What's your job?"

Julia seemed unaffected by the gaff. "I'm an aesthetician."

I reached for my wine, desperate to suppress the eye roll. "Do you do hair?"

She shook her head as though the notion were ridiculous. Judging from her grotesquely long fiery red nails, she certainly wasn't working with acetone or other manicure chemicals.

"I mostly work as an eyebrow technician, but I also do makeup and occasionally general waxing services. I'd be happy to give you a makeover sometime if you'd like."

Everyone else at the table smiled at this sickly-sweet offer. Personally, I felt like vomiting. I glanced to Matteo and realized he was struggling not to laugh, which calmed me immensely.

"How nice of you," I crooned. "Lord knows I can use all the help I can get."

Angelo glared at me, but his doting girlfriend clearly missed the sarcasm in my tone. I focused on my broccoli for a minute, then changed the subject.

"How's business going lately, Dad? Things staying busy at the shipyard?"

He nodded, but was clearly suspicious of my curiosity. "Just fine, Giada."

"So is there a timeframe here for when Angelo officially takes over the family business, or how does that all work? Are there certain projects he's in charge of now?"

My brother and father both stopped eating to eye me warily now.

"Let's leave the shoptalk outside the dining room," my father said.

"Why the sudden curiosity in my life, Giada?" Angelo asked.

I shrugged, trying to act casual. "All that drama at the church makes me think something big must be going on."

I pretended to be completely absorbed in cutting my chicken breast, but I didn't miss the look my dad shot Angelo. So, I hadn't actually learned anything, but I sure felt pleased.

After dinner, I made my way out to the garden. A few minutes later, Matteo joined me. He handed me a tall glass with a green leaf in it.

"It's a mojito," he explained. "Julia made them."

I grimaced, now wondering if it was poisoned. But the night

was hot, and the icy cold mint drink tempted me. I tentatively sipped.

"I hear she's good at waxing pussy too," Matteo said after a moment.

I laughed so hard I nearly dropped my drink.

"You're terrible."

He grinned.

We were both quiet for a moment, and then he asked what I meant about church. I told him what had happened, hoping he'd enlighten me, but either he didn't know why Angelo was arguing with a priest, or he wasn't at liberty to tell me.

"What's with you two lately?" he asked.

I shrugged. "Ask Angelo. He's been a jerk to me ever since Luca…"

"He's always been a jerk. Maybe you're just more sensitive to it now."

I rolled up my sleeve and showed him my arm. The bruising had faded some, and the low lighting with the sun setting on the opposite side of the house meant he had to squint to see it, but he did.

"That was Angelo?"

I nodded.

"You need to give him some space. Stop pushing his buttons."

"He never gives me a break. Why should I go easy on him?"

Matteo patted my leg. "You two are so similar, and I know you hate when people say that, but it's true. And when your temper explodes, someone might lose an eye or get their hair ripped out, but if you push him too far…"

I sighed. I knew what he was saying. *Don't pick a fight you can't win.* Still, I needed answers. "He was so supportive up through the funeral. And since then, I don't know. It's like something changed. What was the deal with him and Luca?"

"What do you mean?"

"Were they friends, rivals, what?"

"I dunno. Both?"

I waited for him to clarify.

"They had a lot in common. Their upbringing, their fathers, you…"

"Angelo seemed to respect me more when I was with Luca."

"I think he just figured you were less of a wildcard with Luca in the picture. Men like him tend to be able to control their women," he said with a snicker. "That's probably why Angelo went for a girl like Julia."

"Is that what you think I was to Luca, a dumb blonde on his arm?"

"Well, you're not blonde or dumb."

"You know what I mean."

"Is that why she bothers you so much?"

I shrugged. "I don't like her. Everything about her rubs me the wrong way."

"She's nice," Matteo said. "And she doesn't pry or ask questions, which Angelo loves."

"He's going to marry her, isn't he?"

"Probably."

I shuddered. I didn't know why it bothered me to think of Angelo marrying Julia. Maybe because up till a few months ago, it looked like I'd be the first Conti to walk down the aisle and now…

"Please tell me you don't have some serious girlfriend you've hidden away from the family for months."

"You will be the first to know if I ever mature enough to settle down."

Oddly enough, that was comforting.

"I'm going out tonight with some friends. If you'd like to tag along, you're welcome to come. I mean, assuming Adrian wouldn't mind."

I relished the thought of escaping the house. After what my brother had just said, I sensed I should tell him about the breakup. But since I couldn't tell the truth of why I did it, my explanation would only involve more lies. "Adrian won't care."

~

Luca

I went to the store in anticipation of Giada's next visit, greeting her with wine and a medium-rare filet. I would never be an expert chef, but I knew meat. Even in my cabin with a simple two-burner stove, I could prepare a steak to mouthwatering perfection. I played music while I worked, an old Sinatra CD. For the first few weeks, I'd been frustrated with the lack of technology in my cabin. But now, I was beginning to embrace its charm. Back in my real life, I hadn't heard a CD in years. And with all the digital options, I wouldn't even consider Sinatra most days. But now, he was perfect.

I heard the crunch of gravel and peered out the window, confirming it was Giada. Then I wiped my hands on a towel and started out the door to help her with her bags, but by the time I reached the porch, she was already there. She dropped her bag on the stained wood plank floor and leapt into my arms, knocking me backwards a few inches.

I hadn't expected that level of enthusiasm, but I certainly wasn't complaining. I placed my hands under her thighs, supporting her while we kissed. The sensations from her legs wrapped around me, her damp lips against my own, and her long hair forming a cocoon around us woke every part of my body, but it wasn't an erotic kiss. It was the greeting I'd expect after months apart, not mere days.

As our mouths parted, I lowered Giada to the ground, but her arms remained tightly wound around my neck. She buried her face against my chest until, suddenly, I realized something was up.

I delicately nudged her backwards, spotting the tears in her eyes that immediately confirmed my concern.

"Hey, what's wrong?"

She shook her head dismissively and reached for her bag.

Sensing her determination, I followed her inside and locked the door behind us. She made her way to the bedroom to drop off her stuff, so I went ahead and slid the steak onto plates. She returned right as I poured the wine.

She stared at the CD player curiously, as though she'd never before seen one, then looked at the plates full of food.

"Wow, you have a whole seduction scene going here, don't you?" she teased. She wiped her eye then came closer, smiling.

"I'm not feeding you until you tell me what's wrong."

Giada shook her head, causing dark strands of her hair to fall over her face. I swept them behind her ear, resenting anything that obscured my view of her deep brown eyes.

"I'm waiting," I said.

She rolled her eyes. "I'm just glad to see you. That's all. I promise."

"You saw me a few days ago."

"Yes, but before that, I thought you were dead. And since then, I can't shake the feeling that this isn't real, that you're not really back." She reached for her wine and chugged half the glass. "I had all these dreams, after you were shot. In my dreams, I always knew you were dead, but then it would turn out that you weren't. Sometimes you were faking, sometimes it was all a dream, but every time, right when I would relax and let myself accept that you were really here, I'd wake up, and you'd be gone again."

I dragged her closer and pressed my mouth to the top of her head. "I'm here now, and I'm not going anywhere. And this is as real as it gets." To make my point, I pinched her ass. She squealed and swatted me, then tucked herself tightly against me again.

I held her against my chest, reveling in the warmth of her breath on my arm and the weight of her hands against my hips.

Nothing felt better than holding Giada in my arms, and after the last couple of months, not knowing if I'd ever again get to hold her, I appreciated the moment even more.

"So will you feed me now?" she asked after several minutes. "This smells amazing."

I nodded and laughed.

We made small talk while we ate, and I was content to avoid any serious topics. I really wanted to know about Angelo, though. Before I'd left my old life, I'd had some suspicions that he was up to no good. I didn't have any evidence and wasn't sure if it was even me that he was double-crossing or maybe just his own father, but I hadn't been able to shake the feeling. Since Giada had shown me the bruise he'd left on her arm, I had grown even less fond of the man.

"How have things been with Angelo this week?"

Giada shrugged.

"He's either working or with Julia, the pussy waxer."

I nearly spit out my wine. "Jesus, Giada. You kiss me with that mouth!"

She made a face. "You say things like that all the time."

"No one ever accused me of having a sweet innocent mouth. Besides, I thought she was a hairstylist or something."

"No, she does waxing, tweezing, makeup application, and maybe spray tans. I don't even think she does nails."

I smiled to myself at the disturbing thought that Angelo's girl may have seen more pussy than him. Still, that was irrelevant. "Have you had any more arguments with him?"

Giada shook her head.

"No more bruises?"

"I've avoided him mostly."

I nodded. That was good, really. Except a large part of me really wanted to garner some intel about what he was up to, and Giada was my only potential informant.

Then she winced.

"What?"

"There was something weird. I was at the church one day, and I didn't think anyone else was in the sanctuary. As I was getting ready to leave, I overheard what sounded like an argument and then saw Angelo storm out of Father John's office.

"Angelo goes to church with you?"

"No, that's just it. He hadn't come with me, and he actually seemed to think I'd come to spy on him or something. And he's definitely not a regular churchgoer, so I don't know what Father John could've done to upset him."

I briefly considered the possibilities, then filed away the information. I'd have nothing but time to ponder the details after Giada left. For now, I didn't want to waste my time with Giada thinking about her brother.

~

Giada

We didn't even bother cleaning up the dinner dishes before retreating to bed that night. We made love, then stayed up talking for hours about the most random things. When I woke, Luca was still asleep, but his leg was wrapped around my ankle like an anchor. It made me wonder if, even unconscious, he feared I'd leave him.

As I was effectively trapped, I let my mind wander. Since I'd last left the cabin, I'd been plagued with questions about the big revelation Luca had shared with me. I'd been so eager to ask him everything and to fill in all the blanks in my head, but as soon as I'd seen him, I had forgotten it all.

But now, in the quiet cabin, brightly lit by the mid-morning sun, it all flooded back to me. The things he had told me made me look at my family differently, caused me to question everything they did. I didn't understand how I hadn't noticed before that they were different from other families. Yet at the same time, I still wondered if Luca was right. Surely, my father wasn't like his.

The story my parents had told me my entire life still fit. My father owned the shipyards. Shipments came and went at all hours, so he worked odd hours. He trusted family most, so of course, a lot of family worked with him. Having strong family ties didn't make us mafia. Carrying a gun didn't make my father a criminal. I wouldn't deny that his business wasn't entirely legit, but to call him a mob boss seemed…extreme.

Luca groaned and wrapped his arm around my waist. He squeezed tightly then cleared his throat. "Good morning, sunshine."

"Morning," I whispered.

He abruptly lifted himself up over me, nudging me onto my back, and smiled as he hovered over me at the crest of a pushup. "Have you been awake for long?"

"No, just a bit. I was thinking."

"Uh oh. We can't have that happening before breakfast."

"Why did you tell me about my dad, about my family? You know, that stuff you said last time, about how he was…" I paused then lowered my voice to a mere whisper. "In the mafia."

Luca quirked an eyebrow. "Yeah, I remember."

He slowly lowered himself down, and I was momentarily distracted by the multitude of muscles rippling in his arms as he moved. He planted one soft kiss on my lips before fully resting his weight on me.

"Why?" I repeated, unwilling to be distracted by the delicious sensation of his body against my own or the tingling feelings he was arousing in my body as a certain part of his body fully awakened and pressed firmly against my belly.

"Because it's the truth, and you deserved to know."

"But you've known for years. Why tell me now?"

He blew out a sigh. "To keep you safe."

"You didn't want to keep me safe before?"

"Amore, I got shot for you. Repeatedly. And I literally shielded you with my own body once before that," he reminded me.

My mind briefly flitted to that fateful day, when I'd hated Luca with all my heart and he knew it, yet he still dove over me when some crazy guys drove by and shot at me.

"You didn't need to know before because I was there to keep you safe. Now, I am out here, and unless you stay right like this all the time, I can't protect you."

"You think I am in danger?"

"Not specifically. But I think if you'd been more aware of the facts, you could've avoided some of the dangers in the past. Your father thinks he's protecting you by keeping you in the dark. I say knowledge is power."

I giggled at his statement. Luca wasn't a fool by any means, but he had never been an overtly academic guy either.

He kissed me again, but I couldn't lose myself in the moment like I usually did with him. He noticed and rolled off of me onto his side. He left his hand on my abdomen, where his fingers traced small circles along my sensitive skin.

"What's wrong?"

"I'm just having trouble believing it all, I guess."

"You think I'm making it up?"

"No. But maybe… I don't know. You're so deeply entrenched in all this that it might cloud your judgment is all."

I paused, but he didn't answer. It occurred to me that I'd offended him, basically accusing him of lying when he'd apparently breached some key code amongst his group by telling me what he thought about my family. But I knew I couldn't go another week wondering about it all.

"I just thought about what you said all week whenever I was around my family. And I can't believe my father is some murderous criminal. He's not perfect, but he's a good man."

"He is," Luca agreed.

"Huh?"

Luca sat. "Everything I told you last week was true. Your grandpa was the head of the most prominent organized crime family in Connecticut. Your father took over when your grandpa Giuseppi was killed. He's been grooming your brother Angelo to take over for years."

I frowned. He said it all so matter-of-factly that it made me want to slap him. "My father isn't like yours!"

I pushed off the bed and stormed towards the bathroom. I'd barely made it to the entrance when Luca grabbed my arm. *Gah!* He had reflexes like a jungle cat.

"I'm not trying to upset you, Giada. That isn't why I told you." He frowned. "Your papà is nothing like mine. I agree with you. I'm not saying he's a bad man. He loves you, and he would never hurt you. I have nothing but respect for your papà."

I stopped pulling away, so Luca dropped my arm.

"But I'm also not lying when I say that his business isn't entirely legal. He's got police in his pocket, politicians on his payroll, and dozens of businesses in bed with him. I guarantee you the feds have a folder this thick on your father." Luca pinched the air with his fingers.

"If they ever got proof, or any witnesses stupid enough to testify against him, they could charge your dad with a dozen different crimes at least. But that's not going to happen because he's smart, he's careful, and he's very well protected. My papà is feared, but yours is respected. They each do things their own way, but at the end of the day, they're both in business with some very bad people."

I turned away from him but didn't move, so he continued.

"I don't want to ruin your relationship with your father or brothers, and I don't want you to be scared. I only want you to be aware of what is going on around you. If these bad people get upset with your father, they won't go after him because they know they can't get to him. They'll go for the weakest link, which is you and Matteo."

I processed his words slowly and in silence "I need a shower," I said finally.

"I'll make coffee."

As soon as the hot spray of water hit my face, I calmed down. I didn't know why I'd been so antagonistic to Luca, especially when he was just trying to keep me safe. He'd made it abundantly clear that he was crossing all sorts of lines by even revealing what he knew about my family.

Keeping my hair out of the water, I ran the soap over my body then shut off the faucet. I toweled off, then grabbed the new lingerie I'd brought. It was a fiery red lace balconette bra, matching panties, and a garter belt. I didn't need the garter belt now, of course, but surprising Luca with the rest of the getup would be a good way to apologize for freaking out on him earlier.

When I poked my head around the corner, Luca was seated on the couch, coffee mug in hand with his eyes focused on one of the magazines I'd brought him. I took a deep breath, then started towards him.

His eyes roared to life when he turned to face me. His lips parted, but no words came out. After a moment, he simply grinned.

"Is the great Luca Marino actually speechless?" I teased.

He shook his head then nodded. We both laughed until he crooked his finger towards me, motioning for me to step closer.

I did, tentatively, happy to draw out this moment as long as I could.

"Wow," he finally said. "You look phenomenal."

"I'm sorry," I said, swinging a leg over his knees to straddle him.

"I can see that," he said. He ran his hands up my thighs, still grinning widely as his lips pressed into my own.

He kissed me until we were both dizzy, then lowered the cups of the bra down below my breasts. He stroked his thumbs across my pebbled nipples until I was sure I would pass out. I pulled my lips away from his, desperate for a full breath of air, and he replaced his hands with his lips. My body swayed towards him, all of my nerve endings on fire from the delicious way his tongue teased my nipples.

When I was sure I couldn't handle any more of his sweet torture, I rose to my knees, giving him space to slip out of his boxer briefs. Luca reached for me, sliding a finger under the thin material, and stroked me twice before retreating. He tugged on the material, again causing me to break the kiss.

"Don't you dare rip my new lingerie," I cautioned, only partly serious.

Luca raised an eyebrow. "Challenge accepted," he whispered against my lips. He scooted the scrap of material to the side and lowered me onto him, both of us groaning as our bodies joined as one. Having been nearly ready to combust solely from the attention he'd laved on my breasts, I probably could've come within a minute. But just when I was nearly there, Luca lifted me off of him and gently nudged me onto my back on the couch.

He tugged the panties down my legs and tossed them behind the couch before diving over me again. We made it a few more minutes before both of us found our pleasure then collapsed against each other, our bodies still entwined.

After we caught our breath, Luca left the couch briefly, stepped back into his boxer briefs, then returned with a coffee mug for me. It felt oddly luxurious, sipping coffee while lying naked on his couch under the soft fur blanket. I expected Luca to sit beside me, but instead, he lowered himself to the floor. He rested his head on my breast and splayed his fingers across my abdomen.

I relaxed for a moment, simply enjoying the moment. Despite everything, I felt completely at peace. I rested my own palm over his hand, then shifted a minute later so our fingers were entwined. Neither of us spoke, both content to sip our coffee in silence. I traced the pattern on the signet ring he wore on the middle finger of his right hand, following the shape of the L, M, and T. Luca Tomás Marino. As I did, I realized he'd worn that ring every time I'd seen him over the last several years, but I'd never noticed it in high school.

"When did you get this?"

He lifted his head and frowned, then nodded when he saw I was pointing to his ring. "You want, like, the exact date?"

I chuckled. "I guess I meant the occasion." I paused. "Wait, do you know the exact date?"

"I do, yeah."

"You said your father gave this to you, right?"

"Yes."

"Graduation present?" I guessed, unclear why his tone had suddenly grown uneasy.

He breathed a laugh. "Something of the sort." He rose, lifted my head, then sat on the couch with my head and shoulders resting on his lap. "My papà gave this to me when I was officially made a man of honor. It's a family tradition, I guess. All of the men in my family have received a signet ring on the day of their initiation."

Suddenly I felt dumb for not having made the connection before. Of course, it was some sort of mafia thing. "But my brothers don't wear a ring. So is it just your family?"

"Yeah, just my family. It's maybe more common in Italy. The history of the signet ring is pretty cool. Originally, they were designed for the actual seal on official letters."

"Hmm. Wait, so like your biological family, or your...other family?" I tried to recall if I'd seen Alessio wearing one, but hadn't really ever checked out the guy's hands.

"Biological." He chuckled. "It might be a dead giveaway to the cops if we all wore matching rings."

Now I was craving more details. "Can you tell me about the whole initiation thing? Is it like fraternity hazing or a formal ceremony or what?"

"No."

"No…what?"

"No. I can't tell you about it. Not in detail anyway."

"Oh. Because then you'd have to shoot me?" I gazed up at him and smiled.

"Pretty much." He squeezed my hand. "It's not like guys apply for membership. You're chosen, you're groomed or trained, you learn the rules, you prove yourself. Then you take an oath, and it's done."

I assumed there was more to it but appreciated that much detail. "It's not like a blood oath?"

"Actually, it is."

"Really?" I chuckled.

Luca nodded. "Why are you laughing? This is serious stuff."

I shrugged. "I just didn't realize anyone did blood oaths in real life."

"It's tradition."

"So…did my brothers do the same thing?"

"I don't know. And I don't recommend asking them."

"What about this ring?" I asked, lifting the thumb of his left hand. A thick platinum band with a thin black line rested on his thumb.

"This one is from my mom."

"Another initiation gift?"

"God no. Just a present."

"But you always wear it."

He twisted the band for a moment, then wrenched it off his thumb and handed it to me. "Can you read the inscription?"

I squinted to read the tiny lettering. "Il sole della mia vita," I read, shaking my head.

"The light of my life," he translated. "Or quite literally, the sun."

I handed the ring back to him. "Wow. Your jewelry is all really meaningful. All that my jewelry says about me is that I like sparkly, pretty things."

Luca raised an eyebrow and ran his fingers along my ring finger. "I predict someday you'll have two rings of your own with a lot of symbolism."

I smiled at the implication. "In this future, do you see yourself wearing an additional ring then as well?"

"If I'm lucky," he said.

I barely had time to register the sweet sentiment before he swiveled to face me and ducked his head beneath the blanket. His hands slipped under my butt, lifting me to his mouth. I cried out when his tongue hit its goal, but then I relaxed against his lips.

I didn't understand how Luca worked my body the way he did, making me crave his touch as if it had been weeks, and not mere minutes, since I'd last found my release. But he was a magician, and by the time his strong hands flipped me onto my stomach, I wanted nothing more than to feel his full length inside my body. He moved slowly this time, as though worried I'd be sore from the last several rounds, but within a minute, the tension coiled deeply inside of me, threatening to explode yet again.

CHAPTER 8

Giada

When I returned home, I held on to the peaceful happy feeling I'd enjoyed during my stay with Luca. I overheard my mother telling Matteo how relieved she was that my father let me visit Gabriella since the visit clearly perked me up, and I began to formulate a plan. Soon, I'd move in with Gabriella, or at least to an apartment near her. Then, I could visit Luca whenever I wanted without raising suspicion. Since he still wasn't offering any estimate of when he planned to rejoin the world of the living, I had to plan on sneaking around for the long haul.

In the meantime, I focused on enjoying myself as I passed the time until my next visit. Matteo proved an unlikely ally, inviting me to hang out with his friends again. I quickly accepted, certain the distraction would be worthwhile.

I stayed out late with Matteo, having forgotten how refreshing it was to let loose, drink and dance. My brother's friends were a fun group, and though a couple of the single guys danced with me, all of them kept it strictly amicable. I wondered if that was because they thought I was with Adrian or simply because I was Matteo's sister, but regardless, I liked it. I had zero interest in flirting or repelling come-on lines. I entertained fleeting thoughts about how fun it would be to have had Luca with me, but even if he were alive, he was unlikely to take me out to such a club.

I slept in the next morning, then dressed to head out on a shopping trip to grab a few accessories for my new room. The furniture had been delivered, and I'd finished the painting, but I still needed to find some final touches. My father asked Enzo to accompany me, which immediately arose suspicion in my mind. Why had they been comfortable with me driving myself for weeks and now, today, I needed a babysitter?

Remembering Luca's request that I not protest or question their attempts to keep me safe, I agreed. Besides, it was nice not to have to look for parking at every store we visited.

My visits to the first two stores were fairly quick and unsuccessful, but I lingered in the third shop, finding a multitude of accent pieces that brought a smile to my face. Apparently, Enzo had grown bored because he appeared to be cleaning the inside of my car when I returned.

"Why is there a gun in your car?"

Enzo's loud, accusatory tone startled me, and I dropped the clutch I'd been holding. He bent and retrieved it for me but locked his eyes on mine as he handed it over, forcing me to answer.

"It's mine. I have a permit for it."

"Why?"

"Because that's the law."

He growled. "Why do you have a gun?"

"Same reason you do, I suppose."

"Giada…"

I nearly had to laugh. His tone had never sounded more

parental. To think I'd almost slept with him. I shuddered at the thought.

"Do you feel threatened? Did someone say something? Do something?" He pulled his phone out like he was going to text for backup.

"Enzo, someone shot at me. On two separate occasions. I don't think it hurts to be prepared."

"You have me."

I was tempted to remind him that he wasn't the one who kept me safe that fateful day, but he already felt horrible enough about that. Besides, I didn't blame him.

"Those men are gone."

My stomach tightened. Did Enzo know how completely gone they were? Surely, he must. Yet he hadn't bothered to tell me.

"It makes me feel safer. End of discussion."

He frowned. "Well, you need to learn how to use it."

"I already do."

This surprised him. "How? I know your father wouldn't—"

"Luca," I said. "Luca taught me."

Enzo didn't speak for a minute. I wondered if this information improved Luca's standing in his mind or knocked him down even further.

Finally, he handed back my purse and walked around the car. "Well, you need a refresher course sometime. The next time we're at your father's, I'll review with you."

I rolled my eyes, but really, I supposed it wasn't a big deal.

The next day, I spent my morning exercising and working on my room, then I went to church. It was a Tuesday, so there wasn't anyone else in the sanctuary when I arrived. I didn't mind, though. I had so much on my mind to work through, what with everything Luca had told me about my family and his own. I selected a seat near the front, clutched my rosary, then shut my eyes. I made it through the full series of rosary prayers and had just begun to let my mind wander when I heard footsteps.

"Giada." The soft voice startled me out of my daze. I turned to see Father Ryan gazing expectantly at me. "I was just about to have some tea in my office. If you don't have to be anywhere for a little while, I'd love some company."

I hesitated, struggling to ignore the voice in my head that told me Ryan's offer sounded suspiciously like a pickup line. After staunchly defending the clergy of my faith to countless skeptics in college, I couldn't put myself in a situation to be proven wrong.

"Please. I have chai," he said, as though that somehow would entice me.

I followed him down the hall despite my better instincts.

His office was a smaller version of Father John's, but I hadn't been in it before, so while he prepared our drinks, I explored.

"Sit," he commanded suddenly, offering me a steaming mug when I turned to face him. The mug bore the logo of the New England Patriots which, for some reason, surprised me.

"You're a football fan?" I accepted the tea and lowered myself onto a hideous floral armchair.

"I'm allowed to have interests outside the Church," he said, sitting on the armchair across from me.

I leaned my head towards my mug, inhaling the spicy-sweet aroma of the tea to avoid cringing at the implications of his statement.

"You've been to confession every day this week, and then you sit in silent prayer after. Yet when you leave here, you look no more certain than when you arrive. I don't know the nature of the confessions you've shared with Father John, but nothing you've told me merits this heavy heart." He paused, blowing lightly on his own drink. "I thought perhaps there might be something else troubling you, something you'd feel more comfortable sharing here rather than the confessional."

Relief washed over me as I decided I hadn't been wrong about Father Ryan. He was not hoping to seduce me but rather to help me. How awkward it would be to confess that assumption tomorrow.

"Confessing our sins is a sacrament," he continued. "We are called to participate in these sacraments, but they bestow benefits on us, too. Reconciliation washes you clean of your sins, and for most people, that brings with it feelings of relief and peace, or even joy."

"This is my happy face," I said, eagerly anticipating the meager responsive smile from the priest.

"If there's anything else you'd like to tell me, it's all still confidential, regardless of where we are when you tell me."

I sighed and sipped the tea. It was curiously strong but tasty.

"It's authentic chai. I did mission work in Mumbai," he said.

I nodded appreciatively. "I'm more of a coffee person but this is surprisingly good."

He didn't reply, and the silence stretched on. I figured I might as well start talking. Priests probably could endure hours of awkward pauses.

"I said everything there was to say in confession. I really try not to do too many bad things, so hopefully there isn't much."

"And yet your heart is troubled?"

"Well, yes."

"Has prayer and meditation been helping?"

I shrugged. Of course, he didn't reply, so I then explained.

"The trouble is that the things that are bothering me aren't my secrets to confess. There are things I know that I shouldn't. Secrets I'll take to my grave." As soon as the words left my mouth, I chastised myself for being overly dramatic, but my language piqued his interest.

"We have something in common then, Giada," Father Ryan said with a smile. "I hold quite a few secrets of other people too. But it isn't our burden to share alone. God knows what is in your heart. Let Him shoulder some of this burden. Let me."

"You don't mean for me to tell you other people's secrets…"

"Anything you tell me is confidential. I won't tell anyone else, and perhaps you'll feel lighter."

"The secrets I know…they'd get a lot of people in trouble. If I told you, you'd be in danger."

"Are you in danger?"

"No."

He frowned, setting his mug on the table beside him. "Forgive me for being forward, Giada, but I've seen you coming and going, I've seen the various men who accompany you here, and it's hard not to form some observations about your situation."

I shook my head, needing him to stop. "Please don't. I assure you nothing good will come from you making assumptions about what is going on with my family."

Father Ryan didn't speak, but I could tell he had a lot more to say. The sadness and concern in his eyes made me feel pathetic.

"No one is hurting me," I offered. "I'm not, like, a domestic abuse victim or anything."

He remained skeptical.

"I have a bodyguard," I blurted out, having never really called Enzo that before. "My father is so concerned someone will hurt me that he pays someone to drive me around and keep watch over me. My father is paranoid and overprotective, but he'd never hurt me. And my brothers, they wouldn't harm me either, but even if they ever wanted to, there's someone else keeping them in check. And no one outside the family would ever risk the wrath of my father and brothers, so if you think about it, I'm essentially the least endangered person alive."

"Okay," he said, his expression making it clear he was no more convinced.

"My brothers…well, have they ever confessed something bigger to you? I mean, I don't even know if they ever go to confession." I paused, then shook my head. "I'm sorry. You can't tell me anything about that. Forget I asked."

Father Ryan didn't answer, and nothing in his expression

indicated whether or not my brothers had confessed their more significant crimes. If they had already told him, I figured it wouldn't hurt for me to talk with him about it. Obviously, he couldn't do that. Besides, it was highly unlikely Angelo had even seen the inside of a confessional since his first communion.

I gazed around the room, eager to change the topic, but something about the setting compelled me to talk further.

"Father Calvin, at the church by my college, he said something once that stuck with me. He said that choosing to follow God means choosing good over evil."

Father Ryan appeared to consider this before nodding. "I don't disagree with that statement. Do you?"

"No. It seems pretty basic, but I guess that's what's troubling me. I think I keep choosing evil."

"You think?"

I didn't answer.

His eyebrow rose to a point. "Nothing you've confessed to me has ever risen to the level of evil. Failing to reach perfection doesn't make you evil; it makes you human. We're all flawed."

"It's nothing I'm doing, exactly. It's a choice though. It's…well, this seems trivial to bother you with because I guess it's basically a dating dilemma."

A look of bemusement crossed his face, but he quickly regained his composure.

"There are two men in my life. One is good. The other is…" I stopped abruptly. Luca wasn't evil. His father, maybe, but Luca, no. His heart was good. He just didn't always make good choices. "He does bad things. I guess I'm worried that doing bad things means he's a bad person."

I wrinkled my nose, wondering why exactly I'd started down this rambling path. Well, it was too late now to go back and keep my mouth shut, so I just continued. "Anyway, every time I have to choose between the two, I feel like I should pick the good guy, but I don't."

I chewed the inside of my lip, suddenly mortified for blabbing my entire love life to a priest.

He was quiet for a long time, then finally shook his head and chuckled. "I'm sorry, that was unexpected, is all. I've been watching you these past couple of weeks, and I thought I'd figured out your problem, but…"

As he glanced down to his lap, I noticed for the first time that a few pamphlets lay face down on his robe. He held them up, showing me.

"I guess you don't need these," he mumbled.

I leaned closer, noting that all the titles were focused on grief and bereavement. Now, I felt like an even bigger fool. Here he was, assuming I was mourning Luca, when instead I told him I was interested in two men.

I didn't say anything for a full minute. I needed to leave, soon. This whole discussion had been a mistake.

"I'm sorry for wasting your time," I said, shifting to stand.

"Giada, wait." His eyes locked on mine, commanding me to sit. "People are rarely good or evil. And if God keeps bringing someone into your life, there's probably a reason. Maybe God wants you to help this man find his way back to the Church. Maybe His plan is for you to help him choose good over evil."

"So you don't think I'm making a horrible mistake?"

He cocked his head to the side. "I didn't say that. I would never purport to be a dating expert. I only meant that our world isn't random, and there is a reason for the things that happen to us. And sometimes, we can discover what that reason is if we search hard enough."

I blew out a sigh. I appreciated the effort but didn't feel any less "troubled" or whatever than when we'd begun this discussion. "I appreciate your time and the tea," I said, standing.

He smiled politely and stood as well. "This man, the one you're not so sure about, is he Catholic?"

I nodded.

"Why don't you bring him in sometime? I can talk with you both, and—"

"I can't," I interrupted. "He's dead."

Father Ryan's mouth fell open.

"Well, that's what the rest of the world thinks anyway," I added, feeling eons lighter already.

I watched his eyes widen in recognition of what I'd just said before I turned and let myself out of his office. I was nearly at the oversized doors exiting into the parking lot when I heard him call after me.

"Stay safe, Giada."

I didn't turn around.

~

Adrian

Single life was easier than I'd expected, especially with Giada gone from campus. The last time she'd broken my heart, I struggled to move on, in part because I literally saw her everywhere. Now, there were memories of her, and lots of places on campus that sparked those memories, but no physical sightings. Besides, between my full-time summer job and my part-time gig for a professor, I was busy.

Scruffy didn't hurt, either. I wasn't going to keep him permanently, but the shelter still didn't have space for him. A volunteer told me they'd probably have more room by fall when college students returned to campus and adopted some of the cuter pets. Without Giada dominating every free minute of my time, I had time for human friends, too. Mostly that meant Ryan, and we spent a few evenings each week together, and he proved to be an excellent wingman. Or at least he would, once I was ready to date. Sometimes we'd meet up with a group of guys, occasionally for poker, more often for trivia. And sometimes I'd even invite the other interns from work to come along.

Speaking of work, it couldn't be going better. Having experienced behind-the-scenes work at the prosecutor's office, it was fascinating to see the other side of the coin. In law school, I'd always assumed defense attorneys were all weasels, looking to nitpick the cops and prosecutors. Sure, I'd read all the treatises on the importance of constitutional rights for defendants, but until I saw it all in action, it seemed like a lot of bullshit. Now, I saw it differently.

Without excellent defense attorneys, the justice system was a joke. Putting innocent guys in jail meant guilty guys were free to continue harming the public. It also destroyed people's trust in police and lawyers. A good defense attorney wasn't cheating the system; he was making sure that the prosecution didn't, either. It was a system of checks and balances at its finest.

Besides, it wasn't like I was letting murderers go free. Most of the cases I worked on involved traffic violations and minor drug charges. They were the sort of crimes that really didn't have any victims. So even if my clients were guilty, which of course, they weren't, society was no worse off for it.

Scruffy and I sure weren't losing any sleep at night over it.

~

Giada

The next day, I went to see Luca. It was a gorgeous summer day, so we took a long walk through the woods. When we'd returned to his porch, I pulled out my phone to show him the photos I'd taken of my finished bedroom suite remodel.

"This looks great."

"Maybe someday you can see it in person." He didn't answer,

so I paused again. "I just wanted my room to be someplace where I felt comfortable and happy."

"Why don't you do this more?"

"I don't have any other bedrooms."

"No, why don't you decorate other places? Isn't that what you studied in school, interior design?"

"Well, yeah, but…" I stopped talking before I said that no one ever expected me to actually work. How had I been okay with that vague, unspoken plan?

"There have to be some design firms somewhere in the area. Look them up, and send them your resume."

"I'm sure they've already done their hiring for the year." The month I'd spent grieving him had eaten up the main hiring season for recent grads.

"You don't know that unless you try. Look, you've got an advantage because you don't need a paying job right away. You can offer to do an unpaid internship. You'll prove your value and then get hired on for a full position."

Luca made it sound so obvious that I wasn't sure why I'd never looked into it before. I supposed it was because I was undecided. My love of fashion design rivaled my love of interior design, and the feeling that I had to choose one passion and forgo the other paralyzed me. Although, I did have to admit I was better at the interior design stuff than fashion design. I loved clothes and accessories and had a natural talent for eying what would look good on whom and in what circumstances, but actually designing the clothes was a whole different ballgame.

"Okay," I said finally. "I think I can do that."

"Good."

Luca looked uncharacteristically pleased with himself.

"But if I'm going to do something that scares me, you are too," I said.

Now he chuckled. "I taught the most easily distractible person I know how to shoot. If that didn't scare me, nothing will."

"You need to tell your mother you're alive."

"No." There was no room for negotiation in his voice. "That's completely different."

"I can't stop thinking about how miserable she looked at your funeral."

"You don't even like my mother," he reminded me.

I couldn't argue with that sentiment. "But I do know how it feels to love you and to think you're dead."

He pursed his lips together but didn't budge. "My father had his reasons for not wanting her to know. He doesn't think she can keep the secret. And besides, it would put her in an awkward position to know the truth and not be able to let him know that she knows."

"Your father is leaving for Italy soon. I overheard Angelo say something about it."

I noticed his expression lighten some and knew this was my chance.

"Luca, your father is cruel to do this to her. You aren't. Write her a note or something, or let me go talk to her."

"What if she doesn't believe you?"

"She will. I guarantee she'll clutch to any hope that you aren't gone, Luca."

He sighed and stared at me for a minute, his eyes filling with sadness. "I honestly thought it would be better for you. When my papà told me the plan, and I was all hopped up on the pain meds, the only thing that I was confident in was that it would be easier for you to move on with Adrian."

"You were wrong."

"So you've said. But the jury is still out on that."

I swung a leg over his thighs. Luca's hands gripped my hips holding me in place on his lap. "I don't understand why you sell yourself so short. And me. I'm not an idiot, so why do you assume I'm wrong when I say I'm happier with you?"

"Because you're clearly blinded by love?" he teased, lightly kissing the tip of my nose.

We were quiet for a few minutes, both of us content to snuggle together. Then, Luca broke the silence. "I live for these visits, Giada. Thank you for finding me, for bringing me back from the dead."

I smiled, but his words piqued my interest. When would he truly return from the dead? I loved hibernating with him too, but I was ready to rejoin the real world. Still, I'd asked before, and he'd been annoyed. We were happy now, so I didn't want to ruin that with the what-ifs.

CHAPTER 9

Giada

I'd fallen into a tenable routine, spending my weekdays at home before holing up in the cabin with Luca all weekend. My family thought I was visiting Gabriella each time. While the web of lies I was spinning had grown massive, I naively thought I was handling it. My family was pleased to see that I was no longer moping around over Luca all the time, and they didn't really question why Adrian hadn't been by the house lately.

At the end of August, Gabriella was headed home to spend the weekend with her family, so I told my parents I'd be with Adrian over the weekend. Since Enzo still hadn't ratted me out about the breakup, he probably didn't plan to. Besides, for all he knew, I'd rekindled things with Adrian. It certainly wouldn't have been the first time. When I told them I'd be heading out to visit him the next day, they didn't question it, so I smiled to myself and headed out to buy some more new lingerie.

Adrian

I cursed myself for accepting the call the moment I answered. It wasn't like I hadn't seen the caller ID; I just couldn't bring myself to ignore the man. He had no good reason for calling, so why I continued to subject myself to his manipulation was beyond me.

Marco sped through the preliminaries with his usual charm, but I wasn't naïve enough to assume this was merely a friendly call. Finally, his tone changed, signaling he'd reached the real purpose of his call.

"I know you're busy with work this summer, but I was wondering if you'd given any thought to what type of practice you'd like to establish after you graduate."

"Um, well, I will probably keep up the research work for the university at least first semester, and then I might look into a summer job at one of the larger law firms."

"Yeah, I could see that being a good fit for you. Listen, if you are interested, I could put in a good word for you at a few of the firms I'm familiar with, maybe get you an interview at least."

"Why would you do that for me?" I asked, aware my bluntness may come off as rude, but I knew that with Marco Conti, everything had a price.

He chuckled. "Well, since it seems things are getting pretty serious between you and my daughter, I figured it would be in her best interest to make sure you secure a good job. Lord knows *she* doesn't have any lofty career aspirations."

"What makes you say that?" I asked, totally stumped as to how he could consider our latest breakup as something positive for our relationship.

"Well, she's made no effort to find a job, and…"

"No, I mean about our relationship. Did Giada say we were serious?"

He paused. "No, I suppose not. But she's been spending a lot of time with you over the weekends. She's headed out to stay with you tomorrow too, right?"

I was too confused to answer quickly. By the time I realized Giada had clearly tangled me into one of her lies, I had already paused too long to play it off. I could almost understand why Gia wouldn't tell her parents she'd dumped me. They liked me. Plus they hated how indecisive she was with her dating life. But why would she tell them she was spending the weekend with me? Where was she going instead?

"I'm sorry," I said finally. "I might have my dates mixed up, but I didn't think she was coming here tomorrow. Maybe she's going to see Gabriella?"

Marco paused. "No, she definitely said it was you."

"Well, she's been scatterbrained lately. You know Giada," I said, tossing in an awkward laugh for good measure. Although, it was funny, really, in the ironic sort of way. Clearly, *none* of us knew Giada. Where the fuck was she going? I had to admit I was curious now.

"Listen, could you do me a favor?" Marco began.

Every fiber of my soul screamed no, but I didn't actually speak aloud.

"I'm worried about her. She hasn't been the same since…the accident. She's become very private, insistent on driving herself everywhere, and Enzo told me she's begun carrying a gun. If there's anything you've noticed lately or that she's told you, would you let me know? I want to make sure she isn't in some kind of trouble."

I couldn't imagine Gia with a gun. She hated guns and everything they represented. She must be in some sort of trouble. "Yeah, of course. But really, she hasn't said anything to me lately. I don't know what could be going on."

Marco blew out a sigh. His concern for his daughter was clear, and for once, it was warranted. "Alright, I have an idea. Don't tell her I called, okay?"

"Wait, what are you going to do?" He'd sparked my curiosity, and I certainly couldn't count on Gia to tell me anything since we weren't actually speaking.

"Not a thing. I won't tell her we spoke, and I'll let her leave tomorrow as planned. I'll have someone follow her and find out once and for all where she's headed."

I started to ask how that was even possible, but then I remembered who I was talking to. Marco probably had trackers in her car, purse, phone… I wouldn't be surprised if he'd somehow microchipped her toe with a tracking device at birth. He was *that* paranoid about his baby girl.

"I'll do it," I said, startled to hear the words aloud. I opened my mouth to take it back, but then stopped. I wanted to know where she was headed just as much or maybe more than her father did. After the way she'd left me with no explanation, I deserved to know.

"Okay," he agreed. He gave me the specifics, and we hung up.

~

Giada

The next morning, I had a lot on my mind as I started off towards Luca's cabin, but as I drove further into the wilderness, I grew lighter and happier. I realized the situation with Luca couldn't go on indefinitely, but there was something wonderful about knowing he was stuck in the middle of nowhere with nothing to do but await my arrival. After years of feeling like he prioritized his work, his friends, and his ego over me, it felt indulgent to be the only focus of his attention.

I was so distracted by my thoughts about what Luca and I would do once I arrived, that I didn't notice the familiar Jaguar in my rearview mirror until I was on the long, winding, single-lane road that covered the last few miles before the cabin. I slowed to a crawl, trying to decide if I should panic or if I was simply over-reacting.

With the cabin barely in sight, I recognized the driver of my mystery shadow. I stopped abruptly and flew out of my car. Adrian shifted into park and stepped out of his car as I approached.

"What are you doing here?"

"Your father was worried."

"So he sent you?"

"He doesn't know we're...not together anymore. I thought you should be the one to tell him."

"You can't be here. You have to go, Adrian."

"Where are we? Why are you here?" Adrian gazed around us. There was nothing but trees as far as we could see in all directions, except ahead. Luca's cabin was clearly the sole destination at the end of this road.

"Adrian, seriously, come on. Let's just go now. I'll follow you back to town."

He stared past me at the cabin. "Whose cabin is this? What is going on, Gia?"

I shook my head. "Please, Adrian. Just get back in the car." I reached for his arm, and he shook free. "How did you find me anyway?"

Before Adrian could open his mouth, a voice behind me answered.

"GPS. Your car has a tracker. So does your phone."

"Luca?" Adrian's eyes widened.

I swiveled to face Luca. He appeared calm, but a small black handgun was in his hand. "Why are you holding a gun?"

"I heard voices," he replied.

"It's just us. He followed me, but he's leaving now," I said. I turned back to Adrian. "Come on. I'll explain later."

"Luca?" Adrian repeated, his eyes still wide.

"Yes, that's Luca," I replied.

"So this is why you broke up with me?"

"I told you it was because of Luca."

"You left out the part about him not being dead."

"You broke up with him?" Luca asked. "I told you not to."

I turned back to him. "You are not the boss of me," I said through gritted teeth. "And why do you still have the gun out?"

He raised an eyebrow.

"Get in the car, Gia," Adrian said. "Now!"

I flung my hands up. Those two were exasperating, treating me like some wayward child they were co-parenting without a game plan. "I'll get in the damn car when I want to."

As the words left my mouth, I glanced from Luca to Adrian then back and realized my car was exactly where I wanted to be at the moment. Not because I worried Luca would shoot me, although Adrian's chances of being a target likely increased simply due to my presence, but because I didn't want to stand here and watch them argue.

~

Adrian

I'd never seen Gia look as frazzled as she did when she climbed into the car to drive off. But what stuck out more was the way she looked at Luca right before she did. Her expression was so tender, so filled with emotion, that it nauseated me to see. It distracted me temporarily from the fact that I was standing in front of a dead man.

Had I encountered him in different circumstances, I wouldn't have believed him to be real. But the way Gia looked at him erased any doubt in my mind. Once upon a time, she'd looked at me that way. Apparently, to stay in her good graces, I would've had to take a bullet—or three—for her, die, then come back to earth.

Kind of hard to compete with Lazarus.

I walked closer, and much to my surprise, Luca shoved the gun into the back of his jeans.

"You don't want your gun for protection now?"

"Protection from you?" he laughed.

Bastard. Although, he had filled out quite a bit. Apparently, he'd come back to life with an extra twenty pounds of muscle.

"So, uh, did you get a promotion? I figured it was only a matter of time before Marco sent someone, but I figured it'd be Lorenzo or maybe one of the boys."

"I don't work for Marco. He seemed to think I was still invested in Gia. He clearly didn't realize she was sleeping with you again." I held my breath, waiting for him to correct me, but of course, he didn't. "So, was it all just a setup?"

"I certainly didn't go to the shipyard thinking I might get shot. It's not a fun experience."

"You seem to have recovered just fine."

His eye twitched. "It wasn't easy."

"How'd you wind up here?"

"My papà and a few of his men knew I survived, but everyone else believed I died. I wasn't supposed to tell Giada, but she came out here one day and found me."

"She just randomly came out here?"

"I brought her here once before, when we were together."

"How long has this been going on, with you and Gia?"

He gazed past me, seeming reluctant to answer. "A month."

I blew out a sigh. The timing made sense. Maybe I should be flattered that she had the decency to dump me instead of just carrying on with both of us.

"Look, I get that you hate me, but you can't tell anyone I'm alive. Ever. Certainly not Marco."

"You don't get to tell me what I can and can't do."

His eyes narrowed on me. "I'm telling you now."

"What if I don't agree? Are you gonna shoot me?"

He appeared to consider that option longer than I'd have liked. But then he shook his head. "You and I both know that I can never touch you without losing Giada for good. But if you want to keep her safe, you'll keep your mouth shut." He stared at me for another minute, then turned around and retreated into his cabin, leaving me standing in the gravel in front of it.

I waited a minute, weighing my options. I wasn't so sure we were done discussing things, but I didn't have the balls to go knock on his door and demand answers. As much as I hated Luca Marino, I feared him more. That dude was bad news, dead or alive.

Fuck.

I climbed back into my car and made my way back down the winding path. I spotted Giada's car parked at the first diner off the road. As I neared, I saw her standing beside her car, looking furious. I sped into the spot beside her. She didn't get to be pissed. I was the one who was angry.

I flew out of the car the moment it was in park, killing the ignition almost as an afterthought. "Are you kidding me, standing here like *you're* mad at *me*?"

"You followed me, Adrian. So yeah, I'm mad. And you know what? I'm pretty sure if I marched into that diner and told anyone inside that you, my stalker ex-boyfriend followed me all the way to my current boyfriend's house without my knowledge, they would happily call the cops on you."

Her words were a knife in my belly. The pain was so severe and yet so unexpected that I couldn't even remember what I'd been so angry about before. I stepped back and wrapped my arms over my stomach.

"Current boyfriend," I repeated. "So there it is. You are with Luca, again."

Her expression softened, and I felt a tangible shift in the mood. "I'm sorry, Adrian. I didn't want you to find out this way."

"You obviously didn't want me to find out at all."

"Well, no."

"You lied to me."

"I told you I couldn't be with you because of my feelings for Luca. That wasn't a lie."

"You let me think he was dead."

She gazed down at her feet and shuffled them back and forth in the gravel for a moment before looking back to me. "I'm sorry."

"Your dad told me to follow you."

"You don't have to do everything he says."

I ignored her insinuation. "I was surprised that you hadn't told him about the breakup."

"That's not really the sort of thing I discuss with my father."

"Lorenzo didn't tell him either? I thought he was your dad's in-house spy."

She rolled her eyes. "I guess he's passed that job along to you now."

"Your father asked me to follow you because he was worried about you. Enzo told him you had a gun, and we all noticed you'd been disappearing a lot lately. Your father wanted to make sure you weren't in some kind of trouble."

Normally, I wasn't so quick to jump to her father's defense, but in this case, he wasn't the bad guy. His intentions were pure. She was the one sneaking around with a dead mobster.

"Well, you can report back to him that I'm completely fine, and that I simply went to NYC to observe some fashion shows like I said."

"You expect me to lie to your father?"

She leapt forward. "You can't tell him Luca is alive. Promise me, Adrian. He cannot know."

I suppressed an eye roll. How could she be so gullible? She'd always been naïve, but this was a new low, protecting the man even as she feared him. The direct approach never worked with her though, so I decided to go about it differently.

"Why do you have a gun, Gia?"

She shrugged and stared back at me like an impudent teen.

"Gia, seriously. Think about this. You recognize he's dangerous enough to justify you buying a firearm, yet you still want me to lie to protect him?"

"I didn't get the gun as protection against Luca. I got it because he told me to. He didn't like me driving through the woods alone."

That was so unexpected that I had no response. She took my silence as a chance to keep talking.

"I know you don't like him, and I don't blame you for being mad that I didn't tell you he survived. I found it out by chance, right before we broke up." She shook her head. "Look, he's not keeping anything from me now. I know what he's involved with, what the risks are. He told me all about my father, too. And Angelo."

I flung my hands in the air. "And you believed *him*? Jesus, Gia, I've been trying to tell you for years!"

"I know, Adrian. And I'm sorry. I should've listened earlier. I just want you to understand that I'm not going into this blindly."

I rolled my eyes so hard that I nearly fell over. "You absolutely are, Giada. Look, you don't have to be with me, but don't go back to him. Please! If you truly understood what Luca was really like, you would never sneak out into the woods with him. Jesus, Giada. Do you realize there was nothing stopping him from hurting you this past month? If you had gone missing, your family would've never suspected him?"

She let her eyes drift shut. "I get why you think that, Adrian, but you don't know the same Luca as I do."

"There's an alternate version of Luca that isn't manipulative, narcissistic, and cruel?"

Giada scowled. "You never met the Luca that helped me organize a charity event for pediatric hospital patients or who did my pre-calculus homework when I had strep throat."

"Wait, there's a version of Luca that can do math?"

She lifted her hands as if confused. "Luca's always been good at math. Pretty sure he aced calculus."

I must have looked skeptical because she continued.

"He never got bad grades, even though none of his classes were taught in his native language."

"Why didn't he go to college if he's so smart?"

"His father wouldn't let him. He wanted him to train full time to take over the family business."

"The mafia," I supplied.

She flinched but kept going. "It's different in Italy, anyway. There's not the same assumption that everyone's goal is a four-year university."

"Fine. So he's smart. If anything, that makes it worse. It means he knows how to make you disappear, and if he does, no one but me would even suspect him."

"He won't hurt me, Adrian. You know that," she said, her big brown eyes piercing me with their intensity. "And I'm well aware of the risks I'm taking and what I'm asking you when I beg you please don't tell my dad."

I needed time to think. Alone. Gia would never let me out of her sight until I agreed to keep her secret, so I nodded my head. "You need to tell him we broke up, though." I said.

She nodded and then frowned. "No, you tell him. Tell him I saw you following me, and it was awkward because we broke up. Then, reassure him you don't think I'm up to anything dangerous."

I hated that I could never say no to her, but I told myself that was the quickest way to extricate myself from her world. I needed a clean break from her and a clean break from her father. It was time to stand on my own two feet.

~

Giada

I watched Adrian drive off before returning to Luca's cabin. He was on the porch as I pulled up, and he came to my car to greet me.

"I'm alone this time," I said.

Luca nodded and slipped my duffel bag off my shoulder. After he dropped my bags in the house, we sat on the porch swing. It was a nice evening, but I wondered if we were simply outside because he expected someone else to come by, and he wanted to be prepared.

"I'm sorry I led Adrian to you."

Luca nodded. "I knew it was a risk. Every time you came here, I knew the chances of someone tracking you."

"So why didn't you tell me?"

He angled his head down at me. "Because you knew it, too."

I frowned. "You should've told me to stay away then."

"Yeah."

I flung my hands in the air. "Then why didn't you?"

Now Luca simply laughed, which was even more frustrating. He reached over and tucked my hair behind my ear. "Because it's lonely out here all alone. And boring. And I missed you."

I sighed and relaxed into his arms, shifting so I could lean against him and rest my feet in front of me on the bench. We rocked slowly for a few minutes, the squeaking of the wooden glider the only sound.

"You weren't truly considering shooting him." I phrased it like an assertion, but we both knew it was a question.

Luca simply chuckled.

"No matter what happens, you know I'd never forgive you if you hurt Adrian, right?"

"Yes," he said quickly. "But it's only a matter of time before I do something else unforgiveable."

I wanted to disagree, to tell him shooting Adrian was the only thing he could do that I'd never forgive...but he was right. There were many other things he could do, and the longer we were together, the more likely he was to do one of them.

"He won't tell anyone," I said. "He's a man of his word."

"He'll tell your father," Luca said. He spoke quickly and with such conviction that I almost wondered why he hadn't shot Adrian if he was so certain of the fact.

"He won't."

Luca kissed the top of my head. "Yes, he will. Maybe not right away, but eventually. I'll be shocked if he makes it a week without telling."

"He said he wouldn't."

"And I guarantee you he will. He'll think he has to. He'll think it's the best thing for you."

"I hate how so many men in my life think they know what's best for me."

Luca's breath battered my head as he chuckled.

A squirrel leapt across the far railing of the porch onto a low tree branch, and I gazed up at the horizon. The sun was starting to set, and the chirping of bugs was beginning to drown out the daytime chatter of the birds. The temperature had dropped several degrees just since we'd been sitting here. Without Luca's arms wrapped around me, I'd be shivering already. But I wasn't ready to go inside yet.

"So what if he tells my dad? You took a bullet for me. You should be my father's favorite person right now."

"It was three bullets," he reminded me. "And it's not *your* papà I'm worried about."

I realized what he meant. "Why would my dad tell your dad?"

"He'll talk for the same reason Adrian will, because he'll think he has to. That's how their arrangement works."

"I'll just make sure he knows your dad already knows you're alive, and then there's nothing for him to tell."

"Giada, sweetheart, that's not what he'll tell. Me being alive is of no relevance to your dad, but me involved with his daughter again…"

"You saved my life. He'll support our relationship."

"I almost died for you, Giada, when you weren't even mine to save. My papà has been clear that I should have nothing to do with you. Your father will support that because he owes me, and therefore my papà, for your life."

I finally understood his point but couldn't ignore how ridiculous it all was. "For years, those two have been trying to force us together, and now they want us apart?"

"Ironic, huh?"

"So, what do we do?"

He didn't answer immediately, but he did tighten his hold on me. "We make the most of the time we have."

"And then what? What happens when your dad finds out?"

"Then I'll head to Italy like I was supposed to in the first place."

I considered that for a moment. Despite our frequent travels to Italy, it had never occurred to me to live in Italy for any substantial measure of time. But why shouldn't I? It was Italy. It was gorgeous and exotic yet familiar and definitely the place to be for fashion design or interior decorating.

"I could move to Italy," I said. The more I thought about it, the better it sounded. Actually, now I wasn't sure why I hadn't opted to go sooner. Moving to Sicily would get me away from my father and his crew of controlling spies, at least.

"No, Giada. I'll go to Italy alone. The whole point is for me to be far away from you."

I slid my feet off the bench and turned to face him. "I don't want you to be far away from me."

"Me neither, amore. But you know it's for the best. We can't go on like this forever."

"Why not?"

His lips smiled, but his eyes revealed that he felt the same way

I did about it all. "That's just not the way we work. Staying together forever is boring. It's ordinary, average. Nothing about what you and I have is boring. We were never meant to be forever, Giada. Besides, I'd rather leave while you still love me."

"I'll hate you if you leave me," I said.

Even though I meant what I said, Luca smiled. And then he kissed me until another brilliant idea popped into my head.

"We could go off the grid for real," I said, breaking off the kiss. "Just like your fantasy, except we'd do it together."

He shook his head. "Giada, you can't disappear. You have too many people who love you. They'd miss you too much. And they'd never stop looking."

"You have people who'd miss you, too."

He raised an eyebrow. "I have you."

I frowned.

"Besides, you'd get bored. And sick of me. And it would be nothing like you're imagining. I don't want to live that way with you."

"You'd rather live without me?"

"I'd rather enjoy the time we do have together and always leave you wanting more of me," Luca said, standing and scooping me into his arms. He carried me into the cabin and set me delicately on the bed. He paused before joining me, wiping a tear off my cheek. "Non piangere, amore," he said. "Don't cry."

~

Luca

I kissed the salty tears staining Giada's smooth cheeks, wondering how many times my poor princess had cried over my death. I hated knowing I'd hurt her, but that hadn't been my intention. I'd thought that by leaving her, she'd be safe. Instead, we'd both suffered.

Giada captured my face in her hands, pulling me from my thoughts as she gazed into my eyes with an intensity that made my heart pound. Only Giada could look at me in a way that felt like my soul was on display.

"I love you, Luca Marino," she whispered. "And I will always want more of you."

Our lips clashed in a tangle of passion that left us both breathless within minutes. When I pulled back for air, Giada nudged me to the side and squirmed out from under me. Her eyes gleamed with a mischievous twinkle as she stood at the foot of the bed. Swaying her hips from side to side, she began slowly unbuttoning her shirt. I scooted back to lean against the headboard, crossing my ankles and propping my arms behind my head. I was certain this was a show I'd enjoy.

Once she reached the fourth button, I deduced the reason for the striptease. She'd bought new lingerie. Again. And I was not complaining, although her father might start wondering how his single daughter managed to spend so much money at high-end lingerie stores. The bra was a sheer white lace, and I was willing to bet the panties matched. When she finally reached the snap on her jeans, I saw that I was right.

I growled my appreciation. I loved Giada in white. It contrasted nicely with her olive complexion and dark hair, but mostly it just reminded me of her angelic perfection. She stopped swaying and gazed at me, smiling shyly as a soft pink hue washed across her cheeks.

"Every time I see you, you're more beautiful than I remember."

"That's the beauty of only seeing me once a week," she replied.

I frowned, but she had a point. When we only had two nights together, followed by several days apart, we spent our days as newlyweds—making love, talking, and cuddling, with only the briefest of breaks for food and other essentials. If we were together every day, surely at some point we'd tire of each other, or at least our bodies would wear out.

Giada knelt on the bed, making quick work of my shirt, then pants. I lifted my hips so she could take off my pants, then I grabbed her while she was distracted, sucking her breast through the thin lace. She moaned as I'd known she would, her back arching to press her nipple further into my mouth. I rewarded her with a gentle nip, then moved on to the other breast. She was panting by the time she pushed me off her, settling between my legs instead.

I dragged my hand through her hair, relishing the way she worshiped my hardened length with her mouth. Giada tackled oral sex the same way she did tiramisu—enthusiastically, pausing to savor every moment. She gazed up at me beneath her thick, black eyelashes, her dimples popping, and I groaned. Later, when she had grown sore from our lovemaking, then I'd let her pleasure me with her mouth. Then, I'd return the favor, too, but for now, I wanted all of her.

I wiggled my hips until she released me, rising onto her own knees again. Before she could make her next move, I inched lower on the bed and grabbed each of her buttocks in my palms. I pressed her against my face, licking and sucking along the thin lace barrier of the thong.

"Not fair," she said, her voice breathless. "If I can't taste you, you can't taste me."

I chuckled at her logic but released her, raising to meet her for a kiss instead. "How about we both taste you then?" I teased.

She shimmied out of her thong while kissing me, then twisted until her back was facing me. I grinned, knowing exactly what she wanted. I leaned back against the headboard and let her slowly lower herself over me. I reached my arms around her waist and hauled her torso to me, sucking her neck and rolling her nipples between my fingers while she raised her hips up and down.

I loved that the position made it so easy for me to touch her. My hands could stroke her clit, her breasts, and her throat, all with minimal effort. And I loved how she relished the control. But I hated that, from this position, I couldn't see the look on her face as her body shattered into sweet release.

I could sense when she was close. Her breathing grew erratic, her nipples hardened into impossibly stiff peaks, and her movements lacked control. That was my cue to take over the brunt of the effort, meeting her thrust for thrust. My fingers reached for her throat right as she moaned. I tilted her head to face me, and the fleeting glimpse of the exquisitely drunk-with-pleasure look on her gorgeous face was all it took to send me over the edge. I pulled her to me as we both caught our breath. She shifted off my lap, but I hooked my leg over hers, trapping her.

She relaxed against my chest and sighed peacefully. After a moment, she turned to me. "How do you do laundry?"

Her question seemed so out of the blue that I laughed.

"I'm serious."

"There's a laundromat like three miles down the road."

"Hmm. So you actually do your own laundry?"

"I'm offended that you seem impressed by that."

She winked and then wiggled away from me, headed to the shower.

We ate dinner on the floor by the fireplace, then played card games until the last embers died out. When we settled into bed, Giada fell asleep quickly, her head tucked against my armpit and her thigh roped around my own. I couldn't help but appreciate the simplicity of it all. Giada and I fit together like two pieces of a puzzle. No matter how we shifted or changed, we'd still find our way back to each other.

I considered what she'd said earlier, about how we could just live off the grid together. It was a tempting idea, and I loved the fantasy of that life—alone in the woods with nothing to do to pass the time except ravish each other, over and over. But it was just that, a fantasy.

In reality, I could never disappear with only Giada. If I did, my papà would retaliate against Alessio, and if we helped Alessio disappear too, well, my papà would likely take it out on my friend's family. Besides, what I'd said was the truth. Too many people would miss Giada if she disappeared.

I assumed this would be my last weekend alone with Giada, so I didn't want to waste a minute. I'd known from the start that this idyllic fairy tale existence we'd been enjoying couldn't last forever, but I wasn't completely sure what the future held for us. I'd tried to sacrifice before, to push Giada out of my life on the premise that she'd be better off without me, but it never worked. Every time, we were pulled back together, like two magnets unable to thwart the simple laws of physics.

I could try to resist her, to stay away, but what was the point? What I needed to do was show my papà I was stronger with Giada in my life. Since I couldn't do that while hiding out in a cabin, I told myself that being discovered would ultimately be a good thing. Once my papà let me re-enter the world of the living, I could prove to him that he was wrong about Giada. She wasn't my kryptonite. She was my strength. She was my reason for trying.

I just had to convince the boss.

CHAPTER 10

Adrian

As I stepped into the lobby of the law school and gazed up, the temperature dropped a good twenty degrees. It could've been the air conditioning, but I suspected it had more to do with Angelo Conti standing off to the side, glaring at me like I just snatched the last steak off the buffet.

"Hi," I said, exerting little effort to conceal my frown. "What are you doing here?"

"I called. You didn't answer."

That was true. "We have nothing to talk about."

"I drove all the way here. I think you could spare a few minutes."

"I have class."

"I'll be quick then." He nodded towards a nearby bench, so we sat.

"I have some concerns about Giada," he began without delay. "She's been acting out and disappearing for days at a time."

"Acting out? She's twenty-two. Let her live her life in peace.

The only concerning thing is how closely you monitor your grown sister's actions."

As soon as the words left my mouth, my stomach clenched. Such audacity was Giada's thing, not mine. I prided myself on controlling my temper and dealing with the ridiculous demands of people in a calm manner.

I braced myself for a look of death from Angelo, but instead, his lips curved into the slightest hint of a smile.

"My father said you offered to follow her last weekend but failed."

"She had disabled all the tracking devices," I said, omitting my thoughts on how odd it was that her car, purse, and phone even carried tracking devices for the benefit of her overprotective family.

"Convenient that she did that right after you were told to follow her."

"If you're suggesting I gave her a heads up, you're wrong. I wanted to find out where she was going just as much as your father and you did, maybe more."

"So it's just coincidence." Angelo's tone fell flat.

"Yes."

Angelo sighed. "I thought you had a class to get to."

"I do." I reached for my backpack. "Are we done here?"

"No. But we would be if you'd just tell me the truth. I have places to be today as well, and I don't appreciate people wasting my time."

"I don't know why you're asking me about her anyway. Giada and I are no longer dating. Her whereabouts are not my concern anymore."

A sardonic grin crossed his lips. "But that doesn't change anything between us, does it now?"

"Yes! I want out. I am completely done with your entire family."

Angelo snickered. "I'm surprised you lasted as long as you did with Giada. She is more than a handful. Can't imagine she's worth half the trouble she causes."

I opened my mouth to say something in defense of Giada but stopped myself. It was not my place to defend her anymore. If I truly wanted out, I needed to stop butting in.

"May I see your phone?"

"No."

Angelo cocked his head to the side. "I hate to sound cliché, but we can do this the easy way or the hard way, Adrian. The easy way has you headed to class in under two minutes."

I resisted the urge to ask for specifics on what the hard way entailed. As far as I could tell, Angelo had come alone, and he couldn't exactly torture me in the middle of the law school lobby. But still, what did I have to hide? I hadn't called or texted his sister lately.

I unlocked my phone and handed it to him. He tapped and scrolled for a moment, then paused.

"Finger," he said, holding it so the screen was mostly covered. I hesitantly pressed my thumb onto the sensor, trying to decide what, other than app purchases, required a fingerprint ID.

A moment later, he smiled. He took a series of screenshots, then pulled out his own phone, presumably sending the information to himself. He handed my phone back to me.

"Giada should have taught you how to clear your tracking history when she erased her own," he said.

"I didn't have anything to do with that."

"Sure you didn't. Just like I'm sure you decided to go for a drive on the exact day and time my father asked you to follow Giada, and you ended up here, in the middle of nowhere."

He held up the image on his phone, and I realized it was a pinpoint map of the location where I'd found her. With Luca.

Shit.

"You're looking a little pale there, Adrian," he said, patting me on the back. He leaned forward. "If it's any consolation, my guys outside just extracted the exact same information from your car, so don't feel bad about letting me catch her this way. I guess it's sweet that you're still protecting her, although some might call it pathetic."

Angelo shifted to stand, and I panicked.

"I didn't tell her a damn thing before I followed her. I wanted to see where she was going, too. And I have no reason to defend her now because, like I said, we are not going out anymore. I don't want anything to do with her, you, or the rest of your family ever again. Tell your father."

"Sure thing, bud. Enjoy your class." He stood and sauntered out, leaving me fuming. My hands were shaking, my head was spinning, and the contents of my stomach were threatening to spew out onto the linoleum.

I had to get to class, but I needed to make a call first. She didn't answer, so I left a message.

"Your brother tracked my phone. He knows where the cabin is, and he might be headed there now. Thought I'd give you a heads up." I hung up, silenced my phone, and hurried to class.

~

Giada

I was driving when Adrian's call came through, but I couldn't figure out how to answer and instead sent the call to voice mail. As I clicked to listen to the brief message, I wondered how long it would take before I could seamlessly multitask while driving.

I played Adrian's message twice, praying I'd heard him wrong the first time. Then I maneuvered a U-turn at the next intersection and called Luca to warn him. He had told me never to leave a message, but he didn't answer, and this was important. I said I was on my way but that my brother probably was too, and that he should lock up and leave. Hopefully, I'd get there before Angelo and play it off like it was someone else's cabin. I had an hour's drive to perfect my story, and if Adrian called right as Angelo was leaving from campus, I should have a half-hour head start over him.

I sped up to ensure I'd have time to warn Luca.

When I was twenty-some minutes away, Luca called. Relief flooded my system until I considered the possibility that someone may have gotten to him first and stolen his phone.

My voice was hoarse as I answered.

"Giada?"

I exhaled with relief at the familiar voice. "Yes. Did you get my message? I'm on my way now. Still maybe a half-hour out, but I'm hurrying."

"So Adrian thinks Angelo is on his way?"

"Yes. I'm so sorry. I guess they tracked his phone. He called to warn me."

"It's okay, tesoro. We knew they'd figure it out sooner or later. You don't need to come here. I can pack up and disappear, and if he gets here before I'm gone, I can handle him. Don't worry."

All the panic I felt moments ago rushed back, nearly choking me with intensity. "You can't leave for good! That isn't what I meant. If you're disappearing, you have to take me with you!"

I pressed my foot harder against the gas pedal. Never before had I needed to reach someplace so quickly. As much as I believed Luca loved me, I didn't doubt he'd pack up and leave without a trace. He still harbored his silly beliefs that I'd be okay without him.

"If you leave without me, I will never stop looking for you," I said. "My life will be ruined."

"Giada—"

"No, just listen to me. Get in the car and go someplace right now. But take this phone and come back when I tell you it's safe."

"I don't want you alone at the cabin with your brother. How are you going to explain that?"

"I'll tell him I'm dating someone, and I didn't want them to know. My family knows I'm not happy about how they got involved with Adrian and me, so they won't question me wanting to hide a new relationship."

He was quiet for a moment.

"Luca, promise me I will see you again this week. Swear it."

The pause stretched on for an eternity, but then he answered. "Yes, fine. But stay safe."

He hung up too soon, but I reassured myself that it was only so he could do as I'd asked.

When I reached the cabin, there was no sign of anyone nearby. Luca usually parked way down the road, so his car wouldn't be visible, and as I approached the cabin door, I noted that it too was locked. I didn't have a key, but peering in the window I saw hints of life inside the cabin. There was nothing in sight to identify the inhabitant, but I figured it would be easier to get my brother to leave if he couldn't access the cabin interior in the first place.

I settled onto the porch swing and opened a book on my phone, but of course, I was too stressed to focus on the words. I swiped from one page to the next without retaining a single syllable. Then I froze when I heard the familiar crunch of gravel as a car approached.

When I saw it was the Escalade, I focused all of my energy on appearing casual and relaxed. As the car rolled to a stop, I noticed my cousin Edoardo was driving. My brother took in his surroundings as he stepped out of the SUV. Eddie remained behind the steering wheel as Angelo approached. I stood, planning to head him off before he reached the cabin steps, but my nerves had rendered my legs weak, so I barely made it across the porch.

"What are you doing here?" I asked, feigning surprise.

Angelo raised an eyebrow, clearly not buying my ruse. "I see Adrian gave you a heads up. I knew I should've taken his phone with me."

"I don't know what you're talking about, but Adrian and I broke up. You should leave him alone."

Angelo brushed past me and jiggled the doorknob of the cabin. When it didn't turn, he went to the windows, cupping a hand over his brow as he peered inside.

"Whose cabin is this?" he asked. "And why are you here?"

"None of your business," I said, measurably braver when he wasn't looking at me.

Angelo swiveled to face me. "Don't play games with me."

I clutched my keys so tightly that the metal cut into my palm. Angelo yanked the keys out of my hand.

"Hey!" I protested.

He inspected the keys, then tossed them off the porch into the gravel. "Why are you at a cabin that you don't have a key for."

"I was reading," I said, frantically eying my keys. My plan had been to leave, hopefully encouraging my brother to follow once he saw no one was there besides me. Now I was essentially trapped until Angelo decided the conversation was over.

"Who are you waiting for?"

"No one you know."

"Giada…" As Angelo glared at me, I was struck by the uncanny resemblance between him and our father, the only difference being that Angelo's expression lacked any of the warmth always present in my father's eyes.

"You want the truth? Fine. I'm seeing someone new. This is where we've been meeting. Adrian followed me here like Daddy ordered because he didn't know I was dating someone else. When he saw us, I asked him not to tell you guys because it is none of your business who I'm dating or what I'm doing. I am an adult. Adrian agreed, probably because he was embarrassed that I'd moved on."

Angelo's face relaxed considerably. I exhaled the breath I'd been holding. He resumed his mission of staring into all of the windows, so I started towards my keys.

Without turning, Angelo reached around and grabbed my wrist. "You're not going anywhere," he said.

"Yes, I am. And you might as well follow. He's not going to come back as long as you're here."

Angelo tugged me closer then grabbed my phone. He roughly pressed my finger against it until it unlocked, then went to my recent calls. I braced myself as he dialed Luca's unnamed number. I knew Luca hadn't set up a voice mail with any identifying information, but since I'd told him I'd call when Angelo left, I worried he'd answer. Angelo would recognize Luca's voice in a heartbeat, and then it would all be for nothing.

I heard the generic voice mail pick up, and for the second time that hour, relief flooded my system. My brother fiddled with my phone for another minute, probably looking through my texts. Finally, he clicked the voice mail from Adrian. I winced.

"A little pathetic that he still cares so much after you cheated on him," Angelo said, handing my phone back. "Did he meet your new man?"

"No."

"You're lying." Angelo paused, his eyes searing into my face. "I bet Adrian could be persuaded to tell me the truth if you won't."

I stepped forward, suddenly emboldened. It was bad enough how I'd treated Adrian; I wasn't about to let my brother abuse him, too. Besides, as cruel as Angelo was, he wouldn't hurt me. Not really, anyway. But Adrian, well, I wasn't so sure what Angelo was capable of when it came to others. I didn't want to find out.

"You will leave Adrian alone."

"Or what?" Angelo laughed.

I tried to think of a viable threat but instead just glared.

"What's his name, your new boyfriend?"

"Eric."

"Eric what?"

"Martin."

"Where did you meet?"

"School. Years ago."

Angelo's expression was blank, so I couldn't tell if he believed me or not. Either way, I wasn't naïve enough to mistake his lack of visible emotion for indifference.

"Any idea when he'll return?"

I shrugged.

"Then I guess we'll wait."

I glanced at my keys. "I'm leaving. It's hot out here, and I'm not going to sit around sweating all day with you."

"Fine, then we'll go inside." Angelo quickly retrieved a handgun and shot a hole in the glass above the doorknob.

I jumped at the sudden explosion as it reverberated through the woods, stirring an uproar from the nearby birds, before leaving dead silence in its wake.

"Jesus Christ, Angelo! Are you insane? You can't just shoot windows."

Ignoring me, Angelo used the gun to wipe the glass out of the way, then reached through and unlocked the door.

"Ladies first," he said.

"No thanks. I've been inside before. I'm going home."

Before I registered what had happened, my back was flush against the wall of the cabin beside the front door. The impact wasn't painful, but the suddenness of it all jostled me. Angelo held my wrist tightly in his left hand and placed his right hand on the wall beside my head, pinning me in place.

"Don't waste my time, Giada. I know I'm some big joke to you, but I'm not in the mood for your games. You may think you're an adult, but until you act like one, no one will treat you like an adult."

He paused, glaring so harshly that I turned my head to the side to avoid staring into his dark, angry eyes.

"I want to meet your new boyfriend, and I want to know why you've been hiding him from us."

"I hate you," I said, boldly facing him head on.

Angelo's lips parted, but before he could reply, a voice from the side of the cabin startled us both.

"Let go of her now!"

Angelo dropped my wrist and turned, his gun reappearing in his hand before I even registered that Luca was walking towards us.

Luca stopped just to the side of the porch, a good ten yards away from Angelo and me. Luca's gaze flitted from us to Edoardo, who had stepped out of the car and was also aiming a gun at him.

My heart stopped beating, and I feared I would pass out. I hated that Luca had blown the plan by returning, but I couldn't help but appreciate that he did so to rescue me. He was an idiot, but a romantic one.

I swung my hand over the barrel of Angelo's gun, hoping at least it would delay him from shooting the love of my life.

"Put it down," I said.

"Giada, walk away," Luca called.

I noticed his hands were both empty and at his sides. I knew he was armed. He probably had a gun at his hip and his ankle, so why wasn't he preparing to defend himself?

"Angelo, please. You can't shoot him."

I tried to say something else, but my voice was gone. I couldn't even breathe, let alone talk. Luckily, my brother's hand slowly dropped to his side. That only left Eddie as a threat.

I took the pause in the action as a chance to look at my brother. Both he and Eddie had the same look of disbelief on their faces. It was then that I remembered. Luca was dead.

"Giada, get your keys and go. I've got this," Luca said calmly, still not moving.

I forced air into my lungs and willed my legs to start moving. I slowly clamored off the porch, but instead of walking to my keys, I went to Luca. I faced him as I approached, but his eyes remained on the men behind me. I stopped when I reached him, turning to face first my brother, then my cousin.

"Can you put the guns down, please?" I asked.

Edoardo glanced to my brother, who nodded, and he lowered his gun to the side.

"Luca, is that you?" Angelo asked.

He didn't answer aloud, but he must have nodded because the next thing out of my brother's mouth was a perplexed "holy shit."

Angelo wedged his gun back into its holster and slowly made his way towards us. As he approached, Luca placed his hand on my hip and tugged me backwards, stepping in front of me.

"You're not dead," Angelo said, stopping several feet away.

"No. Almost died, but didn't. Been here since. Long story, but short version is that my papà found there were some perks to me staying dead. Nothing to do with you."

Angelo frowned. "Except that you've dragged my sister into your plan. That makes it my business."

"He got shot three times protecting me," I reminded my brother.

"I never intended for Giada to figure out the truth. She found me on her own, about a month after the funeral. No one else knows that she knows. No one other than us knows I'm alive, aside from my papà and three of my closest associates."

"And Adrian," Angelo added.

"That's on you," Luca replied.

Angelo stared at Luca silently for several minutes. I wondered if he could even reach some sort of decision without consulting our father.

When Angelo finally spoke, he looked bored. "I'm not leaving my sister here with you."

"I'm not going anywhere with you," I said.

I felt Luca's breath in my ear as he pulled me closer.

"Take your own car, and go home. Angelo will have to talk with your papà. I'll have to speak with mine. I'll call you tonight."

"I don't want to leave you."

"I'm fine. You'll be safer at home."

"I need a minute," I said, praying my eyes conveyed my desperation.

"We'll be right back," Luca said to my brother before motioning for me to follow him behind the cabin. It wasn't exactly the privacy I craved, but it would do.

"I'm not leaving you alone with them," I said.

"I can handle myself, promise. And they'll leave when you do, anyway."

"Promise me you won't disappear."

"Ti prometto," he said. "I promise." He placed his hands on my cheeks and gazed at me for a moment before pressing his lips to mine. I kissed him back, feeling calmer with every second our mouths touched. Luca ended the kiss too soon, then whispered, "ti amo" before brushing a soft kiss against my forehead.

I hated that the moment felt like goodbye, but nothing good could possibly come from my brother witnessing an intimate moment between Luca and me. "You'll call tonight, no matter what?"

He nodded solemnly.

"I'll drive out here alone at night if you don't."

Luca breathed a laugh. "Come on."

He walked me back to where my brother and cousin waited and watched as I retrieved my keys.

As I reached my car, Angelo started back to his own.

"You owe me for a window," Luca called.

Angelo paused then climbed into the car. "I'm sure we'll be in touch," he said to Luca. "And Giada, you are to go directly home."

I rolled my eyes and climbed into my car. I kept watch in my rearview mirror, making sure my brother was behind me as I left. Normally, I would've been offended and annoyed that he followed me the entire way home, but today I found it comforting. As long as Angelo was behind me, he wasn't messing with Luca.

CHAPTER 11

Luca

The awareness that my cabin was no longer secret haunted me the entire night. I dreaded telling my papà that the Contis—most likely all of them, by this point—knew I was alive. But the prospect of waiting and risking him realizing I delayed informing him was even more terrifying. When I called and my papà didn't answer, relief filled my bones.

I busied myself affixing a makeshift patch to the door where Angelo had shattered the glass. I was more concerned about mosquitos than errant mobsters or other human visitors, but I didn't anticipate sleeping, either. I tried to enjoy what was likely the last night of relative freedom I'd enjoy for a while and not to dwell too much on what might happen in the morning.

I was ready to rejoin the land of the living, hibernation having long grown dull and lonely. But I would miss it, too. Just then, my phone rang, startling me from my thoughts. My hands turned icy in anticipation of my first conversation with my papà in over a month. But I recognized the number as Giada, not my papà. I knew there was a chance it was Angelo, or even Marco, so I remained silent as I accepted the call, even though there really seemed no harm at this point in confirming my own existence to them.

"Luca?" Giada's frantic voice whimpered. Then she swore, and I smiled at the thought that she realized she shouldn't have said my name. She was learning.

"It's me, baby. I'm fine. How are you?"

"Oh, thank God," she breathed.

I asked if she'd spoken with her father, but of course, she hadn't. Angelo had followed her home then banished her to her room while he spoke to Marco. The fact that they didn't even include her in the discussion was a fast reminder of how far I'd overstepped in speaking so openly with Giada.

"You can't let them know I told you anything about their… lifestyle," I reminded her. "Or mine."

"I'm not an idiot."

"I wouldn't have told you anything if I thought you were. But the less you say, the better. I haven't spoken with my papà yet, but I will."

She blew out a sigh, reminding me how much she hated uncertainty.

"This is a good thing," I told her. "We both knew I couldn't stay dead forever."

"You saved my life," she said. "I'll make sure my father remembers that and that he knows I only feel safe with you nearby."

Her tenacity made me smile. We spoke a little longer, and when we disconnected, I tried my papà again. When he still didn't answer, I called my oldest and best friend. Despite the late hour, he answered on the first ring. The familiarity of his voice warmed me instantly, and for the first time, I truly believed what I had told Giada. Everything would be okay.

"I'm back," I said without otherwise identifying myself.

"Cazzo!" Alessio swore in Italian, roughly translating to a part of a male's anatomy, but the functional equivalent of the "f" word in English. "It's about fucking time."

"Aww, I missed you too, amico."

"Life has been dull in your absence," he said. "Where should I meet you?"

I'd missed that—the reminder that there was someone ready to do my bidding whatever the hour, whatever the cost. I heard a female voice in the background, and my grin widened.

"You have company," I said.

"They were just leaving."

I chuckled. "You have two women in your bed now?"

"Like I said, life was boring, my friend. I had to do something to keep busy."

As much as I wanted to talk with my friend for hours, I wasn't selfish enough to interrupt whatever he had going on when I really didn't need him yet.

"Don't send them away just yet," I said.

"Oh, you want a taste?" Alessio laughed salaciously.

"Grazie but no. I don't think Giada would approve."

"She knows…?"

"She found me, almost five weeks ago. Angelo caught on tonight. Haven't yet reached my papà, so don't know the plan."

"So you've been back with your girl for over a month now? You dog."

I laughed at the irony of the man in bed with two women calling me a dog.

"Listen, until I know how we're playing this, it's top secret. But if the boss asks you, I should stay on the New York/Connecticut scene."

Alessio groaned. "I miss home. Do you know how humid it is here?"

"Yeah, I'm in Connecticut."

"This whole time?"

"Yep."

"Man, I knew it. I got like this spidey sense that you were nearby."

Now I chuckled even harder. "Where is my papà?"

"He's in town. You want me to reach him?"

I considered that. He might ignore my unknown number, but he'd take Alessio's call. And knowing that my closest friend had spoken to me would offer him some extra incentive not to off me when he heard about Giada.

"Si. Give him this number." I paused, determined to get one last taunt in. "And have fun tonight, but don't reuse condoms."

My friend laughed. "It's all for the environment, man. Alright. Talk soon."

I confirmed my phone was charged, then poured a few fingers of whiskey into a glass. Swirling it around, I had time for only one sip before my phone rang.

"Buona sera mio figlio." My papà's voice was cold as he greeted me formally, *hello my son*.

I braced myself, then told him about the Contis. I didn't dare tell him how long I'd been involved with Giada, as keeping such a secret from him was almost as deplorable as my initial crime of seeing her to begin with.

He didn't have to tell me he was disappointed that I'd pursued a relationship with Giada when I was supposed to be in hiding. We both knew that such a blatant violation of his orders would've had grave consequences for anyone else in his command. My papà didn't tolerate disobedience from his men. Even if his order was wrong, Salvatore Marino wouldn't hesitate to maim or kill anyone straying from the letter of his law.

Lucky for me, I was his son, his only son, at that. Moreover, I was already a fuckup in his mind, so this transgression likely had little effect on his overall opinion of me. Still, I couldn't help but remind him that there were some benefits to our current predicament.

"The Contis are greatly indebted to us. They'll keep this secret while I regain a better foothold on all of Stamford for us. I've been out of the game long enough. We need to take advantage of this while the competition still thinks I'm gone."

My papà was silent aside from his usual labored breathing. I wondered if he'd begun smoking again. My mother always lectured him on his unhealthy lifestyle, but as far as I could recall, my papà lived his life as if he assumed he'd die before any of his bad habits could catch up to him. In our line of work, that was a fair bet.

"Stamford doesn't interest me now. We'll keep a foot in the door there, but for now, that is enough. I am headed back to Mezzogiorno this week. You'll stay in the home here and secure the construction contracts around Bridgeport."

"I thought Angelo was working that angle."

"He is, but he's met some resistance. As you said, you'll have an advantage since no one outside our two families knows you're alive. Keep a low profile, and that will help. If the Conti family is, indeed, as indebted to you as you say, Angelo will have no problem passing this project along to you."

"Well, I don't think—" I began.

"If you aren't up to the task, you'll fly out with your mother tomorrow morning."

I clenched my jaw. My papà was under no misconceptions that Angelo would be willing to help me, or even loosely cooperate. He was forcing me to pit Giada against the heir to her family's throne, and he knew it. It was possible that he believed I was stupid enough to think I could succeed at this fool's task, but most likely he simply wanted to me to admit I couldn't do what he asked. He was probably already booking my flight overseas while we spoke.

"No, that's fine. I actually came up with some ideas right

along those lines over these past few weeks," I bluffed, piquing my papà's admiration for confidence, even when unwarranted. "But I'd like to see Mother before she leaves. Can't let her go on thinking her only son is dead, can we?"

My papà exhaled loudly. "I'll have her arrange brunch. Eleven am at the house? We can talk then."

I agreed, then called Alessio back as soon as I'd hung up with my papà. I hated interrupting his night, but if I was going to convince Marco Conti to force his firstborn son to sign his passion project over to me, I needed someone to brainstorm. I gave Alessio directions to my cabin, then started pacing.

Alessio arrived in record time and greeted me with a hug that could only be shared by two Italian men without raising eyebrows. I gave him the two-minute version of my past five weeks, all of which began and ended with Giada, and he filled me in on everything I'd missed, which took the better part of an hour. Then we got to brainstorming.

By four a.m., having figured out as much as we could at that hour, we decided to sleep.

"You can take the bed," I offered. "It's the least I can do after dragging you away from your own."

He shrugged. "Unless your bed has two willing partners waiting, it's not really an even trade. Besides, your security seems a bit lax right now," he said, pointing at the shoddy patchwork job I'd done above the window. "I'll take the couch and keep watch."

I snorted, fully aware he'd be asleep within minutes. Despite that though, I did rest easier knowing he was out there.

My alarm woke us both at nine thirty, and after a quick cup of coffee, I was ready to launch part one of my plan. Alessio gave me a thumbs up, and I dialed the number Giada had given me for her father.

"Luca, my boy," he said upon answering. "It is a pleasure to hear your voice. I was shocked when Angelo told me the news yesterday, but I have never been so happy to hear a man has risen from the dead."

"Well, I appreciate that, Mr. Conti. And I apologize that my papà didn't feel able to let you in on the secret, but I hope we're able to move past that."

"Sure, sure."

"I realize you're busy, but if you have any free time this afternoon, I'd love to come by and speak with you in person. We have a lot to catch up on."

The older man cleared his throat. "Is this about my daughter?"

I cringed. "Well, no. Although, we'd both appreciate your blessing on our relationship."

Mr. Conti laughed but didn't speak. I wasn't sure if that was a good sign or not.

"I actually had some business matters to discuss."

"I see. Will your father be joining us?"

"I don't think so. I'm heading out to see my parents for brunch shortly. My papà also neglected to tell my mother I was alive, so she'd like to see me in person before flying to Italy this afternoon. But after that, I'm free to come by your house whenever."

"Ah, sure thing, son. I'm headed out to check on some matters this afternoon, but I'll be back this afternoon. I'm sure my daughter will keep you company if you arrive before my return."

"Thank you, Sir," I said awkwardly, hanging up.

Alessio made a face. "That was like watching an awkward scene on the Bachelor."

I raised an eyebrow, unable to decide if he in fact watched reality dating shows.

Alessio returned to his place to shower while I met up with my parents. My mother sobbed the entire meal, alternating between hugging me out of relief and slapping me for letting her think I was dead. My papà, though he hadn't seen me much more recently than my mother, appeared relatively unaffected by my presence, not that I'd expected otherwise.

Since I hadn't eaten food prepared by anyone other than myself for months, I was eager to devour the catered brunch. But between my mother holding my hand and my father interrogating me, that was a challenge. After the meal, I stepped into my papà's office to discuss my plans with him.

"I'm headed to the Conti's this afternoon to talk with Marco," I said.

"Should I accompany you?"

"No need. He's only expecting me." I paused. "Alessio caught me up on some of the things Angelo has been working on lately, so I've got a few ideas on how to do things differently. As you mentioned, Marco is well aware of the debt he owes our family, and when I promise to keep an eye on Giada, he'll feel even more inclined to start repaying the favors."

My papà raised an eyebrow, but didn't voice any disagreement.

"To stay on his good side, I'm not going to ask him to cut Angelo out of the deal. Instead, I'm going to propose a partnership. Asking Marco to put me ahead of his own son makes him look weak, but he'll have no problem cutting Angelo's guys out of it. I'll convince him their time is better served elsewhere. Then, once I'm in, I can squeeze Angelo out in no time and without burning any bridges. By the time I'm done, they'll think it was their idea to leave the local construction scene."

"And how do you plan to achieve that?"

I raised my hands. "I won't bore you with the details. Just know that I've got a plan, and I'm ready to go. I'll ask Marco not to tell anyone outside the immediate family that I'm alive. That's the only favor he'll think he's doing for me."

My papà looked skeptical, but a tap on the door interrupted us. It was my mother.

"Are you sure you don't want to come with us to Italy?" she asked. "You look like you haven't been eating enough."

I wasn't completely sure of the connection between travel to Italy and weight gain, but I had to chuckle. Thanks to an excess of time to work out during my purgatory, I'd actually put on about fifteen pounds of muscle. But to an Italian mother, her son would always look hungry.

"I'm sure, Mamma, but thanks. I'll come visit soon."

She nodded and pulled me in for another hug. The strong floral notes of her perfume infiltrated my nostrils and made me wince. I sneezed right as she angled back.

"Oh! I have the perfect girl to introduce you to when you come visit. Her parents own a restaurant, oh you'd love it, and she is just the most gorgeous thing you'll ever see."

"Mamma, I'm back with Giada, remember?"

She grimaced. "That girl almost got you killed, and she's broken your heart three times now. Or is it four?"

I kissed my mother on the cheek. "She is your best and only hope at grandkids, mom. You better be nice to her."

"You could do so much better, Luca," she said with a sigh.

~

Giada

I eagerly awaited Luca's arrival that afternoon and felt a little giddy when I heard a car drive up. My enthusiasm dampened a bit when I saw he'd brought Alessio with him. Alessio had never been my favorite person, and the fact that he'd known Luca was alive and failed to tell me did nothing to improve his standing in my mind. Still, I hurried over to the car as they climbed out.

Luca grinned at me, but when I rushed to him, he held me at bay then pulled me in for a slow hug.

"Hey, sweetheart. Missed you, and have a favor to ask. Can you just pretend to be one of those girls who does whatever her man asks of her today? I'm trying to prove a point to your dad, and I need him to think you listen to me." He cocked an eyebrow while he awaited my response.

"Will it help your dad agree to let you stay here?"

"Yes."

"Then consider me your most obedient mistress," I said with a curtsey.

Luca snorted and shook his head. "Alright, well, I'm going to chat alone with your dad. Can you keep Alessio out of trouble?"

"Sure." I glanced over to Alessio. "Let's go sit out back."

I watched as Luca went inside with my uncle, then Alessio followed me out to the patio.

"Can I get you a drink?" I offered.

He looked at his watch and raised an eyebrow.

"Iced tea?" I suggested, nipping in the bud his dreams that I was suggesting a two p.m. whiskey.

"Sure. Grazie."

I took my time retrieving the drink, curious what was happening with Luca. The door to my dad's office was shut, though, and I couldn't hear a damn thing, so my intel was limited.

"Who all is in Dad's office?" I asked my uncle Leo.

He glanced across the kitchen table where he was seated towards Antonio, my cousin. "Just your father and Luca."

"You gonna go out with him again?" Antonio asked.

I shrugged coyly.

When I returned to the patio, Alessio had unbuttoned the black dress shirt he was wearing.

"It's hot out here," he explained when he saw me eying his attire.

I handed him an iced tea, then froze, reading the lettering on the grey undershirt he wore.

"Does your shirt say 'Meat is Murder'?" I asked, sitting across from him.

He glanced down, then nodded.

"Is it supposed to be ironic?"

Alessio made a sour face. "No. Every time you eat meat, an animal is killed."

"Are you a vegetarian?"

"Yes."

"Does Luca know that?"

"Yes."

I was literally speechless. I'd always assumed Alessio was some heartless monster, but apparently, he had a soft spot for farm animals.

I chugged my tea, then tried to relax, but I was too fidgety. Alessio remained the picture of calm.

"Do you know what they're discussing?" I asked.

He nodded.

I waited a full minute for him to tell me before realizing he would never actually disclose information with me unless his handler explicitly told him to. Still, I reasoned that Alessio wouldn't appear so relaxed if he was concerned about the meeting going poorly.

"So this is just a routine sort of discussion, right? I mean, there's nothing to be worried about, right?"

Alessio made a face and raised an eyebrow.

"What does that mean?"

He raised his shoulders then quickly dropped them.

"Okay, well, let's start with the easy stuff. Obviously, you don't think my dad will hurt Luca, right?"

Alessio shrugged again.

"Seriously? You think my father might hurt your best friend in the world, and you're just calmly sipping iced tea?"

His face displayed no sense of urgency whatsoever.

Surely he was messing with me.

"I could use a refill," he said, shaking his glass gingerly. "More ice this time."

I gritted my teeth together until I'd controlled the urge to dump his remaining ice on his head. I grabbed the glass and stomped into the house, refilling the drink then lingering on the edge of the kitchen. Of course, I couldn't overhear anything, and with my uncles standing in front of the office, I didn't exactly want to loiter much longer.

I returned to Alessio but held tightly to his drink. Two could play at the withholding game.

It took Alessio a moment, but once he realized what I was doing, he chuckled.

"Luca's right. You are a handful," he said.

"Luca did not say that."

Alessio smirked, but it was unnecessary. Of course, Luca had said that. After another minute, Alessio sighed.

"I do know what Luca and your father are discussing, but I am not going to tell you or anyone else, and I suspect you already know why. I have no idea how your father will respond, but Luca told me to sit out here with you, so that's what I'm going to do. He's a smart guy, and he doesn't need either of us questioning his every move. I trust his judgment, and you should, too."

I wouldn't get anything else out of Alessio, so I slid the drink across the table to him. He thanked me, and we resumed our silence. Alessio was the perfect match for Luca. He was everything Luca wanted in a girlfriend, well, aside from that one major point. I figured I was about as likely to suddenly transform into a complacent, obedient girlfriend as Alessio was to sprout breasts, so probably it was good that Luca had both of us in his life.

I was toying with changing into my bikini to lounge in the pool while we waited when finally Luca emerged from the house. I flew out of my seat, but of course, he went to Alessio first. He whispered something to his friend then came to me.

"Thank you for waiting," he said softly. He placed his thumb and forefinger on my chin and tilted my face upwards, smiling before planting a chaste kiss on my lips.

"Did your meeting go well?" I asked, keeping my voice down since I still didn't know what he was up to.

"It did. Very well. Your father and I are going to be working together some."

Relief flooded my system.

"Let's go for a little walk, and then Alessio and I need to head out."

"But you just got here," I whined.

He ignored my comment and firmly gripped my hand, leading me down the path which meandered across my back yard before heading into the relatively grassy area at the back edge of the property. While it was far enough from the main house to protect any secrets we'd share, there weren't enough trees for us to be completely hidden from sight. So I assumed we were walking back there to talk, not for a quick makeout session.

"Thank you for keeping Alessio company," Luca said while we walked. "I wanted your father to feel comfortable."

"Did you know he's a vegetarian?" I asked, quickly clarifying that I meant Alessio, not my father.

"Yes."

I made a face.

"Why does it bother you what the man eats or doesn't eat?"

Honestly, I wasn't sure. I'd always gotten the impression that he was the muscle behind whatever they did all day, and it was hard to imagine him being too intimidating or tough if he wouldn't even hurt a chicken.

"How's a guy who can't hurt a fly going to keep you safe?"

Luca chuckled softly. "He hates flies and other bugs, actually. You two have that in common. And he won't eat animals because they're innocent. People aren't." He led me to a stone bench just the right size for two, and we sat. "You can trust Alessio. I promise."

I must have looked uncertain because he continued.

"If I told him to eat meat, he would. And he wouldn't hesitate to jump in front of a bullet for me the way I did for you."

Oddly enough, that did reassure me. Not that I wanted to think about anyone shooting at anyone ever again.

"My papà wants into the construction business here. Apparently, he's been interested in that for a while, but he hasn't made a move because your brother has been working that angle. But since everything that went down on your birthday, your father feels like he owes me. So, I was meeting with him to see if he'd let me in on Angelo's business."

"Okay." None of that seemed top secret or dangerous or even remotely controversial. "So why all the seriousness this morning?"

Luca sighed and frowned, and I could practically see the gears turning in his head as he debated how much to tell me.

"Our fathers don't take business from each other. We work together when we can, but we keep most of our business separate. For me to jump into the construction business with your brother, well, he's not going to like it. Having me there will undermine his authority. Some of his guys will get cut out of that game altogether, and some of my guys will get in."

He turned to me, probably trying to see how much I understood.

"I don't think Angelo will do anything because of this. With your dad's agreement, there really isn't anything he can do, to me anyway. But you know Angelo. And you know he's already been…short…with you as of late. This won't help. I want you to be careful."

I nodded.

"I'll be doing some work here and some in New York, so I'll be staying at the house in Staten Island."

"Can I move in with you?"

His expression conveyed his answer before he spoke. "You

know I'd love having you there, but I really have to focus. And I want to show my papà I'm not so dependent on you."

The thought of Luca ever depending on me made me chuckle, but I sure needed him.

"Besides, we don't really want a lot of people knowing I'm back yet, and it'll be easier for me to keep a low profile if we aren't together."

"What?"

"Your father knows I'm not dead, obviously. So does Angelo. But my papà has asked them not to share that information with anyone else. As long as some of the competition thinks I'm out of the picture, we've got a leg up."

I suppressed an eye roll. "This is insane, you know?"

Luca leaned in and kissed the sensitive spot behind my ear. I giggled and arched towards him.

"Think anyone would notice if we snuck upstairs to your bedroom?"

I smiled, certain at least ten people would notice. And I was totally willing to try, except I knew Luca was kidding. I kissed him again, memorizing every detail about him, from his velvety tongue to his sporty aftershave. Already he seemed so much like the old Luca, since he'd shaved clean and trimmed his hair. His arms were still stronger, thanks to his frequent workouts in the cabin, but I wondered if even those would revert to its norm after a few weeks.

Luca made a low growl in the back of his throat then pulled away.

"There's something else," he said. "Since we don't know how your brother or his guys will react, I really don't want you out of the house alone."

"Huh?"

"Can you just lay low for me for a couple weeks?"

I shook my head. I mean, I technically still didn't have a job or anything I *had* to do, but I rather liked my routine of shopping and gym-going and meeting with Father Ryan at the church.

"I have places to go."

He rolled his eyes. "Fine. Just don't drive yourself."

"I like driving," I said, proud that I kept my tone matter-of-fact.

"I know you do, baby, but if I am going to do what I need to do to convince my papà you aren't a problem for me, I can't be worried about your safety. If you need to go somewhere and I can't take you, Enzo will go with you."

"Does he know this?"

"It's his job."

"He has a life outside his job."

Luca rolled his eyes. "Well, that's not really appropriate given his position in your family, but I can't imagine him ever saying no to you anyway. And if he does, call Alessio."

I wrinkled my nose. "This sucks."

He reached over and squeezed my thigh. I suspect it was meant as a comforting gesture, but it sent tingles straight to my core. "No, it doesn't Giada. This is perfect. I'm not hiding out in a remote cabin anymore, and you and I can be together."

"But we still have to sneak around, and you're still treating me like a child."

"The sneaking around is temporary. Eventually, everyone will figure out I'm alive, and then we can go about our lives like normal." He paused. "Although…"

He made a face that alerted me to some lingering problem.

"Although what?"

"Well, come on, Giada. You know what your father does for a living. You know what I do. It's not safe for you to be wandering around alone. As long as we're together, I'll feel better knowing you have a bodyguard."

I sucked in a deep breath. Garnering all my self-control, I decided to shelve that tidbit for a future day. For now, I'd go along with his request that I have a babysitter because I didn't want to jeopardize anything in our relationship. No way was I going to agree to that permanently, though.

Luca tilted his head until we made eye contact. "I love you, Giada. We will make this work."

I nodded glumly but let him kiss me.

Of course, he waited until after the lengthy kiss to tell me he was going to be working tons the next few days and would come Saturday afternoon to see me next. I had figured I'd see him more often now than when he was dead. Apparently, I was wrong.

CHAPTER 12

Giada

As long as the majority of our world still thought Luca was dead or otherwise MIA, I figured I might as well continue my daily routine. Enzo actually looked excited when I relayed what Luca had said, and it was hard not to be offended that everyone seemed relieved that I'd no longer be driving. As a punishment, I signed Enzo up for a gym membership, insisting he go into the gym with me while I exercised instead of lounging in the car outside.

The joke was on me, though, as Enzo hopped right onto a treadmill and jogged the entire time I was on the elliptical. I wanted to be annoyed by that, but it was entertaining to watch. I mean, Enzo had always been hot, and while I wasn't about to make out with him ever again, it was nice to have something to look at while I blasted music on my earbuds.

"Why didn't you tell me you're still a runner?" I asked as we drove home.

He shrugged. "You never asked."

I shot him a look. "I thought we were friends. You can tell me things without me expressly inquiring."

His indignant scowl lessened. "I started running when my dad died. It's a great way to work off stress."

"Yeah, but I thought you'd outgrown that," I said, not sure if I meant running or the stress. "I hate running, so I hope I never have that level of stress."

Enzo chuckled. "Giada, you've had a lot more stressful things in your life than many people have a whole lifetime. I think you're just immune to the stress."

We went home, and I lounged by the pool and read for a couple of hours while Enzo ran some errand for my dad. When Enzo returned, we went to the church. As he pulled the car up to the entrance, I turned to him.

"You're not coming in?"

"I'm not feeling so worthy today. Besides, I have some calls to make."

I shrugged. "Suit yourself."

As expected for a Monday afternoon, the sanctuary was quiet. I took a detour past Father Ryan's office, but he wasn't there, so I went on into the large, ornately decorated room and sat in a pew near the middle. I said the rosary, breathing in the serenity that flowed to me with each prayer.

When I finished, I leaned back and shut my eyes. Images of Luca immediately hit me. I couldn't help but smile, even though I missed him already. I was thinking back to our last weekend on the beach in Palermo, and how nice it would be to simply lounge on a beach with my love, without a care in the world or anyplace to be.

Suddenly, I became aware that I wasn't alone. I opened my eyes, half expecting to see an impatient Enzo ready to go, but instead, it was Father Ryan. He smiled warmly.

"Sorry to interrupt," he said. "I just wanted to say hi."

"It's no interruption. I wanted to talk with you anyway. Do you have a few minutes?"

He nodded, then invited me to his office.

He made us each a mug of chai then sat across from me in the cozy office. "You looked so peaceful and happy in the sanctuary."

"I was just thinking."

Father Ryan smiled. "Yes, but you never used to look happy when you came here." He frowned as though concentrating, then gave me a thorough once over. "You seem lighter. I mean, spiritually lighter, or emotionally."

That seemed to be an accurate assessment. "It's been a good week, I guess. Well, I mean, not really. It was really stressful and hard, but it all seems to be working out well."

"So you picked one of the men?"

I felt myself blush at the silliness of sharing my dating update with my priest, but after soiling his sanctuary with my depression the past two months, I owed him an explanation.

"Well, yes. I did, and he spoke to my father, and it seems everyone is okay with us dating. It's complicated because a lot of people still think he's dead."

"But he isn't?"

"No." I laughed as though that were silly, but then I supposed the whole thing was a tad ridiculous if you didn't know what had happened. "Since this is all confidential…" I began. "On my birthday, some people who had some business troubles with my father tried to hurt me. This guy stopped them, and he got hurt instead. Actually, I thought he was dead, as did the rest of the world, but then I discovered he wasn't. For reasons above my pay grade, he wants some people to still think he's dead. But anyway, he makes me happy, so…"

"That's good," the priest said, smiling. "So no more dilemma."

"Nope. Totally confident in my decision. He is my soul mate." I paused, tempted to ask the priest if he believed in such things, but didn't want to seem trite.

"So, you chose the good guy after all?"

I hesitated, trying to recall how much I'd told him before. I definitely hadn't mentioned names, but Adrian was the man I'd described as the good guy.

"He's not a bad person," I finally said. "It's just, well his father is awful, and then with his job, sometimes he has to do things that you or I might not consider nice."

Father Ryan did a poor job of concealing the disappointment in his face. After a lengthy silence, he spoke again. "The nature of sin is that it's tempting. If it weren't fun and satisfying, at least in the moment, no one would do it. The true test is withstanding temptation, realizing that sometimes, sacrificing some pleasure in the present will ultimately result in a greater, more fulfilling reward in the end."

I tried to decipher his words. "Are you saying I'll go to hell if I stay with Luca?"

"Luca?" he repeated. "Is that, um, Marino?"

So much for anonymity. At least it was still confidential. "Do you know him?

"No. Just heard the name before."

That couldn't be a good sign. "He's not a bad man," I repeated.

Father Ryan's face hinted at a flurry of conflicted thoughts as he parted his lips then pursed them tightly shut several times before apparently garnering the courage he needed to speak his mind.

"Giada, I hope you know you can confide in me. If you are scared, we can keep you safe. There are plenty of resources and…"

"I am not afraid of Luca," I interrupted. "I love him. He would never hurt me. He took three bullets for me!"

The Father's eyes widened.

"He's not perfect, but neither am I." I shook my head. "You were just saying that I looked happy. Then as soon as you hear his name, you assume I'm only with him because I'm afraid?

Think about how hard it is for him to live with everyone making that kind of assumption about him. You're supposed to be better than everyone else."

I stood to leave before he could see me crying.

"Giada—" he started.

But I didn't wait. I bolted out of the office so quickly that I slammed right into someone hurrying down the hall in the opposite direction.

We both grunted upon impact, and I mumbled a quick apology before gazing up. The man placed his hand on my shoulder to steady me.

I recognized him immediately. It was Federico, one of Angelo's closest friends. I thought maybe he worked with, or rather *for*, my brother too.

He frowned, surely recognizing me as well, but before he could say anything, my brother rounded the corner.

"What is going on?" Angelo's voice boomed so loudly that Father Ryan poked his head out of his office.

It must've looked suspicious to Angelo, me sobbing in the hallway with his best friend and a priest. Rico dropped his hand and turned to Angelo.

"We ran into each other," he said. "Literally."

Angelo's frown deepened, and he turned to the priest accusatorily. "Why are you crying, Giada?"

"I'm going home," I said, scurrying down the hall and out of the church. Thankfully Enzo's car was parked right in the front, and he was standing beside it, still on his phone.

As soon as he saw me coming, he ended the call and hurried to open my door.

"Are you okay?"

"Fine. Just drive, please."

"Home?"

"Yeah."

I stared out the window until I calmed myself down. It was

silly to be so upset. I mean, I knew a lot of people assumed Luca was a monster, so it shouldn't even bother me. But Father Ryan…well I'd come to consider him a friend. And the fact that he thought so little of Luca and, in turn, me, well, that was offensive.

As we neared my house, I remembered about Angelo.

"I ran into Rico," I said. "Angelo's friend."

"In the church?"

"Yeah."

"Huh. He doesn't strike me as the religious type."

"No. Angelo was there also."

The crease between Enzo's brow deepened. "That's odd. I was parked there the whole time and didn't see either of their cars."

"There's another lot, a small overflow one by the courtyard," I said. "Although there isn't even an entrance there, so I don't know why anyone would park there unless the main lot was packed." It could take a good five minutes to walk around to the entrance from that lot. I'd only seen it used on festivals, Christmas, and Easter.

"That seems fishy," he agreed. "What did Angelo say?"

"Nothing. I literally just ran into Rico and then left."

I watched Enzo as he drove, noticing how his face tightened the closer we got to home.

"If something was going on with my brother, would you tell me?"

The lengthy pause told me his words would be truthful.

"No," he finally said.

"Luca doesn't want me to be alone with Angelo. He seems to be worried, but not worried enough to let me stay with him."

"You are safe at your house, Giada. There is always someone there who can protect you."

That wasn't the reassuring answer I'd hoped for. "So you agree? You think I should be afraid of my own brother?"

He hesitated again. "No. Angelo wouldn't hurt you. But I do

think Luca is right to be wary. Angelo considers him a threat, and as long as you're involved..."

Enzo blew out a sigh then waved at my uncles as he pulled into the drive.

Luca

*C*oming back from the dead was exhausting. Even though everything with the Conti family had gone perfectly according to my plan so far, my papà seemed determined to watch me fail. I spent my days learning the construction business and my nights managing my papà's clubs. Angelo had successfully crowded out the union guys, so really all that was left for me to do was inject a handful of my guys into supervisory roles.

To the extent possible, I stayed behind the scenes. Alessio was my eyes and ears on the sites. Whenever Alessio reported some reluctance from one of the guys—usually a construction manager — I'd get involved. It was amazing how quickly a midnight visit from a dead man with known mafia ties brought out the spirit of cooperation in people.

In the past, we often had to take action to show people we were serious. Sometimes, we stuck with property damage, but other times, guys got hurt. It was the nature of the business, and I had figured it always would be as long as men were motivated by only two things—greed and fear. But now, my mere presence inspired the same fear that in the past, we wouldn't inspire until a few bones had been broken.

At the clubs, everything was calm. Possibly too calm, I feared, but I decided to let my papà worry about that. The entertainment industry had always been his thing. He adored his stupid nightclubs and everything that went with them—the booze, the sex, the gambling, and the drugs. I really couldn't blame him. It was highly profitable and essentially victimless. Plus, as long as men kept their vices, we'd still be in business.

I was busy enough to miss Giada less than I had when I was in the cabin, but I was still looking forward to seeing her that weekend. She said she was doing fine, but she mentioned she'd seen Angelo at the church three days in a row. With Enzo guarding her, I wasn't too worried about Angelo. He was up to something, and sooner or later, I'd figure out what that was. I was curious about Giada's frequent trips to the church, though. She'd always been faithful, but Enzo explained she now met with some Father Ryan guy daily. When I asked him to describe the man in case I'd met him before, he'd led with "attractive" and "young," which wasn't reassuring.

I wanted to see for myself, so I told Giada I'd take her to mass Sunday.

"You look beautiful," I said, picking her up at her front door. Her hair fell across her shoulders in shiny, loose waves, and she wore a buttercup yellow dress with lavender flowers printed on it. It showed some cleavage and was well above her knees, but still seemed classy enough for church.

"Thank you. You look rather dapper yourself," she replied, accepting my hand as we headed to my car.

"Dapper," I repeated with a chuckle. I was wearing a black suit, fairly similar to what I wore most days, although the pale blue tie was a change from my usual, I supposed. "Do you always dress like this for church?"

Giada raised an eyebrow.

"Enzo mentioned you've been there a lot. Meeting with some young priest?"

I tried to gauge her expression, but we'd reached the car so she lowered herself into the seat. I shut her door before walking around to the driver's side.

"I don't always wear a dress, if that's what you mean. But I assure you I always look good," she said, smirking.

I grinned, certain she did, and I placed my hand on her thigh as we started down the long drive. The church was only a few minutes from her house, but it was enough time for me to realize I'd missed her more than I thought I had. I pulled into one of the distant parking spaces and unfastened my belt, unable to wait any longer without feeling her lips against my own.

Just as I neared her mouth, she spoke.

"Are we back here because you don't want people to see you? I mean, are we still pretending you're dead?"

I paused, close enough to feel the warmth from her breath. "I parked back here because I need to kiss you in a not-suitable-for-church way."

I breached the gap between us, devouring her lips with my own. Giada returned the kiss with the same voraciousness. After a few minutes, her hands wandered from my bicep down my torso and towards my lap. I groaned and pulled away.

"We're at church," I reminded her.

She mumbled a curse word under her breath.

"If you let me come live with you, you could kiss me all night."

"Stay with me tonight," I said.

She smiled. "I'll consider it. So, about you being dead…"

I adjusted my pants then started out of the car. "If people see me, they see me. I don't anticipate this crowd including any of the people I'm hiding from, though. Besides, I think by the end of next week, they'll all know I'm back."

"What's happening next week?"

I shook my head dismissively as we were nearing the entrance. Giada frowned, but accepted my hand as we walked the rest of the way.

Once inside, she greeted a few people politely, and I kept an eye out for this priest Enzo mentioned. I guessed who he was the moment he walked over, grinning at Giada like he hadn't just seen her yesterday. I glanced at her and saw her face bore the same expression.

"Father Ryan, this is Luca. Luca, this is Father Ryan."

"Nice to meet you," the priest said.

I nodded politely while giving him a more thorough once over. Enzo had been right. He was definitely young. I'd be surprised if he were even thirty, but I supposed maybe something about that holy lifestyle kept guys looking younger. He seemed to be a decent build, but I couldn't get a real good gauge on that with the robe he wore. He had a good-looking face and thick blonde hair. Honestly, he reminded me a bit of Adrian.

I reminded myself that he was a priest and that Giada was dedicated to me, but just then, he leaned in. At first, I thought he was going to kiss her cheek, but then he whispered something. She nodded, then glanced around the room, and he whispered something else.

I tightened my grip on her hand and tugged her towards a pew. She followed but gazed back towards the young priest.

"Do you have secrets with all the clergy?" I asked as we sat.

She made a face.

"What did he say?"

Giada shook her head as a choir began to sing. "Later," she said as the congregation stood.

~

Giada

I kept an eye out for Angelo throughout mass, but didn't see him. My parents weren't in attendance, so I couldn't imagine Angelo actually making an appearance, but Father Ryan wouldn't have told me he saw my brother at the church if it weren't true.

Luca gripped my hand the entire service, soothingly tracing his thumb across my knuckles. I couldn't tell if he was simply bored, anxious, or just really missed me. I hoped it was the latter.

The moment the service ended Luca turned to me.

"What did he say?"

"Who?"

His exasperation was adorable. "The priest whispered something to you before the service. I want to know what he said."

"He said he saw my brother here earlier."

"Angelo?"

I nodded. Luca looked relieved, which was odd.

He dropped my hand as we stood. "I'm going to stop off in the restroom, okay? I want you to stay in here."

I nodded, but did a mental eye roll. I wasn't a child, and I wasn't going to get lost in the church. I said hello to a few other parishioners, then as the crowd thinned out, I made my way to the back of the sanctuary where Father Ryan stood.

"Did your friend enjoy the service?" he asked.

I laughed at the thought of Luca ever "enjoying" a church service.

"Well, he's here. So that's a start," he said, correctly interpreting my response. He said goodbye to an older couple then turned back to me. "Where is he now?"

"Bathroom supposedly. He probably got lost, though."

Father Ryan nodded. "That is a pretty dress."

"Thank you. So where was Angelo when you saw him?"

"He was with Father John. Looked like they were coming out of the cellar."

"The church has a cellar?"

He nodded.

"Where?"

He started to explain, then shook his head. "Come on. I'll show you. There's a door up to this back hallway there. Although it has a direct entrance into that back parking lot too."

"That's odd. What's in the cellar?"

"No clue. I don't even have a key."

I was really intrigued. We looped towards the back hallway then under an arch.

"Watch your head," Father Ryan cautioned, placing his hand on my arm to slow me.

"Giada?"

I turned in the direction of the familiar voice, smacking my elbow on the doorway I'd just been warned about. I winced and rubbed my arm.

Luca glared at Father Ryan but softened his expression as he turned to me.

"What are you doing back here?"

"What are you doing? This isn't the way to the bathroom."

"I told you to stay in the sanctuary."

I opened my mouth to remind him that I don't always do as I'm told, but before I could speak, a door swung open behind me, and out popped Angelo.

"Angelo?"

His lips pressed closely together as he gazed at all of us. I was about to ask what nefarious task he'd been up to when Luca stepped forward. All annoyance had disappeared from his face, and he looked carefree and chipper as he extended a hand to my brother.

"Hey, how are you? Good service, right?" Luca wrapped his arm around my waist as he spoke, pinching my side in a way that made me think he wanted me not to point out that Angelo was clearly not at the service.

My brother relaxed a bit and nodded.

"Is Julia with you? Giada and I were going to head out for lunch, and we'd love the company."

"Another time," Angelo said. Then he turned to me. "Can I talk with you alone, Giada?"

Luca made a face but quickly recovered. "I need to make a phone call anyway. I'll meet you by the car, okay?"

When I nodded, he disappeared. Angelo turned pointedly to Father Ryan, glaring until he, too, left.

"What were you doing back here?" he asked me once we were alone.

"Looking for Luca. He took off for the bathroom and got lost."

Angelo glanced around. With his face all tensed up, he looked exactly like our father—tall, broad shoulders, olive complexion. He had the same dark brown hair as the rest of us Contis, but more of it than Dad at this point. I could definitely see why people found him intimidating. He was probably double my weight, and even with the heals I wore now, he was a good six inches taller than me.

"So you and Luca are back together even in public now?"

"Yeah."

"What about Adrian?"

"We broke up. A while ago."

"Does he know you cheated on him with Luca?"

I blew out a sigh. "I should get back to Luca."

Angelo grabbed my arm, but dropped it as soon as I stopped. "I just don't get why you're with Luca. He's trouble. You'd be better off with Adrian. You guys could move back to Chicago or something and get away from all this."

"All what, Angelo? My life is here. And I don't want Adrian."

I could tell he wanted to say something else, but instead, he just shook his head.

"Just be careful with Luca, okay? You don't know him as well as you think you do."

CHAPTER 13

Giada

*L*uca was still on the phone when I reached the car, so I got in and waited while he paced around the midnight black BMW for ten minutes. Finally, I honked, and he hung up, laughing.

"You did not just honk at me," he said, shaking his head.

"I'm bored and hungry."

He started the ignition. "You know, everyone else in my life does what I tell them to do, without question or complaints."

"That sounds really monotonous for you. You're lucky you have me to keep you on your toes."

Luca grinned and squeezed my leg.

He seemed distracted at lunch, but he didn't want to talk about Angelo. I was fine with that, though, having had more than my fill of family drama and mafia crap in my life lately.

"I've got good news and bad news," he said as we finished our meal. He dropped a one-hundred-dollar bill on the table by the check.

"Start with the bad," I said.

"Something came up that I need to take care of this afternoon. Alone."

I suspected he didn't actually mean "alone" so much as simply without me, but I waited to hear the good news.

"But I made some calls—not the one you interrupted, by the way—and got you an appointment for a massage and a facial. I'll drop you off at the spa, and then we can head back to my place for dinner."

"You're ditching me on the day you swore we'd spend together?"

He nodded. "But I'll make it up to you tonight. Twice."

That sounded promising, and it wasn't like I had any say in the plan anyway. Luca accepted his change from the waitress and then pulled four more hundred-dollar bills from his wallet.

"To pay at the spa," he explained.

"You don't use credit cards?"

"Not if I can avoid it. I have cash. Might as well use it."

"The spa won't cost this much."

"You can bring me my change later."

Everything about that seemed odd, but I decided to focus on the positive. Sure, an afternoon at a day spa wasn't the same as quality time with Luca, but I could use some relaxation, and we'd make up for the lost time after.

~

Luca

I dropped off Giada, then drove straight to my first stop —the church. The parking lot was empty compared to earlier, so I parked near the door and walked in. Silence greeted me as I gazed around. I cut through the sanctuary and towards a hallway I'd noticed earlier.

I noticed the younger priest walking towards a room at the

end of the hall and followed. He was oblivious to my presence, so I tapped on the doorframe of what appeared to be a really shoddy office.

He glanced up, his eyes widened, and he flashed me a curt smile.

"Can I come in?" I asked. It was obvious by the myriad of expressions that crossed his lips that he wanted to say no, but instead, he nodded and gestured to an ugly chair.

"Thanks, but I can stand. I'll just take a moment of your time."

"I'm not sure we've officially met. I'm Father Ryan Wilson."

"Luca Marino," I said, extending my hand. The man shook it. "I was here earlier with Giada Conti."

He pretended that jogged his memory, but I was certain he'd already known exactly who I was.

"Look, I'll skip to the chase here. Giada has mentioned that you've been counseling her or whatever for some time now, and we both really appreciate all the uh...whatever it is that you do."

"I'm afraid I can't divulge what is discussed during counseling sessions."

"Of course. I respect that. I'm big on secrets too. Pretty crucial in my line of work that you keep your mouth shut when you're supposed to."

The priest grimaced.

"Anyway, I don't actually care about any of that. I just wanted to let you know that Giada really won't be needing your counseling services anymore."

His eyes widened. "Is she ok?"

I almost laughed when I realized he thought I was telling him she'd died. "She's fine. Great, really. She's at a spa now, and then we'll head back to my place. I'm sure she'll have a...satisfying night, if not the most restful. Athletic, you know?" I chuckled. "I guess you don't. Well, no matter."

"Is she changing parishes?"

"Like change churches? No, not yet. That might be a good idea, though, actually."

Father Ryan opened his mouth several times, closing it tightly each time without speaking. Finally, he shook his head. "I'm sorry, I'm not sure I understand what you're trying to tell me."

"Oh." I could handle directness. "Giada is mine. I'd like you to stay away."

He eyed me warily and sighed. "I apologize, Mr. Marino, if something has given you the wrong impression about the situation here. I've come to consider Giada a friend, and she's certainly a valued parishioner, but that is the extent of it. She's spoken with me about you before during our counseling sessions, and she's never once given me the impression she views me as anything more than a spiritual advisor and friend."

"It's not *her* intentions that I'm worried about."

The man took a step closer to me, demonstrating he did have balls after all. "I am a Priest. I took a vow of chastity. I'm essentially married to the Lord. My relationship with Giada is not the sort you need to be jealous of."

"Well, unfortunately, I tend to be a possessive guy. She's mine, and I don't share. I saw the way you were looking at her earlier, and I didn't like it. I'm asking you politely to stop seeing her."

For a moment, I thought he was truly speechless. Surely I wasn't the first guy to accuse him of a wayward eye.

"I think you should discuss this with your girlfriend," he finally said. "She had mentioned couples counseling for you both, and I'm not sure I'm the right person for that job. Now, if you'll excuse me, I have a meeting to attend upstairs."

I nodded and watched him go.

My next stop was to meet up with Alessio at a construction site. We'd instructed the stubborn ass managing that job to lose a few of the bids he claimed to have received, thus enabling different subcontractors to win the project. I'd gotten word from Thomas that the idiot was claiming he couldn't do that and that

Angelo's guys would back him up. Obviously, we needed to make an example of him.

After the day I'd had so far, with the overly involved priest and Angelo's questionable lurking, I was in the mood to get my hands dirty. I probably should've changed clothes before, but at least I thought to stash my tie in the car.

We were done in under an hour, leaving just enough time for us to drop by one of my clubs, 4th & Main, before I needed to pick up Giada. My papà had signed over two of his clubs to me as a birthday present, but so far the experience of owning them wasn't much different from simply managing. Sunday afternoons weren't very busy, so after we checked on everything, we had time to sit down for a drink.

"Giada is sleeping over tonight," I reminded him. "I don't want to leave her alone, so I told Giovanni and Thomas to call you if anything comes up."

He nodded. "What do you have planned with Giada?"

I raised an eyebrow, certain he had a pretty good idea of what I had planned with Giada.

Alessio chuckled, then I told him about my confrontation with the priest. Normally, I wouldn't share anything that could be perceived as a weakness with one of my men, but Alessio was different. And he already knew Giada made me crazy.

I finished my drink just as one of the girls came over to offer a lap dance.

Alessio turned to me, eyebrow quirked.

"I should head out so I have time to shower before I pick up Giada. You have fun, though," I said to my friend.

Giada

*E*ven though it wasn't what I had planned for the afternoon, the spa had definitely relaxed me, and by the time Luca came to pick me up, I was feeling like my usual care-free, chipper self. He had apparently gone home to shower and change, since he was now in a more casual outfit—jeans and a short-sleeve, collared shirt.

He offered to take me out to dinner, but I opted to head straight back to his house. When Luca's parents were home, I never felt comfortable in the Staten Island house, but when we had the place to ourselves, it was fantastic.

"I love this view," I said, gazing out the window.

"View isn't too bad from here either," he replied with a sly grin, staring straight at me.

I turned back to him, then went and made myself comfy on the couch. Luca brought me a drink then sat beside me, still eying me like I was a hyena just out of reach of his lion cage.

"How did your work go?" I asked right as he leaned closer.

"Hmm?" He looked distracted as he slid the strap of my dress lower on my shoulder.

"Isn't that what you were up to, work?" I asked, shifting so he could see the zipper on the back of my dress.

"Yes. Had to see a couple people about some things and then checked in on the club. Now I'm all yours for the night."

"The whole night?"

"Yes." He tugged the zipper down to my hips then watched with delight as the straps fell down my arms, leaving only my nude bra covering me.

"I feel like we might only need a few minutes at this rate."

Luca grinned. "I'll take my time next round. Promise."

And then he pounced, devouring me with kisses while removing my bra then pressing me onto my back on the couch. I fumbled to yank his shirt off over his head, desperate to feel his flesh against my own.

Heat emanated from his body, searing into my already-sensitive skin. His mouth shifted to my neck, sucking firmly then sprinkling feather-light kisses that tickled my flesh as he dropped lower. His lips wrapped around my nipple, followed quickly by his teeth. An intense mixture of pain and pleasure spread through me as I moaned his name.

"Oh God, Luca."

He growled against my tender flesh before moving to the other breast, repeating the delicious torture. I arched my back, lifting my hips to his, only to realize he was still fully clothed from the waist down. I reached for his button, struggling until he lifted off of me. I pouted at the sudden absence of his weight against me, but now I could unfasten his pants with ease.

I reached my hands down his back, sliding his pants and boxer briefs down over his firm butt in one movement, freeing his erection. I smiled at the welcome sight and lifted my back off the couch, eagerly wrapping my lips around his firm, hot flesh.

Luca hissed through clenched teeth, his fingers pressing into my shoulders. I hollowed my cheeks, sucking him firmly before releasing him and tracing my tongue around just the tip while gazing up. Luca was always good looking, but the sight of him slightly undone, his head tilted to the ceiling, eyes closed, was the most beautiful view I could imagine.

His hand shifted to my head, ruffling my hair as I continued to work my magic, then he pulled me away.

"What you do to me, Giada," he mused, his smooth chocolatey eyes piercing into me.

As he released my shoulders, I dropped back onto the couch. Luca leaned over me, lifting one arm, then the other over my head. He stared at me for a moment, smiling widely as he admired the view, then lowered himself over me. He nudged my legs up so my thighs were folded against my abdomen, baring me fully to him. His head dipped down, and he pressed the tip of his tongue lightly against my clit, then repeated the motion, increasing the pressure each time.

I moaned loudly and brought my hands down to his hair, but then he stopped what he was doing and placed my arms back above my head. His tongue danced across my clit one more time then, raising all my nerve endings to high alert.

Before I even registered that his mouth had left my body, his hardened length was poised at my entrance. Then his hips crashed against me as he filled me fully.

"Luca," I groaned, already dizzy with pleasure.

He withdrew slowly, then gradually pressed back into me as his fingers rolled and pinched my nipples.

I didn't dare move my hands, but as he increased the pace, I lifted my hips, meeting him thrust for thrust. The heat spread through me like wildfire, overwhelming all of my senses and taking control of my body. I was a wash of sensations, my world beginning and ending with Luca. He bucked into me harder, and I shattered, my body convulsing around him.

He wriggled his arm under my back, holding me close to him as he thrust a few more times before finding his own release, then collapsing against my chest while we both caught our breath.

True to his word, the second round lasted longer. And then we ordered Chinese food and watched a movie. After that, we ended up in the shower, which of course led to round three. By the time we finally made it to his bed, we were both exhausted. Luca fell asleep almost instantly, though, and I found myself watching him.

As far as I could tell, Luca rarely slept. To Luca, the need to sleep was a weakness, and he would phase it out altogether if he could survive without it. Even when he did sleep, he generally still looked tense. Tonight though, Luca was completely peaceful, much as I imagined he looked as a child when he slept.

I had wanted to talk with him tonight, to find out his plan for the future, for us. Sure, we'd just gotten back together, but in a way, we'd been together forever. Less than one year ago, we'd been engaged. I didn't need to jump back there right away, but based on how Luca had talked at the cabin, he still wanted a future with me, too.

Since he'd encouraged me to look for jobs, though, I had. But I couldn't exactly apply anywhere until I knew where we would end up. I could see us living happily in Connecticut, New York, or even Italy. I'd follow him anywhere and not resent him one bit. But the job market in Palermo and Rome was very different from New York or Connecticut.

Luca shifted, flinging his arm over me. I settled back against his chest, rubbing his hand with my own. His rhythmic breathing lulled me to sleep before I could overanalyze our relationship any further.

I hadn't been asleep for long when a shrill ringing jolted me awake. Instantly remembering where I was, I cursed myself for forgetting to turn off my phone. I reached across Luca, who by some miracle was still asleep, and grabbed my phone from the nightstand. I intended to reject the call then silence my phone, but I inadvertently clicked to accept the call.

I squinted, unfamiliar with the number displayed, but by the time the phone reached my ear, a man was already speaking.

"The package was delivered," he said.

"Hello?" I mumbled.

The line clicked dead right as Luca sat up, rubbing his eyes. He switched on the lamp, and right then, I realized what I'd done.

Luca swore in Italian and snatched his phone out of my hand.

"He hung up," I said. "I'm sorry. I assumed it was mine, and I didn't want it to wake you."

Luca shot of bed, his phone pressed to his ear as he turned to me. "Did he say anything, Giada?"

"Yes. Something about a package. It was delivered, I think."

He swore again, then started talking rapidly in Italian to

whomever was on the phone as he left the room. I glanced at the clock, noting it was not quite three a.m., so I'd been asleep for less than an hour at best. My head was still fuzzy from exhaustion, but the longer Luca was on the phone, the more anxious I became. I knew he'd be angry about me answering his phone, and I felt awful about it. Before I could come up with a coherent way to make it up to him though, Luca returned.

He dropped his phone back on the nightstand and climbed back under the covers.

"I'm so sorry," I said. "Is everything okay?"

He reached for the lamp, cloaking everything in darkness before settling onto his back. He guided me onto his chest, then kissed the top of my head. "It's fine, amore. Go back to sleep."

"You're not mad?"

"It's not your fault, and I took care of it. They were supposed to call Alessio tonight anyway, not me."

I felt like I should say something else, apologize more somehow, but I was so tired that sleep overcame me within minutes.

CHAPTER 14

Giada

On Tuesday, Luca promised to take me to lunch, but my morning was free. So when I overheard Angelo saying he was going to drop something off at the church, I decided to ride with him and have Luca pick me up at the church.

"Why do you need to go to the church?" Angelo asked, his tone filled with accusation. "You've been spending a lot of time with that Father...what's his name."

"Father Ryan?" I said, adding cream to my second cup of coffee. I didn't understand how my brother spent so much time at the church lately and still didn't even know the names of all the priests. Actually, I still wasn't sure what he did at the church at all.

"I go there for confession and to pray, like a normal person," I said. "But what are you doing there?"

"How is that your business?" he snapped.

I rolled my eyes just as my mother breezed through the kitchen.

"I, for one, just love that both of my kids have such an interest in faith these days," she said, leaning in to kiss my brother on the cheek before doing the same to me.

"What are you doing here this morning?" she asked my brother. He had officially moved in with Julia recently, although we still saw him daily.

"Picking up some papers for Dad and now heading out to drop something off at the church." He turned to me. "If you're coming with me, we're leaving in a half-hour."

I slid off the barstool and went upstairs to change out of my pjs. I'd just finished my hair and was starting to choose my jewelry for the day when my phone chimed. I'd given Luca his own ringtone and text signal, so whenever he contacted me, I smiled before even glancing at the caller ID. I was just so happy to finally have him alive and mine and to be able to just enjoy a normal, happy relationship.

I reached for my phone, certain I was grinning like a schoolgirl texting with her new crush.

"Recommend not talking w the young priest," was all his text said.

Huh? "Father Ryan?" I wrote back.

"Yeah. Avoid him."

What the fuck? Had Father Ryan done something I didn't know about? Why were Luca and Angelo both suddenly so weird about the church?

"I was planning to meet with him," I typed back.

"Don't," came the terse reply.

I rolled my eyes and dialed his number.

"Morning, sunshine," he answered.

The mere sound of his voice, all deep and gravelly, made my smile widen.

"Good morning."

"I'm looking forward to lunch. You really want me to pick you up at the church? It might be a couple hours."

"I'll be fine. So why do you want me to avoid Father Ryan?"

"I may have had a little chat with him Sunday afternoon."

I tried to think back to Sunday. Luca had accompanied me to mass in the morning, but he barely spoke with Father Ryan.

"I went back later," he added.

"Wait, you dumped me off at the spa and then went back to church?"

"It's fine. We talked, and now we see eye to eye. But it's probably better you meet with one of the other guys from now on."

"What did you talk about?"

"You," he said.

I heard voices in the background.

"I just didn't like the way he was looking at you, and I told him that. We're all good now. Baby, I have to go. I'll pick you up later, and I love you."

I gritted my teeth as he disconnected.

Father Ryan was meeting with another parishioner when I arrived, so I left a note on his door then made my way to the sanctuary. I'd gotten about three-quarters of the way through my rosary prayers when the pew rebounded softly from another person sitting. I turned and politely smiled at Father Ryan.

"Good morning," I whispered, not wanting to disturb anyone else praying. 'Do you have a few minutes to talk now?" I shifted in preparation to head to his office.

"We can talk here," he said, gesturing around to the empty pews.

I hadn't realized we were alone in the sanctuary, although that wasn't surprising for mid-morning on a weekday with no mass. The church hosted many daytime activities, but few people used the sanctuary for quiet reflection.

I started to insist that I'd feel more comfortable in his office where we could have some privacy, particularly in light of what I wanted to discuss, but then it hit me. *He* was clearly more comfortable in the open with me, probably for the exact same reason.

"Luca told me he came to see you Sunday."

"He did," Father Ryan said with a nod.

"He didn't hurt you," I said, regretting having asked it the moment the words left my mouth. Luca was a changed person. He didn't just go around hurting people, especially priests.

Father Ryan frowned. "No, but the fact that you would even entertain such a possibility…" He didn't finish his sentence.

"I didn't think before I said it. He's not like that anymore. He's just…some people find him intimidating."

"I could see that." He gazed around the empty room again. Someone was in the confessional, probably with Father John, but otherwise, we were still alone. "He asked me to stop counseling you. In light of his concerns, I think it's best if Father John takes over as your spiritual advisor."

I wrinkled my nose. There was probably some rule about not having a preference about which priest counseled me, but I just didn't like Father John. Whenever he delivered the homily, it was excellent. But something about him just rubbed me the wrong way.

"What all did he say to you?" I asked. I couldn't stand the thought of telling Father Ryan what Luca had told me. It was mortifying to even think that Luca had accused the Father of something so completely off base.

"He questioned the nature of our relationship. I assured him there was nothing improper, but I don't want to risk giving anyone the wrong impression. If he has those misbeliefs, others might as well."

"I'm sorry he came to talk with you. Luca is…well, we have a complicated history, and he is really protective of me. He can be a tad paranoid."

"Giada, I understand the trust that goes into the sort of counseling session you want and it may take some time for you to build that up with Father John, but I assure you he is more than capable of shepherding your spiritual growth. If Luca is questioning the propriety of our discussions, it is possible others are as well. I don't want to risk any other parishioner questioning my integrity or honor because if they have concerns that I'm not taking my vows seriously, they won't be able to trust me."

"I understand, and really, I'm sorry about everything he said. No one else would ever think you're doing anything inappropriate. And honestly, not even Luca really thinks that." I stopped myself before saying that Luca wouldn't have merely asked him to stop counseling me if he really had concerns. It probably wouldn't make my jealous boyfriend look any less crazy.

Father Ryan stared straight ahead, and we were both silent for several minutes. Finally, he spoke. "I've been drawn to the church since I was a young child. I've always felt a sense of peace whenever I'm in a spiritual building, and hearing the words we've been taught to pray always comforted me even more."

"I'm the same," I said.

"When I was a teenager, one of my parish priests was caught stealing money from the church."

I winced. "Like from the offering basket?"

He nodded, a sour expression on his face.

"That's horrible."

"Yes, and yet, some could say his motivations were pure. He took the money to give to a family in the parish that was struggling to pay for their son's medication."

"Oh. Well, that's different then. He wasn't stealing."

"He was stealing. He was wrong, it was a sin, and he knew it. Yes, his heart was pure, and his intentions were noble, but even so, he lost the trust of many parishioners. I struggled to trust him after that, too. If he wasn't able to keep his vows with respect to the offerings, how could I be sure he would keep my confessions secret? And if someone so dedicated to God still made such enormous mistakes, how could I ever aspire to attain glory in the eyes of our Lord?"

"We're all human, right? We all sin on occasion."

He nodded. "Yes, but for priests, those sins have larger consequences. When others are struggling to reconcile what they want with how they act, they need to be able to look at us and know that it is possible to resist temptation and maintain a pure heart."

"Okay…" I said, no longer following what he was saying.

"I consider you a friend, Giada," he continued. "But I also recognize you are a beautiful young woman, and I understand that people might misconstrue a friendship between us as something more."

"But it's not."

"Agreed. And to make sure no one questions that, I think it's best that you seek out Father John for spiritual guidance, at least for a while."

I rolled my eyes. "What about meeting with me and Luca together? You could still do that?"

"I'm not sure Luca would value that interaction. You should see someone you both trust."

"Right. And I suppose we can't even chat like this, in the middle of the sanctuary?"

He hesitated then shrugged. "I don't know. I guess…maybe?"

I blew out a sigh. "You should go. Luca is picking me up here today, and I'd hate for him to see you near me and get the wrong idea."

Father Ryan nodded and left the pew. I felt bad for my snotty tone, but I was annoyed.

I quickly texted Luca that he needn't bother to pick me up. I wouldn't be lunching with him. Then I tapped out another message asking Enzo if he could come instead. Heck, maybe I'd even see if Enzo wanted to go out for lunch.

Luca wrote back first, my phone buzzing loudly despite being set to vibrate. "No deal. Be there soon," he said.

I rolled my eyes, but when Enzo's response came shortly after, informing me that he was busy and couldn't come for at least an hour and a half, I relented and walked outside to wait for Luca.

He pulled up to the curb shortly after, rolling down the passenger window and looking at me. I shook my head.

"You are an asshole," I said.

Luca sighed and killed the engine. He took his time walking around the car to me, offering me more than enough opportunity to check him out. He wore black suit pants, a grey button-down, and a black silk tie. I could barely remember the casual, carefree Luca from only days ago at the cabin.

"Yeah, I am," he said as he reached me. It took me a moment to remember what he was agreeing to. He reached his arms around me and squeezed. "But I missed you."

I wriggled free. "What did you say to Father Ryan?" I held my breath while I waited for him to weasel out of this with a lie.

"I told him I don't share, and that I didn't like the way he looked at you."

"He doesn't look at me any particular way!"

Luca's eyebrows shot up as skepticism filled him.

I flung my hands in the air. "Oh my God, Luca. He's a priest. He doesn't even date. His sole interest in my is for my spiritual health."

Luca bit his lip as though trying to suppress a laugh.

"I don't even know if he's straight," I added. Although, I didn't think it mattered since, as a priest, he would never date or act on his more prurient interests anyway.

"He is as straight as they come, Giada, and he has impeccable taste in women."

"Luca, even if he were attracted to me, it doesn't matter. He is a priest. A good one. He would never act on his desire. And even if he did, which he wouldn't, it doesn't matter because I would tell him I only want you." I paused. "Or I did, before you acted like a jealous psychopath."

Luca reached for me again, this time kissing me as though we'd already made up. I was fairly certain that no one had ever been kissed like that on the sidewalk outside the church sanctuary. When he finally released me, it took me a moment to catch my breath and regain my rational thinking ability.

"You can't stop every man from looking at me," I finally said.

"I can try."

"Luca!"

He shrugged casually.

"You have to trust me."

"I do."

I shot him a look.

"What? Just because I don't think you'd cheat on me doesn't mean I'm okay with other guys thinking about you in that way."

"Well, you're going to have to get over it," I said, walking towards his car. Suddenly, I was hungry and acutely aware that the church entrance was not the best place for this discussion. "You can't exactly lock me up in a tower."

He held the door open for me, his smirk spreading wide. "No, not a tower. But I do have a spare cabin…"

~

Luca

After lunch with Giada, I returned to the club. Giovanni and Thomas were both there, bored out of their minds. I planned to take care of some accounting matters and review a few of the vendor contracts before the evening crowd started coming in, so I went straight to the office.

I'd just begun looking at the vender payments when there was a knock at the door.

"Yeah," I called absentmindedly.

The door opened a crack to reveal Thomas. His sheepish expression signaled that this was no ordinary interruption. "You, um, have a visitor," he said.

He nudged the door open a little wider so I could see. Just behind him stood Angelo Conti, his cousin Edoardo, and some other guy whose name I didn't recall. Not the people I wanted to see today.

I stood and smoothed my shirt. I wished I'd kept my suit jacket on since Angelo and his cronies were all formally attired, but I hadn't planned on meeting with anyone.

"Thanks, Thomas," I said before turning to the men. "How are you doing, Angelo?" I then greeted Eddie before turning to the third man. "I don't believe we've met."

"Mike," he said, not offering his hand.

Okay then. I wasn't about to let them all into my office to intimidate me, so I stepped closer. "Shall we get a drink?" I turned to Angelo.

"I'd rather talk in private."

"Sure. Thomas, can you get a drink for Eddie and Mike?"

He agreed, and after Angelo nodded to his guys, they took off. I stepped back to allow Angelo into my office. We both sat then stared awkwardly.

"Are you here about business?" I asked. "Or…something about your sister?"

He raised an eyebrow. "Both, now that you mention it. What is your plan with Giada?"

"Plan?"

"Well, you're back together again, for now. Is this time for good, or are you going to let her return to the Greek kid another time?"

My stomach clenched at the vicious reminder of Giada's recent feelings for Adrian, but I kept a straight face. "I think Giada and I are on the same page now."

"Are you going to propose again?"

I leaned back in my chair, not having expected the third degree about my love life. Maybe I could've seen Matteo interrogating me, since he actually liked his little sister, but Angelo was heartless. He wouldn't care if Giada ended up with some pedophile in Minnesota as long as it didn't affect him.

"I'm focusing on business matters now. I missed a lot when I was recovering after taking a bullet for your sister. So we haven't really discussed the future, but yeah, I assume that is where this is headed."

"Then we will be brothers?"

I grimaced. As much as I'd wanted a brother growing up, I didn't need any such connection to Angelo. "That's not really necessary. You already have a brother, and I'm pretty good at this only child thing."

Angelo's face hardened. "I think you're using my sister to get closer to our father, and I don't like it. Business is one thing, but involving my sister, that's low, even for you."

I tried to decipher whether he truly did care a little about Giada, or if it was just about the business, but Angelo's expression gave nothing away. "I'm not using your sister for anything, but I don't need to explain myself to you. She's a big girl and can make her own decisions about who she dates."

Angelo glared at me for a full minute without speaking.

"If that's all, I'm rather busy today."

"I see what you're doing with the business," he finally said. "Inching me out and thinking I won't notice?"

I sighed, trying my best to sound bored. "My papà has wanted into the construction business for ages, but he stayed out of it as a curtesy to your father. After I saved your sister's life, your dad wanted to repay my family. That's it. No one is cutting you out of anything. If you could take a step back and think about it, you'd see this can be a mutually beneficial arrangement."

At that, Angelo laughed, but it was the type of creepy, sardonic laugh you'd expect from a serial killer. I had flashes of future family Christmases with him, and it wasn't pretty.

"Cutting my guys out of the deal is the same as cutting me out."

"Except it isn't. Your bottom line hasn't changed. In fact, thanks to the new bids Thomas gathered, you're actually making a higher profit."

"You know that isn't how this works. My guys expect more business, not less. And they don't appreciate me cowering at your feet."

I raised an eyebrow. Nothing about our current positions would suggest Angelo was cowering. If anything, he looked like he was about to stab me.

"Don't make business decisions personal," I said. "You can handle your guys, and I'll handle mine. If we both act like grownups, we stand to make a lot of money here."

He blew out a sigh and stood. "Just thought you should know they're pissed."

"Thanks for the heads up."

"It would make things easier on me if I could at least tell them why they're losing business. If they knew you were back..." he paused, his tone lightening. "I don't like lying to my guys."

"I know. I'm sorry about that, I really am. I honestly don't understand my papà's logic with all that, but I know enough to not question him."

"Yeah, I suppose I get that," he said, reminding me of how much we truly had in common in that respect.

"I'll see what I can do," I promised, feeling sorry for the guy.

"Thanks." He started to the door. "But if I get the slightest hint that you're using Giada..."

I chuckled. "I don't doubt for a minute that a dozen different guys will line up to castrate me if I hurt your sister, but trust me, I won't. She's my princess, and I'm not going to screw it up this time."

Giada

Gabriella had the day off work Friday, so she came to visit in the morning. We spent the day lounging at the pool, reading gossip magazines, and swapping stories about guys. According to her, there were no men of boyfriend standards anywhere in Brooklyn.

"I may never go on another date again," she lamented dramatically, fake swooning on the flamingo float.

I splashed her as I floated past on a matching inflatable, but then I had a brilliant idea. "I'll take you on a dream date," I said, cooking up the plan as I went. "We'll get all dressed up and go to a fancy steakhouse and then head out dancing."

Gabby nodded enthusiastically.

I paddled over to the edge of the pool to check the time on my phone. It was already nearly five. "We should get out now so we have plenty of time to look gorgeous."

My friend laughed. "Wait, you're serious?"

"Yes!" I slid off my raft and climbed out of the pool. "I'm going to shower. When I get out, you better be out of this pool. I'll see if I can get us seven p.m. reservations."

I wrung out my hair then wrapped a towel around my waist before I realized the problem. Luca would freak out if Gabby and I went out unattended. Normally I wouldn't worry too much about ruffling his feathers when he was being ridiculous and overprotective, but life had been so calm lately that I didn't want to risk it.

"Want to come to dinner with Gabriella tonight?" I asked Matteo as I made my way through the kitchen.

"Can't. Have plans already," he said without even looking up from his phone.

"I'll go," my cousin Antonio piped up from across the room. "Is Gabriella still single?"

I wrinkled my nose at the prospect of Tony and Gabby becoming an item.

"Giada, you're dripping on the floor," my mother chastised, coming up behind me.

I ignored my mother and made my way upstairs. I started the shower then texted Enzo to see what he was up to. Then I hopped into the shower. By the time I dried off, I had two missed calls from him. *Oops.* I moved into my bedroom so Gabby could shower, and then I called him back.

"Are you okay, Giada?" he asked after answering on the first ring.

"Yes, fine. I just wanted to know if you had plans tonight."

"Why?"

"I'm taking Gabriella out to Parson's for dinner and then dancing."

"That's fancy. Is it her birthday?"

"No. But Luca will be pissed if I go alone with her. He made me promise not to drive anywhere alone for a while. So can you join us? You could bring a friend or, um, a date, if you wanted. It'll be fun."

He breathed a laugh. "What time do you need me, Giada?"

As it turned out, Enzo didn't exactly join us. He drove us, then sat at the bar nursing the drink we sent him and eating his own steak. Gabriella and I each downed two lemon drop martinis and dished more about our lives.

I wanted to tell her everything to do with Luca, but so much of his life was a secret. It had been bad enough lying to her about the timing of when we started seeing each other again and why he let me think he was dead, but explaining that he thought I needed a bodyguard because of his business dealings wasn't something I was up for.

"Just tell him you need to know the plan," she said when I told her my hesitation about applying for jobs anywhere locally. "It's sweet that you're willing to move where his business takes him, but he can't expect you to sacrifice everything. If he won't decide, you just have to make it happen."

"What do you mean?"

"Pick where you want to be, and get a job there."

That did make sense, really. I wasn't sure what was holding me to Connecticut. Now that I had Enzo babysitting me again and my brothers were being all weird, it was like summer during college all over again. "Yeah, I need to get out of my parents' house. I need to start my life as a grown-up."

"Ooh!" Gabriella shrieked so loud that Enzo turned towards us. "I have a brilliant idea."

I waited for her to share.

"Move to New York. Please? My roommate is trying to sublet her room for six weeks, so I have room in my apartment, and there are tons of design jobs there."

I chewed my lip and thought about it. "It does sound fun," I agreed.

I kept thinking about it while we headed to the dance club, and after one more drink, I was sold on the idea.

~

Luca

*I*t was nearly one o'clock in the morning when Giada called. Alessio and I were just about to head out of one of my papà's clubs that we'd been monitoring that night.

"Give me a minute," I said to him before stepping just outside and answering the call. I expected the line to be quiet on her end, figuring she was in bed and couldn't sleep or something like that. But instead, it sounded like she was inside the club I just left.

"Giada? I can't hear you," I said.

"Hang on," she said.

A moment later, the music had grown fainter. Already I felt tense.

"Where are you? Why aren't you at home? Is everything okay?"

"I'm fine. Gabby is visiting for the weekend. Remember? We wanted to go out dancing."

Shit. She sounded drunker than a frat boy on his twenty-first birthday.

"Anyway, I just wanted to tell you I'm moving to New York. I'll stay with Gabby. And I know you're going to say no, but it's just not your decision. I am an adult. A-D-U-L-T. So you have to R-E-S-P-E-T my decisions. Shit. That isn't right," she mumbled.

Before she could attempt to correct her spelling, I interrupted. "Giada, are you guys alone?"

"No, Enzo is here."

Relief washed over me. "Okay, baby, stay with him. You need to drink some water, go home, and then eat something and have more water. Then go to bed. We can talk in the morning."

"You won't change my mind. I'm moving to Brooklyn. I want to be closer to you, and besides, there's lots of jobs in New York."

After my little confrontation with Angelo the other day, I'd been questioning whether it was smart for Giada to still be living at home anyway. So, her idea of crashing with Gabby wasn't a bad idea, at least until I moved into my own place where she could join me. I was fairly certain Giada wouldn't remember this conversation the next day, but I told her I agreed with her plan anyway.

She hung up right as Alessio came outside.

"Sorry. One more quick call," I said, dialing Enzo as we walked to Alessio's car.

He answered quickly.

"Are you with Giada?"

"Yes. Well, she's in the bathroom, but yeah. Gabby is here too."

"Alright, I want you to get them home now. I don't care if you have to carry them out of the bar. They're done. Okay? And make sure Giada drinks lots of water."

Enzo agreed then disconnected.

Alessio shot me a look as we pulled onto the main street, but I just shook my head. "Giada's drunk and wants to move to New York."

"That's not a bad idea," he said.

"No, it really isn't," I agreed. I noticed a dark-colored car pull out of an alley behind us. The headlights were off, but thanks to streetlamps, I could make out at least two men in the car.

"Heads up. We may have a tail," I said, my tone changing abruptly. I reached for the gun at my ankle, then opened the glove box for easy access to the others just in case.

"Shit. I can't tell who it is," he said.

I had my suspicions, but I couldn't be sure that the driver looked like Mike, the guy Angelo had brought to my other club earlier in the week. Or maybe I just expected more trouble from him. Either way, I wasn't going to mess around.

I quickly called Angelo, certain he wouldn't actually answer.

Instead, he did immediately. "What?" he practically spit into the phone.

"There's two men in a dark blue sedan with no headlights following me. I'm sure you don't know anything about that, but I figured I'd call and let you know that I'll be mentioning it to both our fathers regardless. I'd hate for them to decide to change the parameters of our arrangement."

"Not my guys. I don't know what you're talking about."

"Sure you don't. Have a good night," I said, clicking disconnect.

"Call the other guys at the club and have them meet us outside. I'll circle back, and we can take them out there."

I considered that option, but if the guys following us were going to do anything, they would've done it by this point. "I think they're just trying to scare us. It'll look weak if we circle back."

"Looking weak is better than looking dead."

"Looking weak will get you killed," I reminded him.

"Do you want me to try to lose them?"

"No, but head over to Traverse Street. More streetlights there. I want to try to ID these assholes."

Alessio took the next two turns towards Traverse Street, but I'd forgotten that the cut-through to get there was a dark, empty street. The light was red as we approached, so if they wanted to pull beside us, we'd be sitting ducks.

"Fuck," he mumbled. "I can run it."

"Not yet," I said, craning my neck to get a good look. I tightened my grip on my gun just in case.

"Luca…" Alessio cautioned as we rolled to a stop.

Just as I was about to panic, the car behind us took a sharp right turn into an alley. The light turned green, and we pulled on ahead.

"Shit, shit, shit!" I said.

"They're gone."

"Yeah, and we don't know who it was."

I thumped my fist on the dash, then called Enzo back. I instructed him to stay at the Conti house and to let me know immediately if Angelo came home or if anyone else got near Giada. I was nearly certain her brother would never let anyone hurt her, but I wasn't taking any chances.

Next, we called Thomas and Giovanni, and then my papà. By the time we reached my apartment, everyone was caught up, but since we didn't really know anything, I wasn't sure how helpful that would be.

CHAPTER 15

Luca

Giada said her parents were fine with her decision to move to New York, but the angry phone call from her brother led me to suspect that was a lie. Either way, we were all in agreement that she was not bringing her car to New York. So, I offered to drive her. I'd planned to swing by late afternoon, figuring we could do dinner in the city, but kept getting delays.

By the time I was finally en route to her, it was already dinner time. She didn't seem too upset about the delay, though, and we were happily chatting by phone while I drove.

"I hate seeing Gabriella so miserable," she said, finishing the last of her stories about their weekend together.

"It doesn't sound like she was miserable."

"Well, she's lonely. She needs a boyfriend. Are you sure there's no one in New York you could set her up with?"

I laughed at the ridiculousness of the question. "You don't want her dating any of my friends."

"Oh, come on, don't sell yourself short. You have some nice friends."

One of the things I loved about Giada was the way she always saw the best in everyone. It was a dangerous yet endearing trait, and she was possibly the only person I'd met who was blessed with that particular attribute. Actually, Giada was different from nearly everyone else I knew in many ways. For starters, there was no one else I enjoyed talking with on the phone. But with Giada, I could happily listen to her for hours. Her voice soothed me and never failed to bring a smile to my face.

As I neared the next intersection, I glanced down at my GPS to get an estimate of when I'd arrive so she could be ready.

"Looks like I'm about twenty minutes away," I told her. Just then, I noticed the flashing red lights in my rearview. "*Cazzo*," I swore in my native tongue. *Fuck.*

"Luca?"

Merda. "Shit!" I translated my thoughts aloud. "I got to go, Giada." I disconnected the call and struggled to remove the gun from my ankle and hide it in the glove compartment as I signaled and steered the car towards the shoulder.

I thrust my hand into my pocket, retrieving a roll of cash, and slipped that into the center console, underneath some random items. I glanced around to confirm there was nothing in open view that would give probable cause for a more thorough search. Since I wasn't fully certain why I was being pulled over, I couldn't relax even a little.

I retrieved my license and registration and placed them on my lap as the officer approached, not even wanting to open my wallet in front of him.

The officer, a larger man who looked to be in his early forties, motioned for me to lower my window, then asked for my documents. I handed them to him wordlessly. He glanced at them both, then peered into my vehicle. His face showed no recognition of my name, and he didn't look too interested in the inside of my car, which gave me hope.

"Do you know why I pulled you over?"

"No, sir."

He pursed his lips. "You ran a red light."

I clenched my teeth. It had appeared red in my rearview mirror, but I'd been so distracted by the call with Giada that I hadn't really noticed.

"Do you make a habit of doing that?"

"No, sir."

He frowned again then tapped my license against the top of the window. "I'll be right back. Sit tight."

My phone rang as he walked off. It was Giada. I rejected the call then focused on watching the officer in my rearview mirror. I toyed with texting Alessio so he could get in touch with our contacts on the police force if needed, but I didn't want the officer to see me moving my hands around and get suspicious. Besides, maybe he wouldn't know who I was even after running my license.

My confidence in that thought waned after five minutes when the officer still hadn't emerged from his car. I could see his lips moving, so he was talking with someone, but I couldn't see him clearly enough to determine the tone of the call.

My phone rang again, and this time I nearly jumped out of my seat. I rejected the call, again, just as the officer swung open his door and stood up. He adjusted his buckle and approached slowly this time. His unease was apparent. I instantly regretted not having called Alessio. I placed my hands on the steering wheel, hoping to calm the man who now appeared to think I was moments away from shooting him.

He cleared his throat and leaned in. "Where were you headed in such a hurry, Mr. Marino?"

"I was not in a hurry," I said. "Just heading home."

My phone buzzed again. I rejected the call and silently cursed Giada's persistence.

"I could ticket you for reckless driving, for running that red light," he said.

I didn't answer.

"Have you been drinking this afternoon?"

"No, sir."

"Are you under the influence of any substances of any sort?"

"No, sir."

My phone rang again. *Fuck.*

"Someone is eager to reach you. Business call?"

"No," I said.

Now he frowned and leaned over. "You didn't even check the caller ID. How do you know?"

"It's my girlfriend's ringtone," I said, although it was none of his business. He probably just wanted to catch me discussing some illicit arms trade or whatever he thought I did for a living.

"You can answer."

I suspected it was still part of some trick, but knowing Giada, she wouldn't stop calling until she heard my voice, and I couldn't concentrate on doing what I'd been taught if I was distracted by her. I pressed the phone tightly to my ear.

"Amore, something came up. I'll talk with you in a bit," I said, disconnecting before she could answer.

The officer made a face. "That's how you talk to your girlfriend?"

I suppressed an eye roll. "I don't want to waste your time."

"Could you step out of the car, please?"

"Am I being detained for some reason?" I asked.

He motioned for me to step out.

Shit. I complied slowly. "Am I being detained?" I repeated.

He stared at me, then looked into my car.

"Are you armed?"

"No. And I don't consent to a search."

"I didn't ask."

I crossed my arms in front of my body, keeping my hands in plain view but blocking my car and my chest. The guy was starting to make me sweat.

"Would I find anything illegal if I searched your car?"

"No."

"Then you won't mind if I search."

"Do you have a warrant?"

His gaze narrowed. "I don't need a warrant when I've pulled you over for reckless driving and have reason to suspect you may be involved in a crime."

"A crime? What crime exactly?"

"I know who you are."

I sighed and gritted my teeth. The officer simply stared back at me.

"Since you don't have probable cause to search my vehicle or my person, I'd like to go. Am I being detained or am I free to go?"

He stared at me a moment longer, then nodded. "You may get back into your vehicle. Wait here, and I'll be back with your ticket."

I sat in my car, and a moment later he returned with a ticket. I could tell he was frustrated he couldn't saddle me with anything else.

"Thanks," I said. "Have a nice day."

He glared.

Relief flooded me as I drove away, but the feeling was fleeting. My papà would not be happy.

Giada

*L*uca's mood had tanked by the time he arrived at my house. He told me he'd gotten a ticket for running a red light, but I really didn't see why that was such a big deal. Lots of people got tickets.

"You have plenty of money to pay the fine, Luca."

"It's not about that," he said, his voice clipped. "I should've been paying attention."

The implication made me drop the stack of dresses I'd gathered in my arms. "Are you saying it's my fault you ran a red light?"

"If I hadn't been distracted, I wouldn't have put myself in a position to get pulled over." He shook his head and wadded all the clothes into his arms. I winced just envisioning all the wrinkles.

"I didn't make you talk to me," I reminded him. I waited for him to bring up the fact that I called repeatedly after he hung up on me, which, admittedly, wasn't my proudest moment. But in my defense, I thought something really awful had happened. I mean, he had cursed and then hung up on me. It left a lot of questions.

Luca dropped the first load of clothes into the back seat of his BMW. I nudged him to the side so I could straighten and flatten all the dresses. When I finished and looked up, he still had a sour look on his face.

"It's not your fault. But my papà is going to see it as another fuck up on my part because of my relationship with you." He paused and popped the trunk to make room for the bags my uncle had carried down for me. When we were alone, he spoke again.

"It's not about the ticket or the fine. It's about what could have happened. What if he searched my car, Giada?"

I gazed into his car but saw nothing telling. I shrugged.

"Giada, there are things in my car that would give him cause to arrest me."

"Like what?"

Luca flung his hands in the air. "It's not important. Is this everything?"

I checked the contents of the trunk and nodded.

"Wait, and you said another fuck up. What was the first thing I made you do?"

I could tell from his expression that Luca didn't want to say anymore, but luckily he knew me well enough to realize I wouldn't give up until he told me.

"That night at my apartment when you answered my phone."

"You said you weren't mad about that."

"And I'm not, but…well, it doesn't exactly reflect well on me when my papà puts me in charge of something, and then his guys inadvertently leave the message with my girlfriend."

I gritted my teeth together. If the choice was between Luca secretly resenting me and openly telling me he was pissed, I'd choose the latter. Apparently, no one cared about my opinion though.

"Let me say goodbye to my parents, and then we can go," I told him.

Luca nodded.

~

Luca

Giada did her best to relax me on the drive back to New York, but I was still so pissed at myself that I couldn't even fully enjoy the thank you blow job she gave me when we arrived at her new apartment.

The place was tiny, even for New York standards, and Gabriella already had one roommate. The other roommate apparently was never home, though, as she worked for some traveling theater company, so Giada was subletting the closet-sized bedroom for a while. I was afraid to ask what the plan was once the roommate returned, but I suspected Giada either intended to bunk with Gabriella or move in with me. Neither option struck me as ideal.

Still, Giada seemed excited about the prospect, and her enthusiasm was contagious. The full-sized bed spanned the entire width of the room, leaving space for just a small dresser at the foot of the bed. There was no closet either, so Giada simply sprawled her clothes out over the back of the couch that separated the tiny living area from the even tinier kitchen.

"I'll buy a hanging rack tomorrow," she said.

I opened my mouth to tell her not to, then shut it. She was in a new city, and really no one knew she was here yet. As much as I didn't like the idea of her wandering the world alone, I had to admit there didn't seem to be much risk. She planned to look for a job while she was in the city, which I supposed was admirable, if not frivolous and unnecessary. Enzo wouldn't be available to escort her around town until later in the week.

"I need you to promise to stay safe, okay? You don't know your way around, and New Yorkers aren't exactly known for their helpfulness."

Giada raised an eyebrow and then leaned in to kiss me, pressing her soft, smooth lips against my mouth in a way that made me forget my cares. When we finally broke apart, she smiled.

"If you're so concerned about my safety, we could get our own place," she said.

I swatted her butt, having no rational explanation for why that wasn't a good idea. "Alessio is handling the clubs Wednesday night, so let's do dinner then," I said.

Giada flashed me another sweet smile, and then I was on my way.

CHAPTER 16

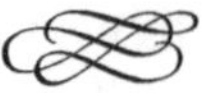

Giada

The Big Apple didn't exactly meet my expectations the first two days I lived there, but I kept an open mind about it. Gabby was rarely home, thanks to her stupid full-time job, the apartment was tiny and dimly lit, and the city was loud. I thought living in a house constantly filled with a revolving door of relatives was noisy, but here, there was music, voices, and traffic at all hours. It was maddening.

Still, I was on my own, and I was close to Luca. I focused on finding a design firm I liked and polishing my resume. Plus, we had a hot date tonight, and I was excited to see him and eager to spend a night in his quiet, luxurious room. Normally I didn't love sleeping at Luca's parents' house, but after a couple of days in Gabriella's miniature apartment, the spaciousness was tempting, and Luca's parents were out of town anyway.

Luca called to discuss restaurant options while I was getting ready.

"Are you dressed yet?" he asked, his tone hopeful.

"No."

"Shoot. I should've done FaceTime."

I snorted. "Okay, I'm dressed, just not wearing what I'll have on tonight. But I'm craving Italian."

"You're always craving Italian," he pointed out.

"True, and lucky for you, you fit that description."

He laughed.

I had just finished my makeup and was starting on my hair when the doorbell rang. I made my way to the door and peered out the small peephole.

I didn't recognize the guy at the door, but he smiled warmly and waved as though we were old friends.

"Giada, it's Tony," he called through the door.

It clicked that he was one of Angelo's friends. That didn't really explain why he was at my apartment, but I figured I could sort that out in a minute.

"Who's talking?" Luca asked. "I thought you said Gabriella would be out all evening."

"Yeah, she's gone. It's just one of Angelo's friends, Tony," I said, as Tony held up an envelope. "I guess he's got something to give me. I'll get rid of him quickly and see you in a few minutes, okay?" I hung up before Luca could protest. I was too eager to see him to risk any more of his excuses.

I unlocked the door and poked my head out. "Hey, um, Angelo isn't here."

He smiled and casually thrust his free hand into his pocket. "Yeah, I know. I live a few blocks over, so he asked me to swing by and drop off some of your mail. You haven't been at home much this week, huh?"

"No," I said, swinging the door open wider to accept the small stack of letters from him. Then, I remembered I'd been straightening my hair when I called Luca. I couldn't risk burning down Gabby's apartment. "Shit, I forgot I left my straightening iron on. Hang on," I said. "You can come in," I added, feeling bad as I noticed him awkwardly loitering in the hall.

I reached over my hairdryer to yank the flatiron plug out of the socket then scurried back to the entry, where Tony remained. He seemed kind of twitchy and antsy to leave, which was fine by me since I certainly couldn't risk him seeing Luca.

"Sorry about that," I apologized. "Thanks for delivering these." I glanced at the letter on top, but couldn't even tell that it was addressed to me as the ink was so smudged. *Weird*, but *whatever*. "I'd tell you to thank Angelo for me, but..." I stopped short of telling my brother's friend that I would've preferred being an only child.

"Yeah, actually, I was hoping you'd pass along a message to your brother for me," he said, his expression changing.

"What sort of message?" I asked, making my way to the door to let him out.

Tony stepped in front of me, blocking my path. "I thought you could tell him I don't appreciate him dipping into my cut."

Alarms began sounding in my head. "Your cut of what?" I asked, trying to sound like I was oblivious to the now predatory look in his eyes.

"Not important. All that matters is your brother did me wrong, and he needs to know that isn't okay."

I inched backwards, trying to recall which objects behind me might be usable as weapons. There was no chance of me getting my gun out in time, and even if I did, could I really shoot a man?

"Angelo is a dick. I don't like him, and he doesn't like me. You're not going to get through to him by doing anything to me," I said.

Tony stepped closer to me, a menacing grin on his face. I panicked, bolting out of the room. I couldn't remember if Gabriella's bedroom had a lock, so I darted into the bathroom, slamming the door behind me. I winced as I twisted the tiny doorknob lock since it didn't look sturdy at all, but it was a moot point. Tony reached the door and kicked it open before I even had a chance to lock it.

I screamed at the top of my lungs.

"Jesus! Shut up, and I swear I won't hurt you," he said.

I paused just as his lips curled up into a wicked smile.

"You'll probably enjoy it," he added.

I screamed again, raising my arm to hit him. He reached for my arm as I flailed, ripping my shirt. I lifted my knee towards his groin, but he dodged the hit and pinned me against the wall beside the sink. The impact of my back slamming into the counter knocked the hairdryer onto the floor.

His laugh came out like a growl. "You wanna play rough? I can do rough."

He moved one hand off my wrists, and I braced myself for impact, but instead he reached for my shorts, popping the button off in his harried attempt to unfasten it. I turned to the mirror, looking for anything I could use as a weapon, and that's when I noticed the little red light still illuminated on my flatiron. When I'd gone to unplug it, I must have yanked the hairdryer cord instead. That meant the flatiron was still 400 degrees of sleek metal.

Tony's entire bodyweight pressed against me, pinning my legs and torso to the wall while he now fumbled with his pants. I tilted to the side, praying I could reach, and barely gripped the cord in my free hand. As soon as he loosened his hold on me to yank my shorts out of the way, I shifted my grip on the flat iron and pressed it against the side of his neck.

He jumped back and roared at the contact, so I didn't waste any time in swinging it at him, this time with all my might. It cracked into the side of his head.

"You fucking bitch!" He lunged at me, but I waved it again towards him, ripping the cord out of the wall but forcing him back just enough for me to run out the door.

I sprinted to the front door, half-dressed and barefoot, and didn't slow until I was on the front steps of the building. I slammed right into someone approaching.

I screamed, then looked up.

"Oh god, Luca!" I said, bursting into tears as the relief flooded over me.

He caught me just as my knees gave way.

~

Luca

The moment I got a good look at Giada, it was obvious what had happened. Her shorts were unfastened, and her blouse was ripped down the front. A surge of adrenaline hit me.

"Are you okay?" I asked.

She sobbed in response. I held her close, not wanting passersby to see her disheveled state. But then it hit me—the way she was running out of the building, she was running from something, not towards me.

"Giada, is he still in there?"

She nodded. I hated the thought of leaving her there alone, but I had to go kill that fucker.

"Stay here!" I told her, releasing her slowly before ducking into the building.

"Luca, no! We'll call the cops. I know who he is."

I rushed to Gabriella's apartment, drawing my gun at the door and slowing my pace. The inside of the apartment was quiet, so I crept in slowly. There were signs of a struggle near the bathroom, but I didn't immediately spot a man. I didn't dismiss the possibility of him hiding, but as soon as I noticed the open window off the main living room, I had to check. Sure enough, the bastard had jumped out and taken the fire escape.

"Fuck!"

I turned at a noise, ready to shoot until I saw that it was Giada.

"I told you to stay outside!"

"We'll call the cops, Luca."

I pulled out my cell phone but dialed Alessio, not the cops. "It's me. Find out Tony Violi's address and call me back when you get it. It's urgent."

I hung up before he could answer, turning my attention to Giada. She was still crying but seemed calmer now.

I stuck my gun in its holster and pulled her into my arms. "Shh, baby, you're okay now." I kissed the top of her head repeatedly before moving to her forehead and then pulling back. "Giada, I've got to know. Did he hurt you?"

The pause before she shook her head was the longest moment of my life.

"Are you sure? Swear on the Holy Mother."

"I'm fine. He would've..." she shook her head as the tears increased again. "I fought him off. I hit him, and then I ran out the door before he could touch me."

"Grazie Dio," I sighed, filled with relief. My phone buzzed before I could say anything else. "Pronto," I answered.

Alessio told me the address then promised to pick me up in five minutes and take me there. That was why he would always be my main man.

"I have to go," I said to Giada. Stay here. Lock all the doors and the windows, and don't unlock it for anyone, no matter what. You understand?"

"Don't go," she said, her voice suddenly calm. "I'm begging you, Luca. Stay with me. I'll call the cops, and they'll arrest him for attempted rape."

I pressed a kiss into her forehead and walked around her. "I'll be back soon."

I pulled the door shut behind me and took a few steps, then paused until I heard the click of the lock. Giada was pissed, but I couldn't help that now. She didn't understand that the cops couldn't do anything, and that she could never call them on Tony anyway. He'd roll over on her brother faster than a dog would steal a bone. No, this was the only way to keep her safe and see that justice was done.

Alessio's Chrysler rolled up to the curb right as I hit the bottom step. I ducked into the passenger seat, and we were off.

"Bastard tried to hurt Giada," I said, even though I knew my friend would do what I asked without demanding any explanation.

"Shit. Is she okay?"

"Fine. She fought him off before he could do anything."

"He have a death wish?"

I didn't answer. Obviously, he must, to have gone after Giada.

"He's one of Angelo's guys, right?"

"Yeah. That doesn't make sense, though."

Alessio slowed the car and leaned forward, pointing. "It's that building ahead. Unit 4C. Want me to park and come with you?"

I glanced around the car, observing our surroundings. "Keep watch out here. I'm going to have a little chat with him first. Then I'll decide if we need to get Angelo involved."

I climbed out of the car, running my hands over my hips to ensure my cell phone and Glock were still in place. I walked around the building first, wanting a good picture of the possible exit routes before heading in. As I turned the corner, though, I saw Tony. He must have walked back from Gabriella's. I flattened back against the side wall of the building so he wouldn't see me as he made his way in the back door. He was rubbing his neck and mumbling to himself, but didn't seem too focused on his surroundings.

I hung back for a minute, but went for the door just before it clicked shut. He was waiting for an elevator off to the side, so I ducked into the stairwell. I took the steps two at a time, quickly spotting the right apartment. I stepped around the corner when I heard the elevator bing, waiting until Tony had unlocked his door to make my move. I walked slowly, not wanting to alert anyone who may be looking into the hallway, then stuck my hand in his doorway right as he stepped through.

His eyes locked on mine, and after a brief flash of confusion, he tried to slam the door on me. I was stronger, though, and more determined. I pushed my way in, kicking the door shut behind me. Before he could make a move or get a hit in, I swung the butt of my gun against the side of his skull, the resulting crack satisfying me more than it should've.

"Ow, fuck," he muttered, stumbling backwards. He glanced up at me, holding his hands in front of his face.

I saw the telltale sign of his problem then, the red blotchy eyes and fully dilated pupils. If he hadn't been high, he might've been harder for Giada to fight off.

"You went after the wrong girl," I said.

"Hey man, I don't have any beef with you," he said, continuing to back up as I held my gun on him. "You don't want to mess with me. I'm one of Angelo's guys. Angelo Conti."

I would've laughed at the guy's stupidity if I hadn't been so focused on killing him. Well, I didn't really plan to kill him, only to make him wish he was dead. "Angelo Conti can't protect you from me."

The guy glanced to the side as I took another step closer. I could tell he was searching for an out, and my instincts said I should just get on with it, but he didn't deserve a quick punishment. I wanted him to be scared at least as long as Giada had been. I wanted him to feel the pain I was going to inflict.

"Who the fuck are you?" he asked, his cavalier tone confirming he truly didn't know.

"Luca Marino," I replied with a grin.

Tony's eyes widened slowly. "He's dead."

"You wish," I said, lunging forward and slamming the gun into his face again. He ducked to avoid the brunt of the impact, so I swung it into his shoulder blades, then followed up with a quick punch to the gut. He crumpled to the ground, his elbows covering his face. I kicked his sides repeatedly, relishing the groans emitted after each blow. I climbed over him and lifted his head by his collar, then slammed his head into the ground. His elbows dropped out of the way, so I punched him.

I vaguely registered voices in the background but was too focused on the stronzo, the asshole, beneath me. His blood was now staining my fingers, with a little more spurting out each time my fist blasted into his fucking head.

I heard my name right as a hand gripped mine. I swung the hand off me then kicked the creep one more time before turning to see who was trying to get in between me and justice for that bastard.

"Stop!" Alessio said, his eyes wide.

He reached for my hand again. Again, I slapped him away, but this time, I sat back on my heels. I took a breath, then gazed at the bloody mess in front of me.

I heard whimpering behind me and turned. There, next to her middle brother, stood Giada. She'd changed her outfit but looked even more distraught than earlier, if that was even possible.

"Shit," Matteo said, pacing to the side.

Alessio tossed a handkerchief over the lowlife's throat, then pressed his fingers over it. "He's still got a pulse," he said, collecting the cloth and wedging it back into his pocket.

Matteo glared at me, clearly not reassured by this, then pulled out his phone. He paused a moment before reciting the address where we were. "I need you to come get Giada now."

Alessio stood and began exploring the apartment, all without touching anything. I turned to face Giada, but instantly regretted it. I should've felt good, and proud. I'd been decisive and brave, plus I'd taken care of a would-be rapist. But seeing the disappointment all over her face, I felt sick.

"He's got meth," Alessio said, leaning closer to inspect another substance, using his handkerchief to lift a magazine out of the way. "And heroin."

"Shit, shit, shit," Matteo muttered.

"Angelo would've just killed him anyway," Alessio said. "At least now you know he won't run anywhere in the meantime."

I caught Matteo shooting Alessio the same pointed stare that I suspected was on my own face.

Alessio still looked clueless, so I nodded to Giada. Alessio shrugged and resumed his inspection of the room.

"Why did you bring her here?" I asked Matteo.

"She didn't give me much choice," he said. "I told her to stay in the car, but…"

I blew out a sigh. Matteo was so different from his father and older brother. I liked the guy, really, but he was the only man I knew who couldn't handle a hundred and twenty pound woman. And while it was convenient having him here now, since we'd have to involve his brother anyway, I didn't count on Matteo being much assistance during the clean-up.

Giada shrieked suddenly. I rushed to her, clamping a hand over her mouth and embracing her tightly. Following her line of sight, I saw that Tony was twitching. I couldn't tell if he was waking up, vomiting, or seizing. Truth be told, I didn't care. I turned Giada's face to me, holding her against the breast of my shirt.

Alessio nudged Tony with the toe of his shoe, and the movement stopped.

Giada wriggled out of my arms, shot me an accusatory stare, then started towards her brother. She glanced down at her shirt, which now had blood over it. She opened her mouth to shriek again, and I motioned to Matteo to stop her. This time, I was the one cursing under my breath.

"Was that Lorenzo that you called?" I asked Matteo, climbing over Tony to get to the kitchen. I used my elbow to flip on the sink then began scrubbing my hands.

Thankfully, he nodded. There was no one else I'd trust to watch over Giada now, well, other than those of us in the room.

"He'll call when he's here," Matteo said.

"Have him bring up some gloves and an extra shirt or two," Alessio said.

As if on cue, Matteo's phone rang. He passed along the messages, then turned to his sister.

"You're going to go with Enzo now. He can take you back home and wait with you until—"

"No, he'll take her to my place," I interrupted. I didn't want to risk her being around Angelo, and besides, we needed to talk.

"I'll go home," she said, stubbornly staring me in the eye.

I slipped off my bloodstained shirt and used the inside to dry my hands. I walked to Giada and reached for the side of her face.

She flinched and curled towards her brother. "Don't touch me!"

The way Giada looked at me turned my stomach. Before I could say anything else, though, Enzo appeared, wrapped Giada in a fresh shirt, and left. Giada didn't look back once.

I stared at the door for several minutes after they left, then kicked the couch. "Cazzo!" I swore in my native tongue, not feeling much better until I repeated it in English, "Fuck!" The whole fucking day was a mess. None of this shit should've happened.

"I'm sorry," Alessio said, already wearing blue latex gloves from the bag Enzo had deposited. "I came up here to warn you as soon as I saw her heading in. I tried to stop you, but you were in the zone."

I glared at Matteo again. If he weren't such a pussy, his sister would have never seen any of this.

"Do you see why you shouldn't have brought her here? Call Angelo," I told Matteo.

As soon as he dialed, I realized he'd probably just fuck up the call. "Say hi then give me the phone," I instructed.

Matteo awkwardly greeted his brother, informed him that we

had a "situation," then handed the phone to me. Rolling my eyes, I paced across the room.

"Hey, so your drugged-out man Tony, does he have some reason to be pissed at you?"

"My guys are none of your business," Angelo replied dryly.

Asshole. "Your guy tried to rape your sister. Matteo and I are here with him now. What do you want us to do with him?"

"He did not!"

"He did. Call Giada and ask her yourself if you don't believe us. She's fine, by the way, but we need to know now how you want us to fix your mess."

"My mess?"

"He's your guy. If you kept him in line…"

"He's on drugs."

"No shit. But again, you should've dealt with that."

Angelo was uncharacteristically quiet for a moment before his next question. "You're positive it was him?"

"Yes."

"And you're certain he intended to hurt her?"

"Yes."

"Kill him."

"Roger that," I said, breathing a sigh of relief that he didn't want to talk with the guy or anything. "How?"

"What the fuck do I care how? Just take care of it."

God. I needed a drink. Giada's brothers were infuriatingly dense today. "Jesus Angelo, I can handle the logistics. I'm trying to help you out here. If you have any loose ends, now's your chance to tie them up."

Fortunately, he figured out what I was offering before too long.

"Send Matteo by the house. I'll have someone wrap up something for you to leave in Tony's apartment."

"Send a courier with it now. What is it?"

"A bracelet, or maybe a necklace."

"Ooh, pretty. Not your size?"

"Fuck you, Marino. It's leftover from a heist. Cops got too interested so we couldn't move the rest of the goods. Stick it in one of his dresser drawers, and we'll pin it on him."

"Yeah, alright," I said, glad I could perform that easy favor since it would, in turn, entitle me to a favor of my own down the road. "Anything you need us to take from the apartment?"

"No, just his cell phone, I guess."

"He's got drug residue all over the place. We'll probably leave that, but take all the electronics and any cash we find, make it look like a burglary related to his smack habit." I paused. "He'd pretty roughed up, so they'll know it was personal."

"How'd he get roughed up?"

"He touched Giada. How the fuck do you think he got roughed up?"

"Is he already dead?"

"Not quite."

Angelo swore under his breath again. "Finish it. I'll send someone with the package within the hour."

By the time we disconnected, Alessio was already aiming his pistol at Tony.

"Hang on!" Matteo said, right as I nodded my approval.

Alessio hesitated.

"It'll be loud," Matteo said.

Alessio tapped the suppressor, already threaded onto the barrel.

"It's still loud," he said.

He was right. Even with a silencer, the gunshot wouldn't be quiet, but it was rush hour in New York. There were dozens of competing noises. Alessio trudged across the room and switched on the stereo with his gloved hand. We all grimaced in unison as some crappy death metal beat pulsed through the speakers.

"He's going to die on his own anyway," Matteo said.

Alessio turned to me to break the tie. Selfishly, I liked the idea of Alessio being the one to officially end this prick's life, but Matteo did have a point. If we were wanting to fully convince the authorities he simply pissed off the wrong dealer, well, maybe we shouldn't shoot him. Or maybe we should. I didn't know how thugs like that operated.

I turned to Alessio and shrugged. Alessio groaned in frustration and crouched down. Rolling the pig onto his side, he then slid his gloved hand under the rug, pressing the cheap fabric tightly around his mouth and nose. The unconscious creep offered no resistance, of course, so Alessio looked bored out of his mind as he waited long enough to ensure he'd suffocated him.

While we waited, I filled Matteo and Alessio in on the plan. I figured we had another hour before Angelo's guy arrived with the jewels to plant, so I called Thomas to have him keep watch outside. Then, we got to work.

I was exhausted by the time we were headed out. Giada hadn't returned any of my texts and had told both Matteo and Lorenzo that she didn't want to see me. So, I didn't bother going to her. I needed a shower, and then I planned to drink until I didn't know my own fucking name.

I went home, standing under the hot spray, watching my skin turn lobster red. When the water cooled to the point of comfort, I began scrubbing with soap. I felt like Lady fucking Macbeth, and it didn't make sense. I didn't kill the guy. And even if I had beaten him to death, he deserved it. He was a druggie and a rapist. He didn't deserve the air he breathed. So why did I feel so dirty?

I'd beaten men before. Hell, I'd killed a man before. The only difference between those instances and this one was the look on Giada's face when she saw me. And I didn't like that one bit.

CHAPTER 17

Giada

Enzo drove me back to Gabriella's apartment and went inside with me so I could pack a bag, clean up the bathroom, and confirm there was no damage to the property. I would've loved the comfort of my best friend now, but I didn't want to tell her that I was nearly raped in her apartment or that I watched my formerly dead ex-fiancé murdered someone with his bare hands. So instead, I left her a post-it note that I was headed back home.

I rode in the front seat with Enzo, comforted by his close proximity. He let me fiddle with the radio stations and didn't pressure me to talk. Actually, he didn't say anything at all until the fourth time my phone buzzed with a text.

"Either respond to the man or silence your phone," he said.

His tone surprised me, and I wondered if he was missing out on fun plans tonight because he had to babysit me. I spoke my thought aloud, apologizing.

"This isn't how I wanted this evening to go, but I didn't have a hot date or anything. I'm just stressed out, same as you. I heard what that guy tried to do to you, and I don't like it," he said.

My chest tightened. Shame washed over me at the awareness that Enzo knew Tony's plans, and then a new wave of guilt hit me over the fact that I felt the initial shame. I knew it wasn't my fault, that I had nothing to feel bad about, but… still my emotions ran wild. I felt nothing if not conflicted.

"If you were my girl, and I walked in on that, I would've done the same." Enzo continued. Then he paused, glancing over his shoulder before changing lanes. "Shoot, I probably would've killed him too, even though you're not my girl."

"I doubt it. You're not like Luca. You don't have that temper. You didn't see him when he was…" I stopped myself abruptly, remembering that it wasn't too long ago that Enzo was on the receiving end of Luca's temper. Although in that particular fight, Luca had delegated the actual hitting. "He was completely out of control," I finally said.

"Honestly, I've never seen him lose it except with you. Luca's usually the most level-headed guy I know. He's calculating, methodical, cool."

I could see that about Luca, sometimes, but I definitely saw the hot-headed side too. After everything we'd been through, I was pissed that he left me when I'd just been through something so traumatic. Enzo shouldn't always have to be the one to pick up the pieces and comfort me.

"He was still alive when you left," Enzo said suddenly.

I wished I could say I cared, but I really didn't. Not just because I couldn't honestly say I minded the guy being dead, but also because it was sheer luck if he survived that beating. Luca hadn't held back at all, and from now on, every time I closed my eyes, I'd either see that perv fumbling with my shorts or my Luca pummeling another human being until his face resembled a chewed-up sushi roll.

Enzo's phone rang, and his eyes flitted to the dash where the caller ID flashed Luca's number.

"I don't want to talk to him or see him tonight," I said.

Enzo ignored the call, then tapped out a quick text a moment later. I assumed Luca replied since there was another buzz of Enzo's phone, prompting Enzo to send another quick text.

"I'm surprised he lets you text while you drive me," I said.

Enzo snorted. "If you'd write him back, he wouldn't have to text me."

We were quiet for a few minutes. Then as we neared my home, I started to worry. "I don't want to see Angelo."

"He's not home."

"Does he know?"

"I would assume so."

"I mean, what happened to me."

"Yes. The guy worked for him. Matteo would've told him."

I winced, mortified by the thought of Angelo knowing what almost happened with that creep. "They wouldn't tell my father though, right?"

"I don't know, maybe."

"Enough people know. I don't want anyone to tell anyone else."

Enzo eyed me sadly. "You don't have anything to be embarrassed about, Giada. You didn't do anything wrong."

"You'll talk with someone tonight, won't you? Either my brother or Luca? Tell them I don't want anyone else knowing the details."

"Okay."

"Will you stay at the house tonight?"

"Don't really have any other options."

"Can we hang out until I go to sleep? I don't want to be alone."

"Sure, Giada."

The house was uncharacteristically quiet when we returned home. My mother was home, but she retired to her bedroom for the night after greeting us. My father was away on business with a couple of my uncles, so the only other inhabitants of the house were my cousins out in the guesthouse.

I showered immediately on our return, then changed into comfortable shorts and a tank top. I tied my hair into a loose knot on top of my head rather than drying it. I wondered if I'd ever again look at a hairdryer or flatiron without panicking.

When I came back downstairs, Enzo was in the kitchen eating a sandwich. "Want one?" he offered.

I nodded, surprised that I actually was hungry. As Enzo compiled the sandwich, I went to the butler's pantry where we kept all the liquor.

"What do you drink these days?" I called around the corner. I mixed myself a strong vodka and club soda while I waited for his response. "You're not working now. You're here as a friend." I paused again. "I promise I won't throw myself at you."

He snickered at this last part. "Whiskey on the rocks."

I poured his drink, going heavy on the whiskey and light on the ice. When I handed it to him, he eyed me skeptically. "Trying to get me drunk?"

"I bet you're a fun drunk."

We clinked our glasses together, then ate in silence for a few minutes. By the time we were both done with our sandwiches, I was ready for a refill and forced one on Enzo as well. Then we retired into the living room. We sat on adjacent couches, and I wondered if Enzo was worried Luca would show up and accuse him of fooling around with me if he sat too close.

I realized Enzo had changed into more casual clothes too, apparently while I'd showered.

"Luca won't come here tonight," I said, needing to reassure myself as much as him.

"Matteo is coming home, though."

I shrugged, indifferent to his whereabouts.

Enzo's phone buzzed, and I glanced over, curious if Luca was still contacting him. The message was from a Sara though.

"Who's Sara?"

He clicked off his phone, masking a grin. "Just a girl."

"A pretty girl," I guessed. "You're blushing."

He shrugged but pulled up a photo on his phone and showed me. The woman was beautiful, with wavy long strawberry blonde hair and hazel eyes. She had the kind of sweet, natural smile that told me she was kind.

"She's gorgeous," I said, returning his phone.

"We've only been out a few times so far, but I like her."

"What does she do?"

"She's a music teacher by day and plays the violin in a local orchestra at night."

I smiled. More than anyone else I knew, Enzo deserved to find a nice woman. I felt the slightest twinge of jealousy at the awareness that I was no longer the main lady in his life, but mostly I was just happy for him.

"What does she think you do?" I asked.

He cocked his head to the side. "What a peculiar question. Why wouldn't I just tell her the truth?"

"Which truth is that?"

"I work for your father."

"Doing?" I felt my eyebrows raise as I awaited his response.

"I'm a driver and personal assistant."

"Hmm. And she naturally just accepts that this job requires a lot of late-night hours?"

"Ships come and go twenty-four hours a day," he said, echoing the explanation I'd always given people curious about my father's hours. He stared at me for a moment, polishing off the remainder of his drink.

"How do you explain the guns?"

"That hasn't come up, but I definitely fill some security roles for your father as well. Sara would understand that."

"The trunk full of latex gloves, cleaning supplies, duct tape, and rope might be harder to explain, though."

"You've never seen inside my trunk." He frowned. "And you never used to ask questions like this."

"We see what we want to see, or not, in my case," I said.

He considered this for several minutes. "Luca told you everything, didn't he?"

I smiled broadly. "I don't know what you're talking about."

Enzo chuckled. "Good girl." He stood and refilled both of our glasses then stretched lengthwise along his couch. I was curled on my side, but our heads were close.

"Do you tell Sara the sort of things you think Luca tells me?"

"No."

"Will you, someday? Like if you got married?"

"No. It's different with you and Luca. You're literally in the family. You can't avoid it." He paused. "And someday, Luca won't have to answer to anyone. That's not the case for me."

I supposed that was true, although I'd successfully turned a blind eye to all of my family's true business dealings the first twenty years of my life. We were both quiet for a while.

"I'm sorry about that night back in college," I said, suddenly realizing I couldn't remember if I'd ever apologized. I had dragged him to the bar that night when I was feeling depressed and unwanted by both men in my life, and I was the one who'd begged for compliments and initiated the make-out session that ultimately led to Enzo nearly getting beaten to death by Luca's guys. "I had no clue anyone was watching us, and I didn't realize Luca could—"

"It's not your fault. I knew exactly what he was capable of." He offered me a conspiratorial smile before continuing. "Even knowing the risks, it was worth it."

I felt my cheeks blush. "What do you think would've happened if you hadn't stopped us?" I, for one, had spent many a night after that fateful evening playing out the details in my mind. Since I'd first met Enzo in my late teens, I'd had a harmless crush on him. But after our little makeout session, when I'd gotten both a taste of what he had to offer and a guarantee that we'd never be together, my thoughts had gotten a little obsessive for a while.

"Are you asking if I think Luca would've killed me?"

I grimaced. "What if we'd gone through with it, and no one ever found out?"

Enzo laughed again, and I could tell he was a little drunk by now. "I think we would've had a very fun night."

I didn't disagree with that. Sure, I'd been drunk at the time, but we'd had good chemistry for sure.

"And then it would've been very awkward the rest of our lives," he continued.

That statement was equally true.

"We never could've had more than just that, you know. It's not like we could've dated."

I wanted to ask why, but I knew. Enzo worked for my father.

"I hope things work out with Sara. You deserve to be happy," I said instead.

"Thanks."

"How did you ever get mixed in with all this anyway? With my family, I mean."

Enzo took his time answering. "My father was killed. He wasn't the target, but he worked at the shipyard, so I guess it was a case of wrong place at the wrong time."

"When?"

He hesitated again. "Same time as your grandfather. Same guys."

I froze, unable to even breathe for a full minute. "But I was there," I finally said as I snapped out of my trance. "I don't remember—"

"You were a child, Giada. You were scared."

I shook my head, uncertain why I'd never learned my grandfather hadn't been the only victim that day. "You weren't much older than me."

"Five years," he reminded me. "Same as now. Anyway, I was mad. My mom became depressed, money was tight, and I lashed out. I went to the marina and blamed your dad."

"Oh no," I said, easily imagining how horribly that would've gone over. My father did not accept criticism well and would never take the blame for something.

"He was kind to me, actually. He told me I should blame the guys that did it, and he told me how they killed his father too. He promised he would find them and make them pay. I liked that. He let me start working at the shipyard, and he paid me well. He became like a mentor to me."

"Was your father…like my father? I mean, you said he worked for him, but was he involved…?"

"I honestly don't know. To this day, your father won't give me a straight answer. He says my dad was a good man. He says he was honest, and kind, and loyal. He also says I remind him a lot of my dad, and that he knows my dad would be proud of me."

"Any dad would be proud of you." I tilted my drink from side to side, watching the ice clank against the side of the glass. I couldn't believe I hadn't asked this sooner. It all made sense now why my dad trusted Enzo so implicitly, and at such a young age.

The full effects of the alcohol had hit me, and I was both dizzy and drowsy. I tugged a blanket from the back of the couch over my legs and yawned.

"You should go up to bed," Enzo said.

"I'm not tired," I said, stifling another yawn. I felt good now, calm even. I knew the second I was alone, my mind would wander to the more pressing issues in my life. Discussing the larger, philosophical topics of my world was much less stressful. "Do you ever feel bad about what you do?"

Enzo took so long answering that I wondered if he had fallen asleep. I was too lazy to lift my head and check, though, so I didn't have confirmation until he spoke.

"Not really. I mean, we all make choices every day. I don't like everything that goes on in this world, but I generally only do things I know I can live with." He paused. "You grow up thinking everything is black and white, right and wrong, but that isn't reality."

I knew what he meant, and actually, I'd heard it all before. "You sound like Luca."

"Ouch," he said, flipping me his middle finger.

I couldn't blame him, but I didn't have a response for that either.

"You know, I was glad he wasn't really dead, for your sake."

"Really?"

"Yep. As much as I want to hate the guy, I get it. You're right, we aren't too dissimilar, Luca and I. And I like Adrian, a lot, but he's not right for you. You and Luca belong together."

I groaned. "If you call me the princess, I'll throw my drink in your face."

"You would never waste good vodka," he replied. "But that's not what I meant anyway. It's not just because of who you are and what families you're from. It's the way you are together. He's got a lot to deal with and a lot of raw…everything, and you're the only thing that seems to get through to him. He loves you more than I've ever seen another man love someone. I think once he starts to feel more comfortable in his own shoes, he's going to make you very happy."

I wrinkled my forehead at the odd expression, but realized I did know what he meant. "I hope you're right," I said.

At the moment, when I couldn't even blink without seeing flashes of Luca pounding away at the unmoving man, blood spurting towards his fists with every move, it was hard to imagine him ever becoming the man I needed him to be.

~

Luca

The inside of the house seemed dead, and Giada's bedroom door was open, her bed clearly untouched from the night before. I trudged back downstairs and was about to call her when I noticed a man seated outside by the pool. As I opened the back door, I saw it was Lorenzo, wearing only a pair of slim-fit shorts and dark wire-rimmed sunglasses that completely blocked my view of his eyes. He didn't move when I stood in front of him, so I gathered he was asleep.

I turned to the side and saw Giada, directly in his line of sight, sprawled on her stomach on a lounge chair wearing nothing but bikini bottoms. Her sunglasses were folded on top of her cell phone, so I was certain she was asleep, but judging from the collection of beer bottles and cocktail glasses between them, they'd had quite the party the night before.

I took a breath to try to calm my nerves, struggling against the urge to crack a beer bottle over Lorenzo's head then throw him in the pool. My stomach churned as my mind flitted back to the night almost two years ago now when Alessio texted me pictures of Giada straddling Lorenzo in a steamed-up car. No matter how many times she told me it hadn't gone past kissing, I couldn't erase those images from my brain.

I knew she was mad at me last night, but this… There had to be an explanation. Lorenzo wasn't stupid enough to seduce his boss' daughter at their home, anyway…was he?

"What the fuck is going on here?" The loud voice startled me, and it wasn't until Lorenzo and Giada both stared at me that I realized I'd been the one to yell. Lorenzo quickly averted his gaze to the side, and as I turned to Giada, I saw why. As she sat, her bikini top, which had apparently been beneath her when she was face down on the chair, stayed on the chair. She had the most amazing tits I'd ever seen—perky, round, and firm. They were slightly larger than fitting for her petite frame but perfect in every way.

Still, that didn't mean I wanted her flashing everyone.

I cleared my throat, and she sighed, reaching for her suit top. She placed it over her chest then stared pointedly, waiting for me to help her tie it. I did so, wondering who would've assisted with this task if I hadn't been there.

"I can tie it myself when I'm on my stomach," she said, apparently reading my mind.

Lorenzo smiled awkwardly and stood, pulling his shirt over his head. "I'll be inside."

"Stop. Explain."

He sighed.

Giada settled back into her chair, this time on her back. "Nothing happened. He's not even on duty today, so you can't boss him around."

"Not on duty? This isn't Starbucks. He's on duty until he's a captain. And even then, *I* can still boss him around until the day I die."

Lorenzo shook his head at Giada. "Sorry, Luca. We were up late last night. Giada asked me to keep her company—in the living room—so I did. I don't think she slept much. She came out here this morning, and apparently Matteo had thrown himself a private party here or something. The beer bottles are all his. Anyway, when Matteo came inside to go take a nap, he asked me to come out here to keep an eye on Giada because he didn't want her to be alone after what happened yesterday."

"So why is your shirt off?"

"I don't want a farmer's tan," he said, as though it were obvious. "And I didn't mean to fall asleep. Like I said, we just hadn't gotten much sleep so I must have just dozed off."

"Nothing happened, Luca," Giada repeated. "If you…"

I cut her off with a wave of my hand. "Whatever. Thank you, Lorenzo. You can leave us."

"I'd feel better if he stayed," she said.

Lorenzo shot Giada an apologetic glance, but left. I wasn't sure if it was worse thinking she'd partied with her driver or knowing she didn't want to be alone with me.

Giada crossed her arms in front of her chest and bent her knees, stubbornly turning her head away from me.

I dragged another chair inches from hers and sat on it, leaning over her.

"You're blocking my sun."

"I'll move after you talk with me." I paused and reached for her hands. "I'm sorry you saw that last night."

Finally, she turned to me. "Are you sorry you did it?"

I hesitated, not wanting to lie. "He wasn't a good man, Giada. He would've hurt you, and, frankly, I probably did him a favor. Your brother..." I stopped myself. Nothing good could come from her knowing Angelo's reputation as a vicious, cruel man in a sea of monsters.

"I asked you to stay, and you didn't."

"I'm sorry."

She turned back towards the pool. The sky-blue lining of the concrete made the water appear blue, and with the sunlight reflecting off of it, it looked magical. Everything about Giada's childhood home was serene and soothing, aside from the residents themselves. She sighed then turned to me.

"I was scared and upset last night. I didn't want to be alone. I needed you, and you left me. And then, in addition to processing what I'd just been through, I had to worry about you."

"You never have to worry about me. I can take care of myself."

"When you run off after some violent criminal, I don't know if you're going to get hurt, arrested, or what's going to happen. I shouldn't have to live that way."

She turned away again, wiping a tear from her eye. She

looked so fragile and small, curled up on her chair. I stood and nudged her forward, sitting behind her on the chair with my feet on the ground on either side of the chair. I pulled her back against me, where she fit perfectly against my chest like we were two pieces of a puzzle coming together.

"I'm sorry," I said again. "I should've waited to go after him. I was so furious at him that I couldn't think straight. All I could focus on was preventing him from ever touching you again."

She was quiet for a minute before speaking again. "Is he dead?"

"Yes," I answered softly.

"Was it you?"

"Does it matter?" I asked, my stomach tightening. Whether or not I was the one to technically end the life, we both knew I wanted to and I would've. So it seemed a moot point. Still, I couldn't live knowing how disgusted she was with me, so I answered. "No. But you can't ever tell anyone that."

She angled to the side, curling closer to me. I wrapped my arms around her waist and closed my eyes. I hadn't slept much, and I had a wicked hangover, but between the sunlight on my face and the gentle rhythm of Giada's heartbeat against my chest, I felt pretty damn good.

"I shouldn't have let him in," Giada said suddenly.

I was dying to know the details of why she did and what all he said, but I didn't want to push. When she wanted to tell me about it all, she would. "It's not your fault," I said. "I'm impressed you were able to fight him off on your own, though. Not surprised, but—"

"Yeah. That whole fight or flight response is no joke, I guess." She paused again. "I'm not sorry he's dead."

"He was a bad man. He would've hurt someone else, and they might not have been as resourceful as you."

"That's not really our place to decide. Maybe he would've repented. He might have gone to jail, met up with a group of missionaries, and ended up saving a dozen Rwandan orphans a decade down the road. But now, thanks to us, the orphans will just die."

"You didn't kill him. None of this is on you. And I don't think it's fair to blame anyone here for those hypothetical orphans."

"My point is we don't know. We aren't equipped to judge other men."

I kissed the top of her head, wishing I could share even a fraction of her blind faith. I'd always loosely believed in God, but justice…well, that was another story. From where I stood, it didn't look like God had gotten involved in his creations for a few hundred years at least. I didn't blame Him; I'd forsake us too. But I certainly wasn't going to count on Him to rid the world of the bad guys while we sat idly by and watched.

"Get dressed. I'll take you to church," I offered, knowing that would cure whatever ailed her. It probably wouldn't hurt me to sit in a holy space for a while either. Maybe some of the goodness would rub off on me. Maybe I'd get the balls to hit up the confessional and speak openly.

I nearly chuckled at the thought. Where would I even start? *Forgive me, Father, I have sinned…I killed a man. I nearly killed another. I've stolen, cheated, and lied. Oh, and I'd do it all again if I had to.* Yeah, that would go over well.

I didn't want redemption. I didn't even regret what I'd done. And I was more concerned about gaining forgiveness from Giada than God.

Clearly, I was doomed.

CHAPTER 18

Giada

*L*uca dropped me off at the church. He offered to stay, and I knew his offer was sincere, but I needed time to think. Luca was a distraction. I needed solitude. I assured him I'd call Enzo when I was ready to leave. I planned to stay at home one more night, but I told Luca I'd head back to New York with him the next day, if only for the night.

"I hate leaving you now," he'd said, and the look in his eyes told me he meant it. I knew he loved me, knew he was sorry, knew I was safe with him. But I also knew there was something inside him. Something I couldn't tame. What I needed to do was decide if I could live with that.

The sky was overcast, which meant virtually no sunlight was breaching the stained glass windows surrounding the familiar sanctuary. For some reason, though, no one had thought to turn on the lights.

It didn't matter, for me, though. I could easily find my way down the far aisle to a comfortable pew, and I hadn't planned to read, anyway. I wanted to say the rosary, needed the familiar words to soothe my terror, to erase the memories of the last twenty-four hours, and to bring my soul the peace I so desperately craved.

I kept my eyes open while I recited the series of prayers, grateful the darkness granted me the privacy I needed without forcing me to shut my eyes. I wasn't afraid to close my eyes. There was nothing to be afraid of. My attacker was dead.

I finished the rosary and sat, staring blankly ahead at the room bathed in darkness for enough time that my hips had begun to ache from remaining still so long. Suddenly, I heard a noise and turned to see a large form looming at the edge of the aisle.

I screamed, then jumped in the seat, startled at the sound of my scream.

"Giada, it's me, Angelo," he said.

With how quickly I flew to my feet and back to the opposite end of the pew, nearly tripping over my own sandals, I probably didn't have to tell him I already knew who he was when I screamed.

"Giada," he said, his voice softer than I'd ever heard before.

Movement from the back of the church drew my attention to a handful of people. I recognized both Fathers John and Ryan and assumed the other people were parishioners who'd been with them.

I sunk back to the pew, mortified at having drawn such a crowd when what I wanted was to be alone. I tucked my face into my palms, flat against my lap, willing the world to disappear by the time I looked up again.

My wish didn't come true.

When I opened my eyes again, I saw that Angelo hadn't moved, but Father John now stood beside him.

"Maybe you should leave," he said to my brother. He usually spoke with authority, but I heard the question in his voice. My brother held some power over him, but what, I didn't know. I only knew that if my brother refused, Father John wouldn't force it.

"It's fine," I said, my tone so uncertain that it conveyed anything but my actual words. "He just startled me. I apologize for disrupting everyone."

"It's no problem. I'm not sure why it's so dark in here anyway. The lights are on a timer, so..." Father John looked away, clearly filled with unease.

"Angelo is my brother," I said, more to remind myself that this man should be comforting to me rather than to inform Father John, who likely already knew that fact.

Father John exchanged an awkward, uncertain glance with my brother, then backed away, clearing his throat. "Right, well, I'll let you two talk then."

My brother slowly inched towards me before sitting a good three feet away.

"If you had something to say, say it. I'm busy," I told him.

"Yeah, clearly," he replied, his tone dripping with sarcasm.

I glared at him through the dimly lit room.

"Matteo told me what happened yesterday. I guess I wanted to say I'm sorry that happened, and I'm glad you're okay."

"Is that supposed to make it better?"

My question clearly caught him off guard. Probably, no one else ever dared question him.

"Matteo said you weren't hurt. I don't see what else there is to make better."

I rolled my eyes, confident he couldn't see my insolence. "Tony said he worked for you."

Angelo was quiet for a moment. "You spoke with him?"

"Yes, before he attacked me. What kind of work do you do that someone like that works for you?"

"Giada," he said, his voice thick with the warning. Then, it lightened, as he added, "Obviously, he wouldn't have been working for me if we knew he was...like that."

I waited for him to make some crack about hindsight being twenty-twenty. Thankfully, he didn't. He was silent for long enough that I started to hope he'd left, but of course he hadn't.

"You shouldn't have let him in the apartment," he said suddenly, piercing the silence.

"Really, Angelo?" My raised voice echoed throughout the sanctuary. God, he was horrible. "Can you just go? I really don't need to listen to you try and explain how everything that happened was my fault."

"It wasn't…I didn't…" he shook his head. "Tony came after you because he was angry, not at me, but because of something Luca did. Luca is the one you should be upset with, not me."

I turned to face him. "Thankfully, I have enough hate in my heart for both of you today."

"Matteo said he thought you were scared of Luca now."

"I'm not afraid of Luca. Luca saved me," I said. Except technically, he hadn't. I had saved myself. All those well-armed men who insisted on following me around like I was a fragile doll, and when it came down to it, I didn't need any of them.

But Angelo didn't need to know that. My physical strength wasn't in question now so much as my spiritual strength.

"Luca is trouble, Giada. You don't know him like I do."

I was so fed up with people assuming I was a shitty judge of character. "Then tell me, Angelo. What exactly does he do that makes him trouble? Is it who he associates with, maybe what he does for a living? Come on, I want to hear specifics." I stared my brother straight in the eye, challenging him to be honest with me for once.

Of course, he wouldn't. He'd rather keep assuming I was an oblivious fool.

"You should just trust me on this," he finally said.

"Right, because you're so different from him?" I shook my head. "Please leave."

He hesitated, then left. Tension still coursed through my veins minutes later when Father Ryan cautiously approached the pew.

"May I?" he asked.

"I don't know. I'd hate for someone to see you this close to the local whore," I replied, coming across even more bitter than I'd intended.

"Oh, Giada, I'm sorry you're hurting. How can I help?"

"Did my brother send you up here to talk to me?"

"No. I figured someone should make sure you were okay. I know you said he just startled you, but you did scream…"

"He's a terrifying guy, but he's not a threat to me now. Something awful happened yesterday, and I just want to be alone and think about it."

The young priest nodded respectfully. "I'm happy to listen if you want to talk about it, but if not, I'd love to pray with you."

It was a nice offer, and usually, I would've found comfort in knowing he was echoing my prayers. But today, I didn't have it in me to even hope for comfort.

"There isn't a prayer for this situation, but thanks."

"There's a prayer for every situation. Prayers for guidance, prayers for comfort, prayers for forgiveness. And if you don't know what to pray for, start with the rosary."

"Already did it."

"Then do it again," he said, his voice pushier now. "God doesn't expect you to have all the answers. He doesn't expect perfection. What He expects is for you to come to him when you need guidance. Eventually, He will show you the way."

I stood abruptly. "Maybe I'm done waiting for answers." I stormed out of the sanctuary and to the front steps of the church. I texted Enzo for a ride just as the sky erupted, dumping buckets and buckets of cold rain on the already-saturated ground. I swore and pushed back through the oversized doors, slamming right into a solid mass.

Of course, it was Father Ryan.

I flung my hands in the air. "Are you following me now?"

"I wanted to make sure you got to your car safely."

"I don't have a car, not anymore. My boyfriend doesn't trust me to drive myself."

"Do you need us to call a cab for you?"

I raised an eyebrow, wondering if there even were still cabs in the area now that ride-share companies had fully infiltrated. "My driver is on his way."

He nodded, then turned, apparently now willing to leave me alone like I'd wanted. Except now, I wasn't so sure it was what I wanted anymore.

"Can I ask you a hypothetical question?" I called after him.

He stepped closer and waited.

"Let's say there's this man, and he attacks a woman. Tries to rape her," I began, struggling to even say the word. "Obviously, that's a sin, right?"

"Yes," Father Ryan answered without hesitation. I looked away so as to avoid seeing the sorrow now filling his eyes.

"Let's say the woman fights him off, killing him. Is that a sin?"

The silence before he answered pained me. "Self-defense is a complicated area for some, who maintain that taking another human life is always wrong. If you want my opinion though, no, it's not."

"What if the girl fights him off and escapes, and then later someone goes after him and kills him?"

"That's a different scenario, both in the eyes of the church and the law."

I blew out a sigh and braced myself to ask the real question. "Which is worse, the original attacker's sin or the guy who kills him?"

My phone buzzed, notifying me that Enzo had arrived.

"Sin is sin, Giada. What matters is how we repent."

~

Luca

I'd fucked up, and I knew it, but even if I could change the past, I wouldn't. Giada would forgive me. She had to. I was prepared to do whatever it took, starting with giving her the space she requested.

Alessio and I went to the gym, where I spent hours imagining Tony's head on the punching bag. Every fiber of my body ached after a half-hour, but I kept going until my muscles cramped too severely to even control their movements. It was a punishing workout, and I relished every second of it.

Once home, I showered, first scalding my skin until it turned beet red, then lingering under the intense spray as it dulled to lukewarm, then ice cold. When I finally toweled off, I was shivering, but I knew what I wanted to say.

I reached for my phone and tapped out a message to Giada. "I'm sorry," I wrote. "I messed up, and I want to do better. I love you. I want to be the type of man who deserves your love."

I clicked send before I could change my mind. Usually, I didn't like putting such sappy shit in writing, but it was the truth, and more importantly, it was what she needed to hear.

Less than an hour later, I was vindicated by her response: "We'll get better together. I love you."

I headed over to Alessio's, figuring I'd feel better on friendly turf than in my family's home, even if my parents weren't there.

With the huge sleep deficit I'd amassed, I wasn't surprised that I fell asleep quickly. What I hadn't expected was to be awakened by my father just shy of eight o'clock in the morning. I knew from the tone of his voice that Angelo had told him what I'd done. And I knew without even meeting with him what that would mean.

I texted Giada that I'd come over that afternoon to talk with her, then dressed to go face the music.

CHAPTER 19

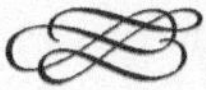

Luca

Even though Papà was in Rome and would have to deliver my lecture via video chat, he insisted I head to our family's home in Staten Island. Given his paranoia about listening devices, that didn't surprise me. But it also made me assume he planned to order me to join him in Italy, and that he needed me to grab some items from the house for him.

The house was cold, as always, but not empty. Lodovico and Iacopo, two of Papá's most trusted guys, met me as I arrived.

"I assume he wants me to call him from his office?" I asked.

Lodovico nodded solemnly, then patted me on the back. The look in his eyes reminded me of the good old days when my papà used to force him to drive me off-campus so his men could beat the shit out of me. Papá had been a big believer in teaching me to take a beating. Fleetingly, I considered whether that might be his plan for today. For all I knew, I was walking into an ambush, and without Alessio or anyone else by my side, I was entirely on my own.

Honestly, the idea of being jumped wasn't the most unappealing, a thought which probably should have disturbed me. A good beating might actually make me feel better for what I'd done that week. It wouldn't help Giada forgive me, but it might make me feel more worthy of her. Plus, if my papà resorted to a physical punishment, maybe he wouldn't insist on as much mental torture.

I peeked my head into the office, noting it was empty. I blew out a sigh, alarmingly disappointed that a high-tech lecture was all that awaited me. I reached for my cell phone, but Lodovico shook his head.

"Use the laptop," he said.

I nodded, then started the call as Lodovico closed the door, leaving me alone in a room where I had nothing but bad memories.

"You're late," my papà said, startling me by speaking English even though I was alone. I wondered if he, perhaps, had company, but he didn't give me a chance to ask.

"I could've called you right away from Alessio's, but traffic coming here sucks," I said.

"I assume you know why I wanted to speak with you," he continued, ignoring my comment.

"You wanted to thank me for doing the Conti family another favor?"

His eyes narrowed into a glare that was frightening even from thousands of miles away.

"You've spent my entire life telling me nothing is more valuable than favors and connections. Your business here is significantly stronger now because of my actions. But if you're calling just to thank me, you don't have to. We have a shared interest in seeing the family business excel, right?"

He blew out a sigh so hard that I imagined he fogged up his own camera. "Luca Tomás, you and I both know you've been distracted. You're reckless, and you've lost sight of your priorities."

He paused as if inviting me to argue, but I wisely kept quiet.

"Do you remember years ago when I encouraged you to settle down with the Conti girl?"

I did remember that, actually. She was still in high school, and my papà had tried to get me to propose. It was such a dumb thought that it was comical.

"Back then, I could have tolerated your misguided, immature, romantic notions. But now you are far too deep in serious business matters for such distractions. If you want a girl to keep you warm at night, or shoot, even for an hour, I have no objection. I'll even send you a list of willing ladies in Rome. But this obsession of yours with Giada stops now. Do you understand?"

I nodded, still too hung up on the fact that my papà seemed to think I needed help finding my own dates to really focus on his words.

"I want you on a plane to Rome this evening. We'll talk in person tomorrow afternoon once you're settled."

"How long am I staying?"

"As long as you're needed," he snapped. Then, he paused, probably realizing there were practical matters I'd need to tend to for a longer stay. "A few months, at least. Bring one of your guys, but leave the rest behind to keep on top of all your dealings in New York."

"What do you need from the house?" I asked.

He frowned, clearly having anticipated more of a fight. "Lodovico has a bag for you to bring to me."

I nodded. "I should go pack."

"Luca," he began, waiting until I made eye contact to continue. "The goodwill you have garnered with the Conti family remains regardless of your continued involvement with their daughter. We will maintain that business partnership, but you will end your romantic relationship with that girl today. Do you understand?"

"She has a name," I said, clenching my abs.

"That she does. But I suspect it will be good practice for us all to stop saying that name. The sooner you get her out of your system and move on, the sooner you can focus on what really matters. And the sooner I can sleep easily knowing you aren't going to do something stupid to get yourself killed over a woman who would just as soon be with another man."

Ouch.

"Go pack your things, son."

I swallowed the lump in my throat right as the screen went blank.

~

Giada

I could see it in his eyes before he even spoke. I should've known sooner, from the moment he stepped out of the car, unable to make eye contact with me and walking without a hint of his usual swagger.

Luca motioned for me to follow him, then reached for my hand to guide me around the back of the house. Alessio had climbed out of the car as well, but he appeared content to lean against the door and wait.

"You're leaving," I said, the moment we reached the semi secluded clearing in the woods behind my home.

He squeezed my hand and nodded as he turned to face me. "My papà thought I was too much of a wildcard with you in my life, and that was before everything with Tony."

That wasn't news to me, but it still pained me to hear.

"You're a liability for me. You affect my judgment."

"That's what your father says."

"No," he said. "Well, yes, but he's right. You do mess with my head. I'm careless when it comes to you."

I hadn't expected that. My knees felt weak already, so I shuffled back until I felt the edge of the stone bench against my legs, then I sat.

Luca's forehead wrinkled, and he dropped to his knees in front of me. I couldn't help but remember the day—ages ago—when he'd assumed that same position as he asked me to marry him. Maybe he'd never planned to share his life with me, but I would've given anything to go back to that moment now, just have a little taste of the carefree happiness I'd felt then.

"Giada, I'm not sure it's a bad thing. That isn't what I'm saying. Before you came back into my life, nothing mattered to me. I never acted on emotion or impulse. I always did what I needed to do to get the job done." He licked his lips. "But now, you're always on my mind. I can't ever focus fully on what I should be doing. I'm so concerned with keeping you safe that I'm reckless."

I understood what Luca was trying to say, and I'd heard it all before—from him, from Matteo, from Enzo. But it was a cop-out. Unless Luca planned to go through life without having any true love outside of his stupid criminal enterprise, he'd have to learn how to deal. Nothing I said now would suddenly make him realize that, though.

"You didn't even try to tell your father no, did you?"

Luca hesitated but shook his head.

I rolled my eyes and let my face slump into my hands. As much as he deserved to see me cry, I couldn't look at him any longer.

"It wouldn't have helped anything. Trying to stand up to my papà would only convince him that he's right, that I can't be the apprentice he wants as long as you're in my life. What I need to do is go to Italy with him, show him I haven't gone soft, and earn back his trust."

"So you're coming back?"

"Of course." He was indignant.

"What am I supposed to do in the meantime?" I asked, raising my head.

"Stay here. Live your life. Have fun with friends. Stop trying to ditch Enzo at every chance you get." He paused and wiped a tear from my cheekbone. "I want you to be happy. You shouldn't have to wait for me."

"What? Are you breaking up with me?" I shoved him backwards as I stood abruptly, causing him to stumble.

"Giada, I'm telling you I'm leaving for Rome in a few hours, and I don't know when I'll be back. I don't want this to be it for us, but I'm not going to tell you to sit at home pining for me. You and I both know you'd be happier with someone who's nothing like me."

"A few hours? You're leaving now?" I clutched my hands into fists so he wouldn't see that they were now shaking.

Luca looked flustered, which only infuriated me more. How had he expected me to react?

"I just found out myself. I'm sorry, Giada, but I think it's best if—"

I pressed my fingers over his mouth. "If you are about to tell me what to do or how I should think, so help me God, I will shoot you with your own gun."

His lips twitched beneath my finger, but he didn't speak.

"I have had plenty of opportunities to live my life without you in it," I reminded him. "There was my last year of high school and more than half of my college years. When you tricked me into breaking off our engagement because you decided I was better off without you, I tried to be happy with Adrian. But when I thought you were dead, I had a really good opportunity to think about my life and what I really want, and finding you again just reinforced that."

I dropped my hand, but Luca still didn't speak, so I continued. "I love you. I don't want Adrian. I don't want to see who else might be out there. I want you. And I'm sick of you treating me like I'm too stupid to understand the consequences of my choices."

Luca's lips were on mine before I could even catch my breath post-rant. His hands clutched the sides of my face like he worried I'd pull away, but as far as I was concerned, the kiss could go on forever. Eventually, he was the one to end it.

"I love you, Giada. And I want you to be happy," he said.

"Then don't tell me not to wait for you. Tell me you'll be back for me soon. Or better yet, don't leave at all. Choose me."

His face fell. "Amore, I do choose you. But this is the only way. Let me earn back my papà's trust. I'll make him think it was his idea for you and I to be together."

I felt sick. "And in the meantime? Are we just going to go back to sneaking around?"

Luca shook his head, cringing. "I'll be with my papà, so you can't call me. He has to believe we've gone our separate ways." He clutched my hands, the look in his eyes almost desperate. "Giada, I want you to be happy, and to trust that I'm working on it. I promise you we will be back together again soon, and this time forever."

"How soon is soon?"

He took his time answering. "Epiphany?"

I scowled, having hoped he'd say Thanksgiving. "Christmas," I countered.

"New Years," he offered as a compromise.

I sighed. As I gazed around us, I realized we stood in the exact same spot where Adrian and I had broken up. *Great.* Apparently, even my own backyard was cursed.

"I don't like this," I said finally.

"I don't either."

"Then don't go. Or take me with you. We don't have to go to Rome. We can go anywhere. Your father won't find us. After what you did for me, my father would help us, I'm sure of it."

Luca shook his head. "It won't work, and that's no way to live.

You are the princess. *My* princess. I am going to see to it that you live like one."

He kissed me again before I could protest. His tongue teased my lips apart, seeking, consuming, and soothing. It was the kind of mind-numbingly perfect kiss that always got me into trouble with Luca. His lips had this magical way of making me forget every coherent argument I still planned to raise.

I wasn't sure how much time had passed when a man's voice interrupted us. He cleared his throat, and I immediately jumped back, albeit only an inch thanks to Luca's firm grip on my head. Luca and I turned in sync to see Alessio.

"Time," he said.

Luca nodded and pressed his lips to my forehead. "Ti amo," he whispered.

Before I even registered what had happened, he was walking away with Alessio.

The End

~

If you enjoyed reading this book, I'd truly appreciate if you took a moment to click the links below and leave a review. Even the shortest of reviews help authors like me tremendously! If you're reading this digitally, here's some links to make it easy.

Retailer Reviews: Mafiosa Princess- Honor

Goodreads Reviews: Review on Goodreads

Click here to join my email list and get a FREE book: Newsletter Signup

SNEAK PEAK OF MAFIOSA
PRINCESS- TRUST

I paid the driver and gazed up at the neon pink sign above the solid black door identifying the popular nightclub as Oro, the pride and joy of none other than Salvatore Marino. Of course, it wasn't Sal I was hoping to see. Unless I'd botched my research, Sal was still in Sicily, which left his sexy son overseeing his clubs in Rome.

My breath hitched in my throat as I thought about finally seeing Luca again. Aside from one brief phone call, my last contact with him had been that fateful day in my own yard, where he kissed me with so much passion that I nearly keeled over. Then, he promptly ditched me to fly to Italy. I'd spent weeks pouting over the separation from my home in Connecticut before convincing Matteo to let me tag along on his trip to Rome.

Even once I'd reached Italian soil, I'd waited another two weeks for Luca to swap locations with his father, unwittingly joining me in the Eternal City. Despite the time I'd had to think, I still didn't know exactly what I wanted to accomplish at Oro. I hoped to not only see Luca, but to talk with him, touch him, and ideally convince him to run away with me. But at this point, I'd settle for any contact at all.

I walked around the lengthy line of patrons hoping to gain entry and flashed the bouncer my sweetest smile, tilting my head downwards in a seductive manner. Just in case my skimpy outfit and pouty lips didn't do the trick, I also offered him roughly fifty dollars in Euros. Giada Conti did not wait in lines, especially on nights like this one. No, I had a mission.

Once inside the club, I stood near a wall, my best fuck-off expression plastered to my face, and I continued to watch for signs of Luca. I was just starting to get discouraged when the crowd parted, allowing two burly guys to pass. They strode straight to me, and before I could even formulate my protests, their hands were on me, nudging me towards the bar, then down a hallway labeled PRIVATO.

Part of me yearned to scream or fight back, but self-restraint and the realization that no one in the club could possibly defend me against Sal Marino kept me quiet. The men opened the door to a room bathed in darkness, holding me still in the entry.

"Leave us," the familiar voice commanded. My heart fluttered as they nudged me into the room, shutting the door behind me.

The light switched on, and our eyes met. God, how I had missed those deep, chocolatey brown eyes. I stepped forward as if pulled by a strong magnet, then stopped an arm's length away. I let my eyes dip to his soft, full lips, which were currently set in a straight line. His expression was intense, yet unreadable. Meanwhile, I probably looked like I was about to pass out from excitement.

The only indication whatsoever that Luca was even remotely affected by me was the rapid movement of his chest. I inched forward again, and this time, my movement broke the spell. His eyes left mine, traveling slowly down my body then back up again.

Luca looked the same as I remembered. He wore black suit pants that flattered his strong, masculine physique and a dark gray button down that I yearned to slowly unbutton while he squirmed against my hands. His dark hair was slightly longer, barely grazing the tops of his ears, and he was cleanly shaven. His shirt clung to the cluster of muscles along his chest as he inhaled slowly and with restraint.

Everything about him screamed power and control. I desperately yearned to tip the balance, to watch him come undone at my hands.

"You're here," he finally said, his voice level and calm.

I tried to come up with a snappy response, but instead I croaked a lame "yes."

He stepped forward, clutching my face in his hands. He held me still as he inspected me then leaned closer and inhaled sharply. I was close enough to feel the heat emanating from his body but not close enough to touch him in the way I wanted. I held my breath in anticipation of a kiss that never came. After a moment, his hands fell to his sides.

"Where's Matteo?"

I shrugged.

"You came here without him? Why would you do that?"

"I saw your car outside. I knew you were here."

"It's not safe for you to be at a place like this alone."

"It's a club, Luca. People come here for fun."

"People come here for drugs and sex," he replied.

"Well, I came here for one of those, but if I can't get my first choice, I suppose I'd take the other at this point."

Luca stared at me for a long moment, like he just couldn't figure out what to do with me. I stepped closer, hoping to hasten his decision, but he held me at a distance.

"Your brother is going to wonder where you went."

"He thinks I'm in bed. As long as I'm back by tomorrow morning, no one will ask questions."

"Giada, this is my papà's club. If he reviews the security footage, or if anyone sees us together…"

I peered around us, realizing that must be why he had someone bring me into the office. It was probably the only place outside of the bathrooms with no security cameras. There was plenty of room on the desk…

"No," he said, always the mind reader. "You deserve more than my papà's office."

"Okay, but I've waited weeks for you to make some progress on figuring out how we can be together, and you've gotten nowhere."

"Not for lack of trying, I assure you. I need to get in my papà's good graces again, let him see I'm capable of whatever he throws my way. Then, I'll tell him I want you back. I just need you to wait for me a little longer."

I bit the side of my cheek, hating the feeling that the person I needed most in the world was rejecting me, again.

Luca bent his head down and cupped my face in his hands. My eyes fluttered shut in anticipation of a slow, romantic kiss, but instead, he pressed his forehead against mine. "Amore mio," he sighed.

I inhaled the familiar scent of his aftershave and smiled. Everything about Luca was familiar to me, yet he was still so mysterious. I could spend years getting to know him and still not understand the way his brain worked.

I shifted my head so I could kiss him, brushing my lips against his with a light, feathery touch.

Luca neither reciprocated nor pulled away, but when I finally ended the kiss, he yanked me closer, devouring my mouth with his own.

I moaned into him, his tongue sending jolts of pleasure through my entire body. Luca ended the kiss too soon, as always.

"I need to finish some things here. Go get lost in the crowd, but don't accept any drinks from anyone but the bartender. In exactly thirty minutes, come look for me," he growled.

I shivered at the prospect, then licked my lips, savoring his taste.

Stay tuned…the fourth book in the **Mafiosa Princess** series, **Mafiosa Princess- Trust** comes out in the summer of 2022!

Click here to visit the **Mafiosa Princess** series page on Amazon and preorder **Mafiosa Princess-Trust** when available: Mafiosa Princess

FREE BOOK OFFER

https://www.LizaMalloy.com/registration

FAMILY TREES

Having trouble keeping track of all these hunky mobsters? Here's a quick guide:

Conti Family Tree

Giada's Grandparents, Giuseppe and Illaria had three children.

1. Marco married Martina, and their children are Angelo, Matteo, and Giada.

2. Sofia married Antonio G, and their children are Gabriel, Giulia, and Giacomo. Gabriel married a woman named Nicole and Giulia married a man named Carlo.

3. Vincenzo married Bianca, and their children are Vinny, Edoardo, Diego and Mia. Diego married a woman named Brittany.

Other Conti "Family"

- Leonardo Ricci ("uncle")
- Giovanni Romano (brother of Bianca Romano-Conti)
- Stefano G. Bruno (Marco's cousin)
- Antonio Ricci (son of Leo and his ex-wife Noemi)

Marino Family
- Salvatore Marino, married to Camille
- Samuele Marino (Salvatore's brother), deceased

Luca's "Crew"
- Alessio Rizzo, Thomas Verratti, Giovanni Costa, Roberto Carbone

Angelo Conti's "Crew"
- Cousins Eddi Conti, Antonio Ricci, Giacomo Grasso
- Friends Federico "Rico" Regio, Giorgio Lomba, Nicolo "Nico" Controni, Tony Violi, Mike Monti

ACKNOWLEDGMENTS

I can't believe how quickly this series is chugging along! I truly appreciate the many people who have helped me along this wild ride.

First, I'm so grateful for all of the loyal readers who have taken the time to review my books. Every review makes such a difference.

Second, thank you to my awesome editor Sarah P! Thank you to my cover artist, J.D. Designs, and to everyone who reviewed early drafts of various covers. Thank you to Kim for helping with my blurbs.

Finally, thank you to all of the bloggers who've supported me and promoted my books. I know you have millions of amazing books you could be reading, so I'm truly appreciative that you choose to read my books!

ABOUT THE AUTHOR

Liza Malloy writes contemporary romance and women's fiction. She's a sucker for alpha males, bad boys, dimples, and muscles, and she can't resist a man in uniform. Liza loves creating worlds where her heroine discovers her own strength and finds her Happily Ever After. When Liza isn't reading or writing torrid love stories, she's a practicing attorney. Her other passions include gummy bears, jelly beans, and the occasional marathon. She lives in the Midwest with her four daughters and her own Prince Charming.

Visit her website at www.LizaMalloy.com

Join her email list at http://eepurl.com/gnuROD

ALSO BY LIZA MALLOY

Sixty Days for Love

For Love and Italian

Forbidden Ink

The Brothers' Band

The Brothers' Band: The Next Track

Hollywood Endings

Hollywood Beginnings

Supporting Roles

Legacy: The Awakening

Legacy: The Revelation

Legacy: The Reckoning

Mafiosa Princess

Mafiosa Princess: Sacrifice

Coming soon Mafiosa Princess: Trust

www.ingramcontent.com/pod-product-compliance
Lightning Source LLC
Chambersburg PA
CBHW030348200726
48286CB00013B/538